Chromium
Birth

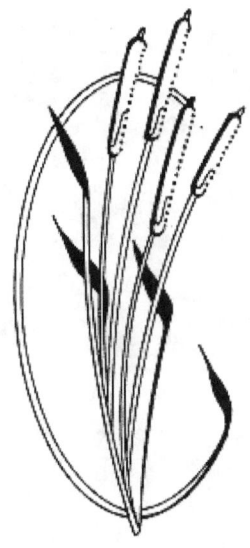

Chromium Birth

by David Talon

Senior Publisher
Steven Hill

ASA Publishing Corporation
ASA Publishing Company

A Publisher Trademark Title page

ASA Publishing Corporation
An Accredited Publishing House with the BBB

105 E. Front St., Suite 101
Monroe, Michigan 48161
www.asapublishingcorporation.com

Copyrights©2015 David Talon, All Rights Reserved
Book: Chromium Birth
Date Published: 12.15 / Edition 1 *Trade Paperback*
Book ID: ASAPCID2380657
ISBN: 978-1-886528-93-2
Library of Congress Cataloging-in-Publication Data

This book was published in the United States of America.
State of Michigan

A Publisher Trademark Copy page

"For my brother Kenneth, and our family of 508."

PREFACE

Imagine a reality of always having to hide in order to attain survival. Now visualize this being kept from you at the start of your own birth.

Chrome, an immature gryphon is subject to a clandestine truth: a fact that his undeveloped mind cannot translate.

Across the frontier, a young vulpine named Forjah is in absolute sanctification. Life is completely the way he has always known it to be—not acknowledging the veil that has enshrouded his upbringing.

This universe is a far departure from the imagined parallels by even the most creative. In a time that is not of the past, nor future . . . This all happens now.

In this universe, developmental maturation is not of age but of change. For young to progressively mature, their bodies and minds adaptively respond to their environments and encounters. This results in them becoming hybrids of various combinations of biological, psychological, and supernatural.

> *"Not from the past . . .*
> *Nor into the future . . .*
> *This all happens now."*

FOREWORD

About eight years ago, a young man stood in the doorway of my pole barn holding a notebook and a pen. All the other scouts were running about, so I asked what he was doing. He said that he is writing a book. "Well alright," I said, and then asked him what it was about. David enthusiastically told his story and I stated that, "If you ever finish it I would love to write your introduction." He said sure thing, and quite honestly I thought that is the last I would ever hear about that. Seven years later, I get a phone call from this same young man and he states, "Well, it is done. Are you ready to write the intro?" So . . ., here we are.

I have known David since that first encounter and watched him grow up into a fine young adult, but we never discussed the book. When you read his story, it is easy to see all the influences on David's childhood come to play in the characters. His family background, his religious life, and his own beliefs, and his own childhood all come into play. David has always had a creative mind and has fought for ways to express himself. All of that is released in his first novel, *Chromium Birth*. If you are a fan of sci-fi fantasy, sit back and enjoy the journey of Chrome from birth as all the adventure begins. When you finish, you will find your appetite only partially satisfied and a hunger for the next chapter in the life of Chrome and his friends. One can only hope that it is not another ten years before that comes to be. I know the next time David tells me what he is working on, I won't doubt him.

– Mr. O

Table of Contents

Chromium Birth

by David Talon

Scenic 1

First Beginning

I awake to the cold air of dawn, my mind had not even told me the day had begun. What had brought me back to this reality is nothing more than a painful throe deep in my body. The same I have been receiving from a biological cause unknown. But the bleakness of dawn is even more irritating on awakening to. Immediately raising myself up, I forced my legs forward and to the outside of my barrier.

Every breeze produces shivers through my fur and plumage while I stretch my six limbs; a task that causes my muscles to cry. I am proven wrong on the assumption of warming myself by moving that seemingly weakens me evermore. This illness has been progressing over a number of days and causing deterioration.

"What is happening?" I voiced in heaving breaths while pressuring my slightly warmer paws to a trek over the frosted earth.

Mist surrounds my sites this morning with chilled water droplets soaking the entire forest. The thorn walls surrounding my barrier glisten in the early light, its construction is for complete safety from intruders. Intruders that have never come to pass because it is claimed the Gryphon has no predator.

A S A P u b l i s h i n g C o r p o r a t i o n

We Gryphons are known as the *Aquileia*, hybrid descendants of the lioness Kyara and her chosen mate, an eagle. It is unknown if she is the only lioness to have born Gryphons, but she and her mate are the first.

In those days, Gryphons had been a viciously fierce race. Using their mother's leonine strength, paired with their father's aquiline power to dominate and overtake many other races.

Eventually these wars became so extreme that the great water being in his disappointment of racial interactions, stretched his mighty arms far beneath the depths and broke away the land which was populated by our ancestors. Isolated from our competition, the Gryphons progressively developed into the peaceful race we are now, a powerful but humble species living our lives as anyone should, coexisting within and outside.

Under the shaded trees, I proceed deeper into the forest to become more secluded. My mind is drawing away from quenching my thirst and to the fatigue that is clouding my senses. It is suggested by my mind to attempt at releasing some adrenaline, but my power of will lacks the motivation.

I am putting no focus into where I am trekking, but right now my surroundings are revealing that I am not alone. The smell of rodents is near; running fresh and wild, but as appetizing as they are I have no energy to hunt for myself. Yet, it would be absolutely inconsiderate to do so because I am within the territory of another, and his scent has come to my nostrils. Having no desire for a conflict I make the sprint of a lioness in realigning my direction to the river.

Now that my adrenals are pulsing into each of my muscle veins, confidence is with me as my ears soon receive the sound of rushing water. Halting at the edge of the river, I take a number of shallow breaths. The acquired internal energy is proving to not be much, for I am lousing it as quickly as I gaining.

"How is it that I lose such energy?" I exasperate out with heaving lungs and a throbbing heart, but these beats I am hearing them with my own ears . . . externally.

"It is not unnatural for an Aquileia of your state to experience."

Turning to the source of this voice, I am in full realization that I have been followed. "Please," I plead to the male emerging from the mist, "I did not mean to enter into your domain. Believe that I was not attempting to trespass or hunt for nourishment."

As if prey escaped my mind, it falls at my paws as the other Gryphon positions at my side. It is the same rodent I had detected earlier, a lagomorph.

"If you hunger for this it is yours to feast," he offers.

I am hesitant about this, but hunger is overtaking me, so I drive my beak through the hide and devour the fresh internal meat in only a number of moments.

"Will you oblige to give me your name?" he requests when I have finished and began to groom.

"Hollice," I revealed while preening a feather on my breast.

"I am glad to meet you, Hollice. If you lack knowledge of myself, I am Moonsight." My ears jump at the name. Gazing up from my grooming, it truly is the silver-eyed Aquileia.

"Moonsight! I have no explanation of how I did not recognize you."

He bows, "There is no need, Hollice. I am not here to judge your loyalty. Only here on my duty of congratulating you."

I gave him a puzzled look.

"Congratulate me?" I repeat stunned and reading his expression as unsure as my own.

"Hollice, would it be feasible for you to divulge your health to me?"

My tail twitches in reaction. "I am not against it, but by the way you are speaking it seems that you already know." He grants a bow of confirmation. "Then please," I ratify, "use your abilities to form a diagnostic and tell me what you know."

He agrees and so begins.

"I assume that your sleep has been disturbed lately. You feel ill along with an increase of appetite, but this frailty comes as an obstacle in providing for yourself. But the overwhelming fear that your physiology is diminishing is what brings you down entirely."

I do not need to interject or make any correction, for his revelations are purely definite. "Are you capable of learning the health of any Gryphon? Just by the use of your mind?" His feathers shake with hesitation, but then he opens his beak confirming.

"I am."

"But why myself in particular?"

My leader is silent, but he is now lifting his forepaw at my chest level, then rests it over my feathered breast and traces the talon tips down into my furred belly.

"My apologies for gifting you a great number of questions, but it is my rite for answers." I demand thrusting his paw away with my own. His silver enshrouded pupils return to my own encased in gold.

Moonsight is one of the only living Gryphons to be elemental; physically capable of manipulating certain forces using what is known as natural magic. Inheriting this through his own genetics, he is known for his healing abilities and knowledge of one's mind.

"Hollice, do not worry about the fact that I know thought process. As soon as I leave you it will be forgotten, for it is of your mind and not my own. As your leader it is my duty and obligation of concern for the health of every Gryphon in the Aquileia. If you wonder why I was feeling your body, I am only assuring myself that you are well on your way, yet I am most intrigued that you do not have the knowledge . . ." for a moment he digs a talon into the soil while tracing his metallic gaze off into the rushing river, "of what you are becoming."

Now I am aggravated by how much he is gaining and all that I continue to lack. "Moonsight," growls vibrating passed my beak, "I do not approve the fact that you are invading my life. It does not matter that you will not remember my thoughts. You know something I do not."

"I do not know if I should be the one to divulge such a revelation, yet I am still amazed you have not discovered it on your own."

His statement only makes me ever more disgusted. "As one under your leadership, I demand you reveal every fact you know of my health matter. It is mine to know."

I suffer a mood-alter at his words, not having experienced a wave of emotional shock in an extensive while. But the information, the phrase Moonsight gives me is not the result of a tragic cataclysm, but enrapturing joy. My mind will never cease to recollect this.

"Hollice, you are becoming a mother."

Scenic 2

Forge Ignited

I am alive within this moment somewhere between icefall and blooming season. Will it snow again tomorrow or will it continue to melt? I really do not know because this demesne is the quiet unpredictable home for a young Vulpine kit gathering firewood.

"I am so looking forward to a rewarding smoked meal," I voice while driving the saw through the last section of the trunk. Its friction is beginning to make me hot, but that only raises my desire for baked meat this evening.

Aligning one of the cuts vertically upon my splitting stump, I take the wooden ax spine into my black skinned paws and raise it high over the target and above my ear points.

With sight set upon the cut's center, I pair it with my mind to form proper coordination. Without initiating an additional thought, I bring the blade down in a 90° degree drop as it snaps the cut in two with a loud . . . "BANG!" The trees carry its echo as a beat from trunk to trunk before distantly dying away far off out into the meadows.

Before making departure, I gather the splits into a roped bundle and conceal my ax in its brush pile hiding place. Raising my safety goggles to my scalp, I spread my limbs and flex the extensions in preparation for the remainder of this day.

"Maybe I will need to summon my adrenaline to carry on." I put out to Lola, while grabbing the wood bundle. Always careful to keep my horse companion at a distance from the saw as well as the ax. Whenever I bring the wedge blade down upon stumps; the two halves and sometimes more, go flying in opposite directions, if not completely different directions. This is why I also wear goggles for extra safety because small splinter shards always fly around, especially when I must make several splits in a large or knotty stump. Thankfully, Lola and I have never harmed ourselves in firewood duty because of our safety.

This mare and I share a bond, but its depths are far deeper than being the firewood team. Whenever she carries me upon her back or rubs her head against my own, she is communicating by opening up to me in her own special way.

"Hmm," I purr, "a wild Vulpine kit and a full wild mustang becoming close allies upon our first meet."

In response, she gives that "Are you going to feed me?" look.

Barking in hysteria, I confirm, "Yes, as soon as our task is done."

"I am so hungry," she might say, "You and I have both worked hard labor this day, your belly must be the same as mine."

"That it is," I agree.

Stopping directly before the tree she is tied to, I climb its lower branches while gripping the free end of the rope in my paw. Focusing on keeping my paw pads gripped upon the branches, I make my way up to where I am now perched upon the branch before Lola's arching, blanketed equine back. Gently touching my toe claw upon it, I step from the tree onto the horse.

Hoisting up the bundle of wood presents the challenge of securing them over her saddle blanket by forcing her belly into deflating with a punch of my paw.

When she cooperates by pulling in her gut, I swing the rope underneath her and catch the end as it returns at the opposing side, then securing the wood bundles by tying off the free end with precision of not splintering her from above the saddle blanket.

As always, a great feeling of satisfaction comes over me as we depart because it is another challenge successfully completed. My panting breaths are strong from all the energy burning through my body. I am warming up just as is the season.

"Icefall is ending." I breathe out to Lola.

Despite the little bit of chill left in the air, I am breathing hard from working up a heat and my temperature is even affecting Lola; for I am able to feel the sweat on her back after mounting her. Ignoring that my rump is going to smell of equine, I make a sacrifice and massage my long bushy tail up and down her back, soaking the sweat into my thick fluffy hairs. Patting her side with my paw, I reassure "Not far now."

My sheltered home is located within great rocky cliffs of the region, consisting of not one den but many. Long before any of the living generations of Vulpine, we lived separately, divided by each individual immediate family. But then, a new time cycled in as unexpectedly and as suddenly as a stray's pregnancy: Predation of an entirely new species, the cat-raptors known as *Gryphons*. For the first time, predators were becoming prey because the Gryphons wanted the territory's largest meat, my Vulpine ancestors. Despite being omnivores as we are today, those Vulpine were top predators in the region until they became the prey to the new hybrid species. Gryphons grow to the size of their big cat mothers and fly even more ravenous than their bird of prey fathers.

The many broken Vulpine families eventually found each other in this most desperate time of need by coming together to form a single skulk. Breeding, hunting, and raising their kits; they claimed refuge of a maze-like interior of a rocky mountain cliff we now call the Labyrinth.

We were the first to discover the deeply dug dens and tunnels out of pure rock. But what was never discovered, is who carved them and with such smooth shaping. Like us Vulpine, the Gryphons could not dig through stone and are much too large to even enter the labyrinth; providing us with the security we so required.

"Yea, that is how my race of this region lives," I tell Lola. "There are other Vulpine out there who still live the majority of their life secluded. Personally my companion equine, I as a Vulpine prefer a life that is a hybrid of both social and solitary."

She may not understand everything I say, but she does read my emotions whenever I am positive or even negative. Yet, I am so much more to her than a link to delectable treats, and she is so much more to me than a large beast who hauls firewood. The first moment she and I met, we both knew at the same time that our friendship was meant to be as it is now. No one ever expected a Vulpine dog and a mustang mare to be so compatible. It has even occurred to me that no one understands our bond more than she and I.

Trotting out from the shaded forest, we enter into the remaining light of day. Casting its last rays upon the familiar cliff face of my labyrinth home. The underside of Lola's blanket is damp with the same sweat that is soaking my underside. I have learned that perspiration is how horses cool their warm blooded bodies by releasing "sweat" from their pores. I am unaware if I even have pores because we canids cool ourselves by panting in breaths.

"I work up a heat with cutting and splitting firewood, and then your humidity increases the warmth of my body temperature even more." It is only a tease, and she takes no offense on knowing that exactly.

Not only are the day's final rays illuminating all that can capture it, my sight catches the radiant shimmer of one who is viewing me with welcoming eyes.

Skylar, a fellow female Vulpine perches at the top of the cliff ledge just outside the high mouth opening. She is one of the few red Vulpine who has a golden coat, if she really is a red at all, which I am not sure of specifically.

I highly admire this vixen for she is both kind and beautiful. I cannot help but see her as a sort of authority or master because of her loving and knowledgeable nature. As I see her up there now, I feel greatly sheltered.

Upon approaching our destination, another Vulpine emerges from the dark labyrinth that I call my home den. This is not just one dog, it is Sparrk, our Prince and Lead Defender. His coat of traditional copper and white from the muzzle to the belly is most distinguishing. Behind this Vulpine's neatly groomed coat, I am informed a powerful warrior lies. Though I do not acknowledge the meaning of this dictation and have not bothered to find out.

"Fox, Lola," my Prince greets, "Your allegiance as the firewood crew is strong; just as powerful as the fire that will consume it this night." His stern but gentle paw brushes against Lola's side, and what a paradox it is to be both serious and docile at the same time. Untying the rope from around Lola and the bundles, I allow it to loosely descend to the earth below. Observing that Sparrk is able to rub Lola's belly arises the fact that I still have much maturity ahead of myself. He can easily extend his paw and touch it to the side of her torso, while at the full extent of my limbs, I cannot reach even the underbelly of the mare that is fifty times larger than I. Jumping clears that distance height, yet I still must rely on her or a tree climb for access.

Taking the first bundle by its tether, I easily lift it from Lola's tired back and then lower the splits into Sparrk's paws. Taking care in not splintering Lola or ourselves. We each take a load into the clutches of our paws and place them at the tunnel's entrance so to be ready for the night.

Returning my eyes to the high point that is now directly above me, I view that Skylar has set her focus upon a great distance high out over the treetops; she does this so often whenever deep in her personal thoughts, but even from way down here my strong eyes identify a change in her mood. It appears to be a mix between worry and austerity, but should it really be of my own concern? I am about to turn back to Lola when the sound of pattering feet reaches our ears, accompanied by a vocal announcement of . . .

"Hey! I am either late or just in time," a little blue-gray vixen frantically approaches on her hurried feet, baring a single fruit in her paw.

"Thank you, Tia," I respect in gratitude, "I had her pick this especially for you, Lola." She promised the largest available from the tree. Extending my arm directly before her, she dips her great head down to me and encompasses the malus with a touch of her lips surrounding my leathery paw pad. Once she consumes her treat we begin exchanging a quick goodbye.

Unexpectedly, she repeats a habit that has been going to quite the extent of time. She is viciously rubbing her head upon me in a vertical fashion as though attempting to rid away bothersome insects.

"LOLA!" I command with a strict bark from my muzzle and a slight thrust away with my paws, "None of that!" I declared. I have yet to gain the knowledge of why she does this, but all attempts have resulted in failure.

When the two of us have calmed down, I brush her forelock away and press my muzzle to the star in a sweet kiss. She is now taking an easy trod toward her own territory on the plain, and I let her off with a departure call of . . .

"Into the meadow and the maze until we meet again."

Scenic 3

Life Anew

Just as the disc casts its rays through the mists, shivers begin to ripple through my feathers and into my fur. I take a breath in pursuit of calming myself but cannot reply to Moonsight. Yet, I must force a rush of confidence and ask. "You would not deceive me. How long have you known and how did you gain the knowledge even before I?"

His silver eyes give me a serious stare as his wing feathers stand on end. "I didn't realize you lacked the knowledge until this morning. I even assumed you learned what to expect once conception took place."

"How many kits am I to expect?"

"If you would like, I will listen to your womb."

In ratification, I immediately accept his offer, "Yes please."

Gently he places his paw against my lower belly, feeling for any vibrations and any sound that may come up. "I feel life force apart from your own. Just as when I first felt the presence of my own kit within my mate."

"You are to be a father?" I inquire.

"I already am, once the youth is conceived that makes one a parent."

"So, you feel additional life within the body of a

mother?"

"Yes indeed," he confirms in the kind of voice I know to not forget. "And Hollice, I must now congratulate the remaining new mothers. So as my final question before departure, you do have a mate of your own?"

I bow, "I do, but I am outside his territory at the time." Offering to guide me back, I cannot refuse his obligation.

"Thank you," I return.

Draping his wing over my back and taking the lead away from the river, a frenzied emotion is arising deep from within me. The signals my body is receiving from my mind is stirring up the excitement of what I have been becoming from the first moment of conception; a mother, I feel it deep within me.

My mate, Evaron, always comes to me early in the morning, but I believe I was not here when he had. How am I to reveal that he is now a father?

"However I am to do so, it cannot be done here in the barrier." Rising from my bedding and returning onto my paws, I give my spine and six limbs a great stretch before departing back into the wilderness. The coastline and its sandy shore is my destination, as it is part of Evaron's territory. I have hopes I will meet him there, attending to Adelhied and her daughter by bringing them prey.

I am his chosen mate but he also includes Adelhied under his guard. She had given birth to her first kit only a short time ago with no one to call her mate. I do not understand why the father would not remain once she had conceived. The discovery of her pregnancy motivated her to come to us and request Evaron for a barrier to raise her kits. Of course he obliged to his longtime friend, dating back to before even I knew him.

The sky disc, with its warm touch cleared the mist by the time I arrive upon the western shoreline. As always, the repetition of waves comes upon Chromium's sand. Padding through the rough minerals, I make my way around the great cliff to where Adelhied's barrier is located. Within the thick rock it lies and the entrance opening being located before the shoreline.

Shuffling my tired paws through the sand brings back just about every previous occurrence of maneuvering through the thick soil. Kicking up the grains into your companion's eyes or even your own is quite the vigorous disturbance. As a kit, my sister and I experienced it first paw when we attempted to play here. After the mess left in our coats of fur and down, our longing for flight feathers greatly increased to our desires to become adults. But flying at the moment is neither in my strength nor motivation. The distance is unnecessary along with much of my energy being devoted to the kits now growing within my womb. All, or a good amount of it must be conserved for their upcoming future, and that of Evaron and I becoming parents. This same joy I will soon share with him is arising within me and even summoning some vital adrenaline. My devoted honor is so high right now I almost pass off a small figure catching my eye.

In the morning illumination, a kit is leaping away from the waves as they came for her on the sand. Avalon, Adelhied's daughter, alone and on her own? Having only met her once before, she is sure not to recognize me. With ears still quite flat and undeveloped, she does not take in the sound of my forwarding through the sand mounds. Most definitely, she has her auditory tuned into receiving the water's waves. As all kits are, she is grey with down in place of where her adult feathers will eventually grow.

"Avalon," I greet as she turns with a frightful gaze,

"I see that you have become successful at leaving your den, but without your mother?"

The kit does not answer whether she understands me or not. But the fact she is not looking directly but pass me is setting off my instinctive alert. The sound of wings on air swiftly approaches as it fills my ears with its recognizable sound. Yet, there is no call of announcement and no thud of a landing; meaning that the wings of the host are still airborne, coming at us to an extent of . . . stealthy silence.

I instantly reverse to see a dark figure descending upon us with talons unsheathed, ready for mutilation. The closest thing to prey in his path is the two of us. With sudden instinctive reaction I throw myself up with my paws spread and unleashing my own talons. This is the one way of defense against a mighty rival, by interlocking with your own predator claws.

This assaulter's strength really surprises me as he picks me up in flight and drags my form along in his painful grip. His points pierce into the tendons of my digits and I can only respond by giving him the exact same incisions. Upon releasing me, I collided over the face of a shoreline stone and dropped over the side into the cold shallows. Pulled into the shallows, chilling surges pulse out more adrenaline; the inducing adrenaline to protect my friend's kit.

Fighting the newly formed pain is a task all on its own as I force the return to my paws. Assisted by the onset of a wave, I return to the sand with blood now running between the digits of my newly scarred forefeet. Avalon and I spring forward and meet upon the sand where I accept her under my drenched wing for cover.

Refocusing my sight upon the attacker, I find him gliding out over the water and shifting back to our direction in means of making another assault. The four limbs set beneath the quadruped body with the mighty raptor's wings present the impossible.

"An Aquileia!"

Why, why is one of our own attacking? I have always been peaceful to my fellows, but here is another Gryphon making a deadly assault upon his own with advances exactly of predator upon prey.

I am ready for this next strike. With my battle-scarred form, I make the leap of my lioness ancestors and sever my talons into his neck. This causes him to collapse as feathers come away in my grasp and flutter into the air.

"I should not be battling," I realize, while my heart throbs heavily within my breast. "I am not fit in the maternal condition."

In truth I should not be locking talons with any Gryphon. We are not enemies toward one another, but here I am defending myself and Avalon's life. The moment I left the sand to meet the dark Gryphon in combat, she made for the cliffs in a slow but determined running crawl through what are sand mountains to her.

"Please reach your mother," I thoughtfully pray.

In the attempt to follow up and carry her in my beak, I am prevented as another set of paws crush me into the grains with a forceful gravitational impact. Quickly my enemy's shadow blankets over me, fresh wounds flow with blood that drip out from under my feathers and over the side of my beak. Moving at a speed my eyes cannot follow, he forces the tip of his beak into my neck; followed by my screeches echoing from the trees and into all proximity. I forced him off with a desperate thrust of my opened talon hind legs; but with one punch of his paw I am returned to the ground.

Fresh scars burn beneath my eye and near my throat. The exposed barbs had been included with the punch and now my golden feathers are fluttering in the shore's breeze. Coming to their final rest upon the sand where I now am. I do not know where I just found the energy to run, let alone the power to rise up; but I must use what remains of my strength to spiritually empower my body. Blood is now seeping from my own neck. I may not have long to live but neither will my kits.

With my physical form fueled by adrenaline and spirit, I clam Avalon in my beak and begin a steady bound toward her barrier . . . yet, that dark Aquileia pursues us at a greater speed. In my side vision I see its wings spread as he throws his massive figure upon me, bringing me back down upon the shoreline. Avalon slips away and runs the remaining distance, calling loudly to her mother. This will surely alert Adelhied.

Rolling over, I again thrust my hind legs into my foes belly, partially getting him away, but this villain is still going strong. The way his restlessly scarred body holds its ground is supernaturally creepy with its nauseating charge emitting in an electrifying way. I am so weak that everything feels peculiar, as though I am losing connection with my physical form.

My rival continues his creeping toward me with pit black eyes, feathers of discolored grey, and fur texture appearing still and inorganic. This is my last sight before my final passing. I can feel my final moments slipping away. This evil, tranquil Gryphon is here to take me out of this reality and painfully sending me into the next. Maybe it is best that I close my eyes and allow it all to happen. As afraid as I am of dying, I wonder how much harder it will be for my kits.

I hear them now, crying out from deep inside me, "HOLLICE!"

"No, please call me Mother," I plead in these last moments.

"HOLLICE!" My name yes, but not upon a voice from

within me, but a voice I know better than any other.

"Evaron!" I manage to voice upon the air of my remaining strength. He is only there for a moment before beating the silent Gryphon out of sight. Then another emerges from the trees, Moonsight. In only a number of moments, the fighting ceases as both males bring down my assaulter.

"Hollice," Evaron pants when arriving directly at my side. I breathe hard as he begins to fade to the point of no longer being able to hear him. The scent of the fresh water has vanished as well as its evaporation from my tongue. All colors are darkening as imagery passes into shapeless values.

Now they are brightening as the glare of the sky shines radiantly, in the exact opposite way it blacked out. Both scent and sound of water are returning and my body's pain depleting. Once new air fills my lungs, I rise from the sand.

It appears that I have lost much of my body heat— because right now I am frantically trembling with shivers.

"You almost lost your life." Moonsight breaks in, coming into view. He looks nothing like when I had seen him earlier in the dawn. Feathers are in need of preening. Colors are faded with a presentation of fatigue.

"Do not worry for me," he assures, "I have given an amount of my energy in order for you to live. I will regenerate just as you will." Adelhied had emerged from her barrier with Avalon and a belly bulging with the remainder of her kits to bare.

"My kit awakened me by coming into my barrier crying, I had no knowledge she had left." Whether or not this is anger, it all boils down into fear. Moonsight relays to her all that has happened and I add in my part for completion. While our voices carry, Evaron cleans my bloodstained feathers.

"I give you great thanks, Hollice. For defending my daughter. . ." Once Adelhied gives her gratitude, she transfers to Moonsight and questions, "Why was a Gryphon after Hollice and Avalon?" She strikingly demands with a worried glance over to the body of our attacker.

"Forgive me, Adelhied, but I do not know." Moonsight's eyes open and come to rest on me. My own eyes fall to my belly . . . are my own kits in danger as well?

"This Gryphon is not of our Aquileia," our leader informs, "his scent and body are far different from our own."

"A rogue outsider?" suggests Evaron. The first to answer is our leader, who responds, "Perhaps, or something more." He continues to calm and reassure Adelhied after my mate leads me away from the shoreline and into the trees. I agree with what was exchanged. This enemy is now dead and he can be buried and forgotten altogether. Our leader volunteered to take the task upon himself.

As painful as it is to flex my paws and endure my hot convalescing scars, I press onward at Evaron's side knowing it is time.

"Evaron."

"Yes, Hollice?" he replies keeping at close distance with a wing draped over my shoulders.

"Now is the time for a joyful relieving revelation."

Scenic 4

Instinctive

"Do you feel something?" Eternity inquires when she and I fall into conversation. The blue-gray vixen has her mind in strong focus at the moment with eyes fixed on something I clearly cannot see.

"Please Tia, specify." I invite by use of her condensed name as she is occupying her paws with pulling up grass blades. With gentle precision, she knots them into jointed chain and brings the ends together to complete a ring. Then she places it over the white tip of her tail, which is quite motionless with obvious physical behavior of fearful agitation. In an attempt not to pressure her any further, I hold my sight within the forest tree line. Patiently awaiting her revelation by holding my knees against my chest and chin rested overtop. Nightfall is nearing and the climate has passed out of its maximum and into the chilling drop. Unlocking the folds out from against my back, I open my wings and wrap the membranes around my folded legs.

"It is the adults," she continues, "They are so silent and withholding a single subject on their minds. A subject that burdens their hearts."

"And the subject is?" I plead with newfound - heart throbbing curiosity.

A S A P u b l i s h i n g C o r p o r a t i o n

"I only know it is the exact same thought they are sharing."

"Most astonishing," is my single response. Tia has had this advanced sensory as long as I am able to remember. Whether it is another's thought process, emotion, or foresight of the upcoming, she is always in preceded alert.

"It is, in fact, miraculous that you can feel such supernatural energies," comes an approaching voice of interruption, "Anyone within or outside the Vulpine sees that."

"I thank you for the admiration," Eternity says with a glance as Vykan emerges from the southern meadow.

"If you do not mind me commenting." He trails on, not waiting for permission. "The Prince is most secretive right now. I believe he plays a large part in all this."

"I am amazed you can see that," I mock with a drawing of his competitive gaze to me. His tail limply hangs to his ankles with the annoyance I have just induced.

"While we are blessed. Fox, you possess a curse. A pair of flightless wings upon a Vulpine is pointless with waste of conception. What creature gave birth to the freak you are?"

Now my spirit rages like the fire yet to come. I respond by leaping to my paws and unfurling my third set of limbs. Naturally territorial and instinctive, I set myself in a defensive stance before my opponent.

"Fox, you do not have to do this," Tia advises.

I know her well enough that she will not go any further than a suggestion. This is a battle both challenging and personal. Nothing rages in me more than one attempting control over me.

"I will not be taken advantage of," I tauntingly growl to the copper dog.

"Why is it dogs enjoy competition?" Eternity

inquires??

"The independent vs the territorial?" Vykan taunts with the domesticated raise of his opposable digit.

"Dog dual is approved." I snarl, followed by my great lung; forcing him off his paws at a speed not even I anticipated. However, he quickly reacted by nipping my wing, just enough to shock me out of focus. Then he takes the advantage and kicks me so far out, Eternity has to dodge out of my path. Rolling over back onto my feet, an action arises in my mind that is most clever. My hard intuition now fuels me with new energy as my mind links properly to my body. Muscles shift within my limbs and I transition to my four legged form. With my arms having become legs, I am gifted double strength and speed.

Galloping forward as does a horse, I advance upon Vykan, greeting him with a gracious leap and wings outstretched. His expression of astonishment only lasts a moment before I land upon him like a bird of prey, tightly wrapping him in my wings and restraining him almost entirely; his forfeit is closely followed.

"Defeated," he pleadingly struggles, "you win freak."

"Freak?" A new voice brings out. At its recognition, Vykan and I break away and come to attention before Sparrk approaches behind the gold pelted vixen, Skylar.

Dropping down to a single knee, she fixes her eyes upon either of us by being claimed in her sincere focus. She is a gorgeous Vulpine with a strong fertile body that shines of divine light, as well as a voice that seems to neutralize ones' negative emotion. Skylar is only a normal vixen, but her personality acts as a high power of authority to us kits, myself especially.

But right now, I notice that everyone has their eyes upon me: Tia, Vykan, Skylar, and Sparrk. Bowing my head, my eyes fall upon my paws, for I am on four legs while they are only on two. I had completely forgotten.

"What are you . . .?" Vykan begins, looking down on my quad stance in disgust. "You are nature's monstrosity."

"Vykan!" Skylar hisses with a head turn exposing her clenched teeth. By meeting her disciplined expression, my fellow kit instantly retreats back with head hung in shame. We always respect our females, but not because of their fragility; the reason is who they are.

Our fathers pass their life forces onto their mates where we begin deep inside their wombs, and later coming into their loving paws. As a dog, I give full submission to them because it is they who are the final key into life. This is what I have learned in my own life so far and why Vykan has given his own submission. But this is the first time I am connecting to the criticism of my form. Now, even I question why I am a Vulpine who bares flightless wings and can function on two or four legs.

"I do not know what I am." I declared to Vykan, "for I am like the single weed in a mass of grass."

I have no desire to make eye contact with anyone right now, but my eyes lock onto Skylar against my own will. But the emotion I see in her is apart from the awkward expressions of the others. Plus, I am producing my own surprise toward her charm. Why is she so positive while the rest are negative?

But in the midst of my fellow Vulpine, she is not softening my mood all that much. Not trumping on how embarrassed I feel toward Vykan's disgust, Tia's fear, and Sparrk's wide eyes and gawking mouth. This humiliation is negatively empowering while it burns through my spiritual side. Pulling my eyes away from them, I throw myself back into the forest as far as it will carry me away.

Scenic 5

Two Within One

The succeeding days are more at peace, yet I have no complete knowledge of what to expect from unborn kits. But then, what had Kyara done? The lioness, our foremother and the first of Aquileia. She must have been able to manage them, let alone being the first to mother Gryphons. But that time would have been much different compared to the present. Kyara is a lioness who fell in love with the eagle who became our forefather. What did she experience when carrying them in the womb that may have been the first to conceive a hybrid? I cannot envision carrying young that I would only share some physical appearance with. It must have been like giving birth to a bird from a mammal's body. However, we Aquileia have always been mammals. Many assume we are so because Kyara had the dominant gene compared to her mate.

My battle wounds have healed, but I am showing little development with my own womb only partially expanded. I have also taken notice of another great change; have not endured much pain since I had been attacked that night.

Proceeding out from my barrier, my temperature takes a slight drop just as I sing my voice out into a call carrying its echo through the trees. Only a number of moments pass before a shadow casts over and I sight wings through the tree branches, followed by Evaron landing before me.

"Hollice," he greets with our lovers' embrace, though we have long advanced into a mated pair. The purrs he now produces are drowning out my own thoughts and pulling me away from reality. Right now I feel that he is all that matters and there is nothing else I will ever want or need but my oakwood Gryphon.

"Your calling," he confirms, "is it of distress?"

"Evaron . . . I cannot feel them." Needing no further explanation to digest my meaning, he bows low and presses his ear between my flanks; listening for the life I dearly hope we have not lost. Only when returning with a rise does he meet my eyes again.

"I hear them Hollice. It is there, they are there." My head drops and I voice through a clenched beak.

"How can you be certain when I am the one who should be feeling?" Engulfed in his wings, he pulls me close and I trace my beak through his feathered chest. Taking in his scent, severely desiring his reassurance.

"You are still at an early stage of developing into a mother. You will improve, that is my promise."

My only reply is by deeply breathing in acceptance of his word. Guiding my return into the barrier, he allows me to collapse into my grass bed. "Please stay with me, just until I return to sleep."

"Certainly," he obliges, lying with me as I hold him close; embracing me in the comeback to my slumber. My mate passes his tongue beneath my eye, softening and preening the feathers. Only now do I feel another; another who cannot be seen.

The days now go by at a pace that slows time. I do

nothing but cast my ears out and listen to the birdsongs cooing from dawn to twilight, the squirrels chattering up and down trees, and even the waters of both the river and shoreline.

The fish Evaron brought me is all I have eaten, but the kit's dependence on nourishment is a great portion of my appetite. I have retired to the den until he arrives again with additional prey, but my body informs me that the time is near, whether a number of days or moments.

Sleep is a major priority and at times I am unsure whether if I am slumbering or awake. My nights are accompanied with infectious visions of seeing the same Gryphon who attempted death upon me. His sharp, prickling talons combing over my belly in bloody marks. I have no time to cry as they scar through my hide and into my womb. All desires are to reawaken out of this reality and into the one I have always known.

Rising to my haunches only grants more pain while pressing a paw to my belly and feel fur instead of open wounds. The pain is real however . . . and here. Lifting my body from the bedding only returns me to collapse out of balance by the eruption in my pelvis. The impulsion of pain is familiar as its source, my womb.

I am not prepared for this time but my adrenaline builds despite the fatigue. The many spasms pick up while I pace between the sides of the barrier. Each of my grunting breaths are for every throe pulsing from within.

"I am not ready, but my kits are."

Now comes a throe so strong, it brings me down instantly. Bravely spreading my hind legs to the unbearable pain, elongating my tail and digging my talons into the earth of the den, a final great bellow escapes my throat as something warm lands beneath me.

Breathing as I have not before, adrenaline continues

to pulse through my sore body. I almost feel too numb to hurt, but it is over—my womb is free.

A wail breaks the silence through the throbbing in my ears. I fall into the grass bed as the cries carry on and the scent of blood intrudes into my nostrils . . . my blood. My vision refocuses as my eyes rest upon a dark figure crawling through the grass in attempt of reaching me.

"How can it be over?"

There it creeps, the kit. The source of all the endurance of preparing for motherhood, is begging for the first time. Taking it in my beak for the beginning grooming is the result of our first contact. A Gryphon it is of six limbs and full of life.

"One kit?" I state in agitation while cleaning the liquids away from the infant, "Who only bares one, this is it?" I disgustedly protest, "Everything I have endured, for this helpless bundle?"

For so long it had been nothing but a disturbance, causing me nothing but depression during the carry. It prevented me from living normally, restraining sleep and rest, making me feel sick and helpless. Also, if I had not been hauling it around in my womb I would have been properly able to defend myself when Avalon and I were attacked. My reward is one ungrateful kit wailing like an entire mock to all my suffering.

I always knew I would fail against my denial. This kit is a burden, signifying this has all been a mistake. Believing I could raise one after having no knowledge of being a mother was plain ignorant.

"How have I been so foolish and psychotically insane? I am cursed with a single kit who proves to be my ultimate mistake."

How can I take pity for a creature that has caused me so much? The only good it has brought is no longer taking up space inside me; For these reasons, I have no love toward the bundle at my belly.

I have made the decision of giving it up. Once it is older I will grant it to another who can put up with it themselves. Until that time comes, I have to attend to its needs.

Flipping the kit over causes it to wail from being pulled away from its nourishment.

"Be patient," I order, "You're just a little agitating creature, aren't you?" It of course, cannot hear me with the reason being deaf and also blind. After a quick inspection, I allow it to continue nursing.

"A male, I have born a son. Now he needs a name, because I am tired of calling him it."

Now what is a proper label for a lone birth? He is on his own in isolated deviance, just like our region of Chromium.

"Chromium?" I suggest. No, that does not feel right. But after some minimal moments, I fashion a new name that is similar, yet different.

"I Hollice, name you . . ." I breathe out with it upon my tongue, ". . . Chrome."

Evaron is of course enraptured at the sight of our son. Even my sister Camira comes and comments on how much he resembles me. All Chrome does is sleep and nurse at a continuous pace, but I assume every Gryphon has at their newborn age. I am now producing a large amount of milk just for him, but it is natural if I bare again in a number of days, just as Adelhied did. However, my womb feels empty and I am not sure if I am disappointed or relieved.

The fact that I must remain in the barrier is by far the most dreadful part of all. I find that it is best to leave during his slumber or else he will wail and draw attention from the whole forest.

Evaron is now around more frequently and I prefer him at my side than patrolling the territory; however, I also prefer that he does not enter the barrier. I always enjoy being with my mate over suckling our son.

"You really should not leave him," he advises, "Chrome is totally dependent on you."

"As I am dependent on you," I bring up and give him a nuzzle, "we are only just outside, so I am not worried about him. I must stretch my limbs while he sleeps. I do wish I were able to fly, my wings are so restless."

"When Chrome is older," my mate offers, "I will remain here with him while you can enjoy some freedom from your demanding motherhood."

I bow, "It has only been a number of days since his birth. Already I am so irritated of being confined in the den. He does not even speak but remains a burden."

"A mother must make these sacrifices for the life of her kits," he reassures. "I cannot possibly inform him of my choice to give Chrome up."

"His eyes have not even opened. When they do I will allow you to be with him." With these final voices exchanged, I return to my vexatious life as a mother.

The days are now long and enduring but I am satisfied with my son's progression. Taking his first steps is a skill he has mastered easily. Being only a newborn, I am already taking notice of the masculine personality developing outward from within him. Any Gryphon would know he is full of courage and determination; but, what really intrigues me is his eyes, which seemed to be a random happening.

I had awoken late that day finding the dark spheres

open before me, seeing me for the first time with underdeveloped irises. Making me the first to ever cross his vision. In time, his eyes will color which can be quite diverse among every Gryphon. Wondering as he explores the barrier with his new sense if he might hear me. I breath steadily to call across to him in a soft voice.

"Chrome?" His ears lift at the new sense, along with the short tail flaunting in astonishment and downy draped wings trembling at their shoulder roots.

"Chrome," I call again, resulting with him making a jump. His eyes land on me with wings raised in a defensive manner. In moments he realizes that I am the source of the sound. With ears rising, the small paws now begin shuffling forward as they carry his small body over in my direction.

"Chrome!" The dark eyes gleam at the sound, "listen to my voice." Bowing low, I rest the tip of my beak upon him with continued verbal passage.

"Your name is Chrome and you are my son. I am Hollice. I am your . . . mother." In truth, he may be completely unaware that I am attempting communication with him.

"Will you ever understand?" Before now I had not given thought on how long it would take for him to learn by imitation. When my voice changes tone he immediately notices with a signifying arch of his head. "Well then," I begin, "you will learn our ways from another. Whether you understand that or not, I am stuck with you for now so just learn from observing me. You can be someone else's problem whenever I find the opportunity to get rid of you."

He is now massaging himself against my chest, pressing his ears to my breast and listening to my heart. Burrowing into my feathers he takes in the sound as though it is a continuous chorus of melodic beats. My son then begins to purr, possibly for the first time as well. Gazing down at him causes our eyes to meet. He is expressing what looks like complete confidence.

"Do not be deceived, Chrome." I divulge. Of course, he shows no sign of understanding. Running my tongue over my chest, I groom the feathers he had just ruffled up.

"You have no idea," I scoff, "how annoying you really are." Pushing him away with my paw I lay my head back down, "Please leave me alone!" I order, "I am in great need of sleep, possibly more than ever before." His only response are a few whimpers and I have no idea what the meaning is.

"You are going to have to learn that I cannot always be awake, plus, I thought kits slept a lot anyway." Closing my eyes, I use all the will within me to ignore his annoying behavior. Doing my best to rest, I put up with his beak pulling upon my ears and the excessive climbing upon my body like a hill.

"Come to me!" I call in an easy but demanding voice causing the small legs to carry him across the grass and over roots ascending uphill. When he produces a cry for me I realize it is caused by our growing distance. My pace is much greater because his squirrel sized legs are no comparison to that of my leonine limbs. He must learn to use them properly, so I am having him overcome every obstacle in his path. There were second thoughts this day about revealing him to the outside but I really needed to escape from the enclosures of the den.

I observe the kit while he draws a short distance away to a blueberry patch. Shifting his beak through the leaves and slipping his tongue out, he plucks a berry from the branch and takes it into his mouth. We Gryphons are carnivores but I have nothing against sampling other food sources. His ears and tail rise into a vertical position that reveals his simple enjoyment. He now knows of the sweet scent and taste because these berries are strong and literally block and conceal all other scents.

"Mother?" The distinguishing voice startles me, having only been the third time I have been addressed by the term. So far, mother is the only bit of tongue he knows.

"Did you enjoy the berry?"

His wings rise and the dark eyes scrutinize me. "Yes . . . Mother." Gifting a low bow, my son returns in act of imitation.

"You are very perceptive, Chrome, learning the ways of the Aquileia at a pace I did not expect." The limitedly developed mind is unable to translate my compliment; yet, I have recently learned of the kit's adoration to the sound of my voice, in constant awe at every vocal I make.

The blueberries granted me the opportunity to give Chrome a test that all kits must undertake. I have hidden deep within the plants, leaving a scent trail for tracking. The goal is to find me among the strong masking scent of the berries. It may be a complicated task to achieve with inexperienced senses, but the purpose is to develop sensory. Leaving the gray bundle alone in the shaded maples is the hardest part because we have never been so far apart.

Truthfully we have been together my entire life. When I had been no more than a kit myself, he was an egg within me. The days I had nursed alongside my sister; growing to reach full maturity to the time Evaron courted me. Chrome had been there, deep within my body waiting to be brought to life.

Out of the hundreds I have, only his egg had been fertilized. The life it has become is now here in this forest seeking me. After a time of remaining as calm as I am capable of, I begin to wonder where he now is. I hear his distant paws stepping through the plants and even saw them tremble from his movements.

I am still not making any movement until his cry echoes into the air. Leaping to my paws at the speed of a lioness, I tear through the brush and onto the source's location. The call produces adrenaline throughout the time my ears are receiving it. But why be afraid, why should I feel guilty of his harm?

I find him crouched in the vegetation with dark pelt almost concealing his entire presence. When the dark eyes find me, the form reacts by jumping at my arrival; every one of his breaths is accompanied by a tremble. Judging by the whimpers; he had been much too afraid of being apart from me. How had I not realized the fact of being too young for such a task?

"I am sorry, Chrome. I did not realize your inexperienced self." His shivers then become streams of purrs huddled close to my flank.

"Do not worry," I grasp, "I will find you a proper mother."

To not know my own son is proof of my failure as his mother. I am no more than Hollice, a Gryphon who had been wrong for baring a kit.

Scenic 6

Biologic

I am not sure of the last time I physically cried, for the hurt I now feel is withheld within painful absorption. I have returned to a place I love dearly, a great hill set between the forest and the prairie where I enjoy staring off into the distance in both the far and near. This is when I combine my mind with the environment and open it free, where I desire it to be.

But as serenely as I intend of unleashing the guilt and hurt from my brain, it clings upon my thought processing like a thirsty tick feeding off my guilt. That tick may as well be all of them who witnessed my alien stance. It was always meant to be secret after I discovered it by instinct alone. As comfortable as I am upon four legs, I knew others would view it far differently. But on the cause of my careless stupid mistake, I wonder if returning to the Labyrinth is even a wise option.

Sliding my forearms out from beneath me, I let my paws catch my muzzle as it lands in their cradles in shame. Functionality on two and four legs has great advantages, especially speed and maneuverability, but a pair of flightless wings is pointless to the extreme. I was taught to not take criticism and allow its downfall, but that task is so complicated when I have no one to share and relate with. Lola comes close but she knows as little as I do.

"I did not realize before that you meditate." I could have jumped at her silent approach but I knew she was there before the announcement. Skylar kneels at my side and takes a position of comfort as well. I prefer resting on my belly and supporting my head over my forearms. My tail is motionless because I am not in a happy mood even as I gaze off into the peaceful prairie sky with the descending disc. My eyes remain concealed behind their lids while I have not given her a single vocal; but she knows I am only faking sleep. Is it out of my fear or embarrassment? Well, they are the same emotion so I assume it does not matter.

But the moment she strokes the tips of her paws against my back, all focus breaks away. Her gentle massage slips between the roots of my wings, immediately healing my emotional stress. The vixen has a peculiar control over me, so strong that I always give in to her.

"I know you are disturbed," she clarifies, "and you may have none who can share and relate, but I offer to do my best in their position."

I may not know how to react to that revelation, but I can choose how. Communicating to her I begin our conversation with . . . "I feel you are only making that claim to ease me. Meaning that you are only pressuring from dull desire to comfort me." She now becomes silent just as I was, "And you are not succeeding," I add.

"I do not know then what to converse," she states in proving her direct honesty. She is not a complete psyche manipulator as I know many adults to be. Again, there is nothing I hate more than the attempt of control over me. I want to take charge and reject all who wish to enslave.

But Skylar is different. She may act as a master but there is something more to her higher authority. Her intent is serious, but that is paired with emotional love. The connection between us has been strong since my first beginning. It began with sharing the warmth of her body and the security of both the den and her emotion. When I was that immature she was everything I wanted.

When blind I relied on feeling her soft furry figure to reassure she was there. Before my ears could pick up sound energy, my nose guided me to her. Now I am a matured kit placing his paws forward to fulfill the dog's self-actualization. One of my greatest desires is to be self-independent and I feel I am working mighty hard toward that goal.

As much as I wish to separate from my homeland there is someone I just cannot let go of. One I care and love so dearly as she do for me. Impossible it is to shake both her emotional and psychological connection with me.

This Vulpine is Skylar and at times I ask myself, why? Oh yeah! She is my mother, my biological mother. But I do not believe such factorial based only on claim, it is literally inconceivable. But the stronger that question taunts, the more I desire to ask it. So I now start the conversation.

"I appreciate your honesty, Mother, and I wish for you to answer this question with only truth. Who is my 'real' mother? Whose son am I?"

Now she meets me with neutral intent as the question has startled her, yet she holds firm and remarks.

"Even if I choose to reveal her identity you will not believe me." There is a definite hint of sarcasm in her voice, but it is granting a calm mood.

"You are teasing me!" I accuse. Her taunts are strong as the gold vixen's binding have me in their grasp.

"I am taking advantage of your desire to solve my own mystery," she jokes, scratching her claws between my ears, a production of the rather playful mood she is in. Then the barks start passing through my muzzle.

"I barely believe you are toying with me like a game." As terrible as it may be, I feel like a pawn.

"Life can be rewarding when made into a game," she enlightens, "when presented a challenge, put all you have forward in order to triumph over it."

"A nice concept," I comment after giving her verbal some considerable thought. When a brief moment passes I repeat my question.

This time, Skylar returns to her feet and motions the tip of her golden tail for me to follow. Rising upon my own paws, I reverse and follow her down the hill. I only wonder how she feels right now, seeing me rise up on what are just arms to her; yet, a second pair of legs to me.

But I follow her in silence through the woods. I dearly hope no one sees me like this trotting along in quadruped, led by the biped vixen who I have called mother for quite some time. Of course, that is excluding my folded wings locked against my back. Most certainly, more than ever, do I feel we are not related. I wonder if I am even a true Vulpine.

I believe we have reached our destination once she stops before a great oak tree near the middle of our forest territory. Skylar changes position, now settling upon her haunches by bending her fore legs and resting her folded paws upon her knees. She elongates her tail and begins to drum it against the ground like a heartbeat.

I set myself in the roots to rest my back against a tree trunk and position my ears toward the vixen, ready to take in her revelation.

"I deeply assumed my mother is someone else. I have only partially accepted that I am different and desire to know my origin," fidgeting by scraping my claw points over the tree roots, I now conclude, "I believe you have the true knowledge."

"I do," the female acknowledges, now focusing sight and ear directly upon me. I remain under the tree as she holds out her paw and obligingly receives my own. Guiding it to the tree's roots it lands upon a series of deep scratches in the bark obviously made by claws of another.

"These were made by her when baring you," she then presses my paw against her lower belly and reveals, "It is here you began, Fox. 'I' am your mother. You fell from my womb into your father's paws and then into my own. As I cleaned over your blooded figure, I found your wings and was so remarkably astonished that a third pair of limbs conceived by my own womb."

Intentionally releasing a heated breath, I prepare a simple reactive action. "You are right, I do not believe you." This simple revelation is giving me an even greater astonishment. It is quite possible she is making this up in attempt to deceive me to a greater extent. But deep down out of my own common sense; I know she would not do so. Only her kit could know that, and I am he.

I feel like crying but as I said before, my tears are almost never physical. I came here to escape the humiliation of my quadruped secret thinking Skylar was rejecting me as well.

"Quadruped behavior is nothing to be ashamed of," she assures, "it is only a sign that you are as I intended you to be."

Right now my understanding toward her is quite limited.

"You must understand that it has meaning, just as everything else."

In silence, she lifts me from the ground and into the limbs she only calls arms. Mother does not yet want to break our chat so I carry on with a breath into her cat-like ears.

"I continue finding it hard to believe I even came from your womb. How could you produce me, how could a freak be conceived in a Vulpine's body?"

I am launching questions like bullets flying from the artillery of my brain, but mother, as she is now officially, returns on a most gentle breeze of a breath.

"The only true freaks are those who choose to be. By being immoral and following paths of evil and departing from what is truly right or against nature. Belief only has meaning when it is belief in what is right.

"Then what am I?" I beg in desperate anxiety.

"I have not raised you to be a that, but rather, the miracle that life is."

There is true wonder on how she is turning all my negativity around, granting me an entirely new perspective of not just myself but existence as well.

"Life is only a curse when you subject yourself to wrong. Only when you lead yourself into right is it a blessing."

"But how can I make flightless wings a blessing? A wings only purpose is to fly, right?"

"Only time and endurance will answer that question," Skylar concludes, "but I assure you that answer will be given and received."

I am about to continue the conversation but am interrupted when she takes notice that night is approaching. As the sky grows darker she is growing brighter; this is her most unique feature. Each individual hair upon her gold and white pelt is of a different texture than others. Each hair is translucent and allows a natural light to filter through. This light is what we call supernatural for it shines from inside her through every strand of white and gold. It makes the vixen appear to internally glow like a star in the night.

"I really am proud to have you as my beginning. Though I do not completely understand your love for me." Her folds produce a grin and expose the mighty canine jaws. Too embarrassed I am to grin back with my undeveloped teeth.

"The time will come when you understand love, Fox. I am in gratitude to reveal that I understand my own for both you and your father."

"Then I want to be like you!" I announce, throwing my arms around her neck into the welcoming embrace. I know that even my eyes are shining with excitement, accompanied by my tail wildly flinging about with revived joy, "May I learn and be strong as you are, mother?" The sensation to call her by this title is strengthened relief.

"Absolutely!" The vixen declares while I plant a gentle kiss on the side of her muzzle. My whiskers brush against her own and for the first time I notice they are her only hairs of black. Even they are illuminated in silver from her internals.

"Will I ever shine as you do?"

"That is another possibility you may inherit," she agrees, "I may have passed it on to you."

I will not argue and want only to please her. Along with my arms gripped around her neck I unlock my third limb set to extend outward in wrapping them around her shoulders.

"I do not want to be your burden, mother. I want to be your gift."

"That is who you are. But do not make yourself only my gift, but also to others."

"Like your illumination and my quadruped."

"Yes, there are even blessings we all share. Such as the power to bare new life from our own bodies as you were." Skylar's expression changes to a serious but calm mood so I instantly kick into high listening intent.

"Then there are the Vulpine bestowals we share, but are unique to each dog and vixen."

I give her no take, because I have no understanding of that last factorial phrase. Mother's voice has always entered my ears with ease; filling an empty space in my mind with something new. But now, my mentality cannot process nor translate this new meaning.

Finally, we touch noses and she finalizes.

"You will be receiving many new answers this evening my son. Have your senses open and I will do my best to help and prepare you. For tonight you will be opened to a new reality."

In my instinctive comeback I give a low but conforming bow. Hoping I understand her at least enough.

We depart from my birthing tree and make our return to the labyrinth, which grants the opportunity of showing her quadruped vs. biped. The amount of bliss on her expression clearly shows the high admiration.

"She is proud of me," I close out. But my head is burning with cold sable enigma, what is the meaning of being opened to a new reality?

Scenic 7

Role Play

The night is quickly approaching, Sparrk and I are preparing the wood I cut this afternoon by arranging the small kindling into a cabin style. This will give us the advantage in allowing it to catch. There is also something else clinging to my mind.

"I can now declare that your suspicion is correct," I tell Eternity who is separating the remaining wood in two piles.

"How?" she inquires.

"My mother and I had another chat. She says that this night I will be opened to a new reality. Do you understand that, because I cannot make sense of it."

My friend gives a twitch of her ears once receiving the message.

"I feel we will know the answer soon," Tia asserts while her figure sulks down accompanied by the deep bow of the neck.

"I detect your fear," I imply but fail to break her silence. She brings her tail around across her knees, remaining in a depressed state. Leaving Sparrk to finish the wood structure I approach my friend with incentive act of comfort.

A S A P u b l i s h i n g C o r p o r a t i o n

"I have known you long enough to understand you are extremely perceptive." That simple line of dialogue brings her head up and is followed by a teething grin.

"So you have faith in my instinct?"

"Absolutely! But are your feelings detecting something negative?"

Her eyes pass to one side the moment my question reaches her, knowing her unique mind is gathering its required data.

"My mind is working like multiples desperately attempting to form a unity. What I see about this subject is both good and bad." Placing a forepaw against her frontal lobe, she adds, "I feel totally psychotic at the moment, and just need some time alone. My brain needs to process this on its own."

"Mental pain," I enlighten, "It must be hard to do such advanced thinking when your mind and body are still early in development. You are still a kit as much as I, Eternity." Amongst all this stress, her expression turns to emphasis.

"Who explained that to you?" Now I go completely blank, for I know that out of my own common sense. There is no harm thinking beyond my capability as a kit. So to Tia, I honestly answer.

"Those are my own productions of the mind."

"Son, you reek like a horse. Lola always rubs off on your own hide." In a return off topic, I bring up.

"You are empowering my curiosity to solve the mystery?" Skylar hurriedly runs her tongue over me with intent to refresh my appearance for the night.

"Why, is there still another mystery, Mother?" I intervene as she continues grooming with bordering ignorance, "You have been secretive for as long I have known time. This time however, the level feels so different from all previous." Finally, she pulls away, tongue retreating back behind their black lips.

"Instinct," is all she murmurs in a tone I cannot decode. My estimated guess is praise or satisfaction. Once again, her tongue slips out but this time upon my leathery folds. I flex them out for proper cleansing that I cannot match. Her grooming is of expertise when compared to my lack of skill.

"Show me how you are able to shift between quadruped and biped," Mother pleasingly requests and receives my welcoming response. Distributing the power into my legs I rise up on my hinds and stretch my joints out far. When properly balanced a deep pop sounds in my knees followed by fully elongation my legs into the biped stance.

"There you are," I present. Her grin spreads out, visible even in the dim light of our den.

"Most remarkable, you prove me proud of your creation each new day," she continues on by coming to my side and running her soft paws over my knee joints, "I find that many of your muscle joints change whenever you shift. Your bones do as well?" She takes notice of all this while holding a blank tone. I think she is more mesmerized than disturbed. Maybe this closer inspection will give her a second thought to whether we are related.

"Yes, my bones shift."

"Wild and adaptive," that is what comes next in her voice. It is creepy as her claws run over the curve of my spine.

"Are there any other kits like me?" I ask.

"None that I know of."

"What about the kits you had before me?"

"No, you are not alike at all. The way your body functions is neither new nor unexpected." Now I am directly connecting to her with hungry eyes.

"Mother, you are conceiving so many questions in my brain. I am becoming overwhelmed with all the mysteries associated with you."

"There is so little I am able to reveal," Mother instructs, now cocking her head and narrowing her eyelids. Only ever seeing her do this when her attitude is suspicious. Instead of throwing out more questions like a crowd of spectators, I stay silent and remember that tonight many questions will be answered.

Wishing to depart from the subject all together, I free my mind and clear my senses with an utter of, "Will you please groom around my ears? I have the need of purification there." She approves at once and sets her tongue to work, massaging it forcefully against my scalp in a scrubbing but gentle caressing touch. I am clinging to her now, gripping my paws around her back with muzzle resting at her breast. The warmth and satisfaction she gives is the same energy I have known since my first beginning. Because she is my beginning. Only just today did I learn I am her son and my faith agrees to the full extent.

Upon entering into the night, I am welcomed by both the raging fire and tender venison I have craved all day. Selecting a deer leg for my meal I take to the fire ring to roast the tender morsel on the end of my crimsophilite. It is a unique tool made of metal telescoping blades which can be split apart to reveal a string and cables when transferring into the archer's bow. It is a gift my father passed on to his mate whom Skylar presented to me when the time came.

"Another gift I have," telling Lola only days prior, "is my memory." I did not know him, my sire dog, but his memory is one of the clearest my mind documents from my early days as a kit. He held me in his arms one last time before making departure, my eyes had only been open for a number of days and this just might be when I first received his visual. His masculinity is empowered by the firm cradle made by his arms withholding my minuscule self. The cheek-ruffs spreading out from the sides of his muzzle are a signature for us dogs, yet my visual traits are an inheritance from Skylar. I have her fur of gold and tinted silver white, but as I mature and transfer from a pup into a dog, my own furs will thicken out to expand into cheek ruffs.

When my meat is hot and tender, I remove it from the blade tip and crunch the points of my teeth into its moist flesh. Not caring how my pads and mouth are parched with burns; for I love my prey in this challenging way. The reward is an absolute overlay to the irritated skin. While I take in the much needed feed, all my content is in synch with mesmerizing the night fire burning away my wood cuts; loving the paradox of how something so dangerous is so pleasurable. Too much would destroy almost anything, leaving nothing but soot and stone it its place. Yet these flames are providing an addition to the taste of prey and the warmth many around are sharing with their mates, kits, siblings, or parents. Taking in the thermal waves and inhaling the burnt wood is joy filling my senses.

This fire is like a trustworthy companion here to comfort and protect me as a guardian. Only lasting until it has nothing to consume.

"What are you thinking about?" Mother intrudes.

"I want the fire to last." I divulge, "To me it is a close and comforting guardian burning away all concern into ash. Just its light touching my retinas calms my spirits into satisfying content. There is nothing I would change whether good or bad. If only there was an everlasting fire."

"Envision onward," she recommends.

Vulpine are a quiet race on the account that we just want to live on as much as anyone. Our skulk has had many fires such as this before, except the tranquility I am witnessing now is far different from any I have known. Mother has been this way as long as I can remember, now it feels her secretive behavior has filled the hearts of other adults as well.

Eternity and I have always wondered what takes place after the night's fire, and Skylar has not left my side or suggested I return to the labyrinth as she had demanded in the times prior. She is not alone with kneecaps supporting her thought processing head. Every dog and vixen settled in circular formation around our bonfire are grouped significantly together. Mothers and fathers sheltering their young in facial expressions I can only read as hurt and regret. Now my own facials are turning to suspicion. I do have the option to question Skylar but some supernatural feeling tells me not to, despite whether she would answer or not.

All I really desire is the pleasure of the flame's refreshing heat touching the bridge of my nose. The warm glow penetrates my eyes and fills my soul up in fiery sensation. Even the smoky smell of the tinder does not bother my sinuses. Conclusively, the result of these presences causes my tail to motion in true expression of a canid's excitement. Being that I am Vulpine, my tail is large, fluffy, and acting more like a flag in the cross winds.

Another part of me awakens, rising up and falling in tune with my tail motions and heart beats as though I'm not in control. For it is my sails that open up and miraculously begin to respond by fanning the fire. Many of my fellow Vulpine jump as it instantly flares up from excess oxygen, presenting its inferno touch against my black leather folds.

I feel I could truly fly.

Every one of my digits begins to uplift with

empowered desire, then advancing from an instinctive idea into immediate action. The fire rages up, its embers again at the same moment as I lift my whole form off the now descending ground. Roaring in delight at the feeling of first airborne with outstretched paws feeling nothing but smoke and ash.

But the moment my adrenaline heats up, everything backfires even quicker than it happened. Instantly I am overtaken by gravity and land in the catch of Skylar's arms.

The outburst of the Prince announces his approach at incredible speed. I am expecting a discipline or an angry rejoinder for the dangerous accident. But High Prince Sparrk only takes a relieving bow while placing a paw over his heart, then resting its digits again over my own. This is custom in Vulpine, touching heart to another's.

Sparrk then turns his tail and resumes position before the bonfire, ignoring any glares he is meant to receive. He and my sire are powerful allies and bonded friends. Whether he or Skylar is my closest connection to him, I do not know.

Many of the vixens are licking the soot clean from the brows of their young. There is no one harm beyond a few irritated eyes, but again my instinctive action was risk of danger. Thankfully, it did not result in the fire shifting from comforting to incinerating.

"You uplifted." Skylar praises by planting the strongest sort of kiss on my brow.

"You were right mother," my purrs mix with her own by forming a melodic chorus joining the crackling fire."

"Remarkable!" comes the frenzied voice of Vykan, Tia only a step behind.

I am at a loss for choice of reaction, so proclaiming in honesty, "The rush is just so much."

"You bet it is!" Tia agrees, "You are finally in control

of each of your limbs."

"Also," Vykan adds, "you dog, really are not the freak I thought you were." He is speaking to both Skylar and I directly as I follow his eye line to her. "You really impressed me just now."

"Thanks," I return with a toothy expression, "I am proud of what I achieved. But I will remain on the ground . . . for the moment." Skylar relieves me from her grasp to where I return thankfully to the transitioning earth from icefall to blooming season. My dosage of adrenaline has left me panting, leaving my cardio heaving with recovery.

Scenic 8

A New Reality

An odd tranquility has set over as many of the Vulpine retire to their dens in the labyrinth. Continuously, the circle diminishes leaving only Vykan, Tia, their parents, Skylar, and myself with Sparrk. Now noticing each of us he projects out.

"Have you chosen this to be the time?"

"Yes," they all agree at once by resting their paws upon our shoulders.

"Confident your kits are ready?" again they agree, but Skylar is silent.

"Do you feel your son is prepared?" he questions.

"I do not believe he is," she remarks, "but he must know regardless of readiness." Only a small moment passes before Sparrk contributes a bow of acceptance.

"Please come," he beckons us with a twitch of his whiskers. Drawing us alongside the fire where we position our bodies into comfort.

"With the approval of your parents, I now regard the three of you are at correct maturity level to learn our truth . . ."

I have known this peaceful life of simplicity as long as I am able to recall, but according to the adults I have only lived a small portion of it so far. This is what Sparrk is now enlightening upon.

"The lifestyle you have known from birth is all you have had up to this night."

I feel this to be a most significant revelation. Proving once again that both Tia and Vykan's feelings are true of something totally new taking place this night.

"I am ready Prince Sparrk," I affirm, "I feel we cannot progress any further unless you open us all into this new reality." That phrase had just now filled my mind, filling up my throat and flowing off my tongue.

"It is by far a different reality to you," he directs with a motion of his paw digit, "but it is far from new; having gone on long before anyone here was born."

"So," Vykan suggests, "we are about to learn a history from you?"

"I wish it were only history," Sparrk foretells to the dog while progressing out of disclosure:

"In the beginning, the demense were created for the purpose of life. The Vulpine were among the races to be brought into existence. Upon our arrival we were granted a special blessing that we each share: Advanced Adaptability. This means that we have an incredible ability to accommodate to almost anything natural or supernatural.

Some develop infinite advancement of their senses; to hear and see the unlimited into the extent of interactively communicating in ways beyond imagination. This bestowal is named the Vulpine Instinct."

Others did not modernize into domestication by almost entirely remaining feral and rejecting the change into tame creatures. They found life with artificial machines and unnatural styles too different. Choosing not to evolve into civilians, they continue nature's wild tradition of being retro.

These Vulpine who continue to live naturally wild have developed their gift of Wild Inheritance.

It is through these three bestowals that we mature and develop. Growing not by maturity alone, but by hybridization."

This one phrase, a simple five syllable verbal is bringing the nightly cold touch of this new revelation. Skylar explained that a new existence would be opened this night, but that nor anything else could have possibly prepared my mind, body, or spirit.

"We . . . hybridize?" Tia pants with awestruck eyes.

"It means we bond with another force to mature. As you progress, your mind, body, and spirit usually develop with one of our three gifts and you merge with that specific force to become a hybrid. You may be unable to control it immediately because it will happen when you are not ready. The hybridization is specific according to which of the three blessings."

"Are you a hybrid, Sparrk?" Vykan consults with absolute excitement.

"Not yet," he resounds, "we do not hybridize until the right moment. It is not yet my time; however, two friends here have hybridized."

Everyone instantly follows his eyes where they land upon Skylar and I.

"So, these are the result of my hybridizing?" I gesture with slight flex of my gliding limbs.

"Most definitely!" the Prince ensures, "there is an entirely new race of winged Vulpine out there in the demesne who have named themselves Actyx. However, the fact that you were 'born' with them is quite unusual. For it is within your mother's womb," he relays by giving her an approving glance, "that you hybridized all entirely before birth."

We are all accepting the incredible fact that Skylar was able to form membraned appendages inside her, yet have others done so in their own wombs?

"I have also hybridized," mother brings out. "Allow me to reveal exactly how I did."

Is she going to detail us about how she adapted into bringing me forth?

"My internal illumination is how I have advanced through the bestowal of adaptability. Every one of my hairs has become translucent, allowing my internal star light to shine forth. It is by the sorrow I have carried through life, that I gained the ability. Because I wanted to become a shining hope."

"So, you became exactly who you wanted to be?" Tia pesters in interest, "Getting exactly what you chose?" In admiration for curiosity, mother details.

"I am not sure we hybridize in that exact way, but I have become who I desired to be. We cannot always control how we transform, but we can control on how it affects our lives in becoming who we want to be."

"The one way to do so, " Sparrk carries on, "is to bond with the correct force meant for you. Once you are joined you will become hybridized; however, the body, mind, and soul require time to mature and become stronger."

"What happens when bonding with more than one force?" Vykan barks. Our Prince raises his brow addressing.

"I am most pleased you have brought this forth. When a hybrid bonds with yet another force they become a tribrid. This can also happen if a non-hybrid bonds with two or more forces at the same time. Tribrids are many while hybrid is only two."

Already, from what Sparrk has revealed in his short speech is of absolute fascination. But the little joy of his is only a forced type, why is he so down about it when these bestowals are most special? How was this so hard for him by needing to emotionally prepare?

"Our adaptability made us strong, powerful, and prosperous. We took life to a challenge no race had ever before. Rising to our own personal authority; many believed we were to dominate the demesne. But we did not want that power."

Sparrk takes a breath seeming quite sorrowful. Everything he has divulged to us kits is definitely positive. I can now even see that both Tia and Vykan have this . . . Vulpine Instinct, while I am sure I have the Wild Inheritance.

"You're sad," Tia brings out by taking notice of the Prince's change in mood.

"What is it that is wrong?" Vykan requests in concern.

"I have no way of preparing you, but never have I been unsuccessful with the generations preceding you. The only way I can prep you is by first giving you this knowledge. Information that is new to only yourselves. Revelations from a past deeper than any of us here, now to be incorporated in your lives for the first time."

"If you do not feel fit to do this, Sparrk . . . we will tell it ourselves." It is Tia's mother who offers to the Prince as he makes no immediate answer.

"Feel free to add anything to what I am about to convey." He approves with a bow and an exhale escaping into the smoky air, "I welcome any of your participation."

"Our blessing struck fear into other races. Becoming so powerful caused others envy, leading into hatred." Sparrk reassures that we are granting full attention before clarifying.

"The final outcome was genocide."

I do not need a reference from anyone to know this meaning.

"Extermination was plagued on us just because of covet?"

"Yes," he clarifies in verifying Vykan's declaration. "Whether fearful, jealous, or with hatred; few wanted us around. Our great eradication came into existence with the desire for us dead, or for our power."

"Are there none who respect us?" Tia pleads with fearful desperation in her voice.

"Those who accept us, are minimal. Hiding out and only helping us in secret. If caught, authorities do away with them in similar retaliation. That is why we live outside the city of Gauntlet where many domestics help us, whether among them or here in the wild." Yet, as good comes out of even the most terrible of events, our attempted extermination was no different." Now our Prince has captured our attention by famishing our curiosity.

"Oh what could this be?" I ponder while impatient as never before now.

"I remind you that we Vulpine are the creatures of adaptability, and our miraculous adaptation kicked in when the genocide began. Something that fought against death itself."

The three of us are lock jawed, for we do not have an idea what is coming next.

"The Vulpine adapted to immortality, the immunity to death." His phrase is much like an electric charge conducting a current between my body and soul. It is Vykan who breaks this most awkward silence.

"You are presenting, Sparrk, that we cannot die?"

"That is the way we now know it to be. Our bodies develop from the smallest kit to a full hybrid or tribrid. But our physical mass refuses death."

"But our minds, bodies, and souls continue on." Skylar adds in, "Refusing death because of our endangerment, and also continuing our developmental hybridization. By becoming stronger while our vessels remain alive."

Sparrk gives a validating bow and details. "Many have a hard time robbing us of our lives because our bodies reject death and cling to life. Wounds that prove fatal will almost always heal. A Vulpine who is stabbed through the heart will indeed pass out but once that blade is removed, his flesh and bone will regenerate and heal. Later on when it's convalescing is through, he will awaken and continue on."

"That is great to know!" Tia brings out, "We will live forever as long as we remain endangered. Either way, we will prosper."

"I wish it were that simple, young vixen. But Castige proved our immortality is indeed limited. He somehow was killed, possibly because he gave everything of himself to defend the innocent."

Sparrk now tells of Castige, the first Vulpine ever to use his gift of immortality by rebelling against the genocide. Using anything and everything he had to defend, the dog fought to his last end. How his immortality expired is totally unknown.

"But if we really are immune to dying, how is it that he did? What reason does our eradication still exist if they know we cannot be killed?"

"Our enemies have shifted to another motive. That being to have total control over our supernatural powers, enslavement, but especially, sterilization."

Tia's question is the one I also have, and most likely is the same for Vykan. None of us know the meaning of the term our Prince has just used.

"They have a hard time killing us, so they see to make sure we do not breed. By taking away our fertility and reproductive ability."

Okay, now I am frightful.

"Couldn't . . .," Tia falters in tongue, "our bodies just heal and regenerate?"

"Not if it is removed entirely," barks Sparrk. "That is the meaning of sterilization. They cannot kill us so they make sure we cannot repopulate. This is why you all have been raised far and hidden from all this. So we can protect our future generations."

Our Prince now brings his paws together in final conclusion along with a gentle motion of his tail. Relieved he is, to have overcome and passed all this information onto the three of us.

"Now that the three of you know our history, as well as our survival lifestyle; it is time for you to decide which blessing is your lead." Something is prickling down my spine by causing a twitch of my tail. This is a final request from our Prince who is obviously closing with his final action for these great revelations. I am as sure as the Vulpine Instinct apprises me so. "Wait!" I rebuke, "I have the wild inheritance."

"There is a great refuge for us remaining Vulpine. Its name is Scorpula and it is there in this great city we are building up our hybridized strength to rebel against our enemies. Vulpine and those in allegiance travel there and train their gifted selves into skilled hybrids and even tribrids. Continued adaptation to what only strengthens us is the solution to our survival."

Taking the nail of his paw, he traces in the dirt depicting three rings side by side. Once adding a line spreading over top, he expresses.

A S A P u b l i s h i n g C o r p o r a t i o n

"Every Vulpine has the three gifts, but we usually develop only into one. It is up to you to discover which is clinging with you." Beckoning us forward, Sparrk touches each of the rings by identifying, "Vulpine Instinct, Wild Inheritance, and Advanced Adaptability."

"Test yourselves and touch a paw to your specific ring."

Vykan and Tia both touch Vulpine Instinct, confirming my guess. Her energy awareness and his strategic mind are definite proof of their empowered senses. Now is my time to place my paw in the Wild Inheritance circle. Flexing out my arm of a leg at the shoulder and elbow, I hold it overhead in immediate preparation for decent. But the whole process is halted as an entire charge of paralysis overcomes me. Beginning from within my soul by traveling into both my mind and senses. I attempt at Vulpine Instinct, followed by Advanced Adaptability; but neither feel right. All their eyes are on me as I falteringly struggle with the supernatural sensation, only when I instantly retreat back does the numbness do the same. Feeling returns to my limbs by a charge transmitting from my paws tips and into my abdomen. This sudden reclaim of motor control is as quick and unexpected as when it retreated. I may have collapsed if not caught into my mother's arms for a third time.

"What's wrong, dear?" She is the only one to bring it up, but everyone else has equally questioning expressions.

"I do not know!" I bark with a growl, but it does not satisfy their hunger for answers. So I detail "Honestly, I do not know which gift I am growing with." Before anyone else, Sparrk breaks the tranquil atmosphere with . . .

"You may be the most unusual Vulpine I have seen brought to life," he comments, "but that also means you will mature differently as all of us do. In time you will gain the knowledge you desire." This advisory declaration is closely succeeded with, "I have revealed to you just about everything, but you must progressively learn the remaining yourself. Additionally, give yourself time to think and choose if you would like to advance in Scorpula, remain here, or even another choice. Yet right now, I see you need to rest your growing bodies. Put them to sleep and gain the energy you need for your next awakening." Sparrk's finale follows with everyone retreating into the labyrinth to get the rest he has advised. But I am remaining right where I am; Skylar has not left either.

Scenic 9

Adventurous Curiosity

Frenzy pulses through me as I trek in Hollice's path.

"Chrome, keep a steady pace. You and I are both required to attend this gathering."

"Yes Mother," I announce in understanding. From what she earlier explained, the description was most accurate. Fellow Gryphons are all circled before a stone ledge jutting out from what mother calls a mountain. It is an expanding mound of stone ascending high up into the clouds. Despite the loose appearance of the numerous stones scattered along the slope, they all remain motionless right where they are.

"Chrome!" comes her call from the place she has taken among the others. With a motion of her wings to bring me forward, I react by sprinting to her side.

"Stay close!" she orders.

As the mountain releases its chilling breeze, shivers ripple through both my fur and pierce through the down of my wings. Attempting not to fret over the chills, I instead focus on my surroundings. Learning that many other Gryphons exist outside our kin really came as a startle, but I had not imagined so many.

"Mother," I bring up, "how many different

Gryphons are there?" From above, she lets out and irritated breath with a dip of her head.

"If you really must know, we gryphons are the result of large cats and raptors. Tiger Gryphons are the largest with striped pelts, gold lion Gryphons such as you and I, leopard Gryphons with spotted coats, then the smaller species of cougar and jaguar with solid brown and black pelts . . .

"Is that all?"

"No," she continues. "we also inherit from our raptor parents as well. Whether eagles, hawks, falcons, or owls, it is their feathers and beaks we get. At times our fur and plumage colors blend together into each other."

Making use of what I have just learned, I begin to take in the many around us. Though I do not remember specifically all of them, I at least define their appearance.

The tiger descendants are noticeably larger, with pelts designed black, white, and orange stripes. Many other Gryphons are solid colors, such as different shades of brown, black, and gold. I also notice the different combinations of both fur and feathers—both of solids and patches spreading across their heads, necks, and into their wings. The owl Gryphons have noticeably smaller beaks with wide set eyes apart from the others who have the exact opposite.

Comparing myself to the mature Gryphons, I find that I bare the gold lion pelt of Hollice. Currently my feathers are of grey fluffy down that will not give color until after my fledgling feathers develop. How long it will be until I have a bright plumage is completely unknown.

It is not long before my chills reach the extreme and my trembles intensify, resulting in my being clamped in Hollice's beak and carried to the ledge Moonsight will occupy. It acts as a shield against the breeze that mother seems absolutely unaffected by – as she settles her golden body in the grass. My father told me that I must rely on Hollice until I am able to control my body temperature. Chromium, Hollice calls our region, is never defined as warm; but I hope to bond with the climate as I mature.

The bleak flesh penetrating air is only reminding me of my hunger. My body has exhausted its calories and I require both shelter and restoration. Crawling beneath my mother's wing, I press myself to her body with intent on sharing her warmth. She has always been my heat source, but I also loved to lie at her belly because of the milk rich mammary I have nourished since birth.

It is easy to recollect the first time I learned of her presence. I had been exposed to the cold for the first time and the only senses I had were touch and smell. With her scent first coming to my nostrils, I became dazzled and immediately knew I needed to reach her.

Wedging myself beneath her belly to quench my thirst causes mother to roll on her side, finding me with aggravated disgust.

"If you must nurse," she scolds, "get it over with."

I have angered her again with a plead of, "I did not intend to wake you mother." I know how tired she has been lately, despite her golden eyes turning hostile with strengthened rage.

"Then cease your chatter," she viciously suggests, "that would really help me get some rest." I shy away, stared down under the piercing gaze. To quarrel against her is wrong as well as making her mad. With no more exchange, I latch on to my favorite nipple and begin to nurse. With the little bit of satisfaction to my hunger; I continue to wonder when Moonsight will arrive from his mountain dwelling. How is it even feasible for a Gryphon to live in a region so different from that of his own race? The idea of living alone is even more depressing.

Time has gone on even before coming out of sleep into consciousness. Still warmly compelled between the wing and body of my mother; It is the echo of her voice that has awakened me.

Leaving the protection of her wing, I return into the chilly mountain air. The disk has now passed over close to its midday high point. More Gryphons have arrived, emerging from beneath the tree branches as well up from over the tops. Some are quiet or socializing with each other, yet my attention is already claimed cause my ears are receiving high frequency vocals; that of other kits.

Beneath the shadowy branches settles a tall female accompanied by three surrounding her. For the first time I am seeing kits apart from myself. Do I look as they do with discolored spherical eyes and beaks of black? It is alien for us to know our own image, only a few times does the sky disk shine accordingly over a rain puddle, presenting us with a true but rare reflection. My day to see myself is yet to come, but I am focusing on one particular kit definitively shimmering out among her playmates.

Shining radiant, pouncing upon her companions with speed that of a warrior. My eyes are also having trouble registering her value, being this is the first I have taken in a color my mind is unfamiliar with. It almost hurts my irises along with the strenuous task of filling it in the documents of my brain. Her appearance dazzles me so much that I am feeling the palpitations of my heart returning the heat to my body.

"Chrome," Hollice voice intercedes into my thoughts. Drawing my attention; I realize her notice of my occupation, "Does she amuse you?" Mother pesters.

"Yes she does," I validate in honesty, "but what color is she? It is not like the tiger Gryphons, this is a different shade.

"Crimson, which is indeed a rarity in Aquileia. She in particular is irresistible to your eyes with unique appearance further filling your attraction."

I gift a bow revealing my understanding. "Her color, it . . . passes through me like a divine wind," I admit with somewhat of a blush, "though, she may not be as beautiful as you, mother." A breath now escapes her.

"Chrome, there is absolutely nothing wrong with your affection toward her. It is only your natural intention." For the first time her mood shifts into humor, accompanied by a glow in her eyes I have not ever seen before.

"She may feel the same way toward you," she mocks. "Oh yes, I would not at all be in alarm if her heart leapt within that small breast just from the sight of you, the same way you are reacting."

I give no verbal response by transferring away to resume watching the kit prowl upon the others. She truly possesses the strength and speed of our ancestors. The largest of these kits is feminine by the appearance and I really take notice of how she resembles the adult.

"They must be mother and daughter," I conclude. "Yet, where are the mothers of the other kits?"

"I know her," Hollice brings up, breaking into my concentration.

"Who, the kit?" I return.

"No, the mother, Adelhied."

I settle before her in arisen interest as she proceeds.

"Adelhied has been a friend of Evaron since the two were kits. A time before you were born, she came to us and revealed that she was expecting. In fact, she was alone with absolutely no support."

Had I received that correctly?

"Mother, how can she not have a mate? You just brought up her own motherhood."

Her golden gaze turns fierce with a penetrating glare. In the short time we have been mother and son, I have learned anger is the emotion she uses most frequently. She hates my disobedience and constant pestering, but her hatred toward interruptions is exceptional.

"Forgive me mother," I apologize with the deepest bow I can physically make, she continues after a brief pause.

"Adelhied begged your father for a dwelling within our territory. She desired a place to raise her young."

"Another mother within our territory, with a kit," I am now joyful to the full extent of excitement.

"She now lives on the far side of the territory along the shoreline. "If you wish; we may visit."

"Please mother," I beg again with a low bow, "I really want to be with other kits."

"We will," she promises.

"How are you Chrome?" requests a gleaming, pine green eyed Gryphon settled on the opposite side of mother. Her bronze feathers and the golden pelt are easily distinguishable by baring a likeness to Hollice. While I hold my gaze to her own, a recognizable scent comes to my nose; yet, I still do not know her.

"I am not sure, I have not thought about it."

"Really, that is a most interesting reply. Do you know how he is, sister?"

"Sister?"

"Yes Chrome, your mother is my sibling."

"Sibling?" When she takes notice of my misunderstanding, she enlightens, "We share the same mother and father."

With a raise of my ears, what slips past my beak is . . . "I had no knowledge one could bare more than one kit. In truth, I do not have what you call a sibling."

"I am aware of that," she acknowledges. "Chrome, do not feel depressed that you are alone. Your mother will have many more chances to conceive, you are only her first." My heart jumps at her words. Turning to Hollice with my wings raised I plead.

"Mother, is what she claims . . . true? Will you conceive again?" Her eyes seem to darken their value at my approach, and I feel grief radiating from her.

"Mother?" she turns away from my gaze.

"It is . . . possible. But my lifeless eggs are not of any concern."

"Lifeless." I realize. Her eggs are not living as I am, but I desire that she give them life. I want kin, another kit to mature alongside me. Those kits are not only companions, they are siblings; sharing Adelhied as their mother. A life I cannot help but feel really left out of?

At times I desire to be suckling from Hollice with another to share with. Worst of all is when I am left in the barrier alone. Whenever mother departs, I burrow beneath the grass bed to where I shiver beneath the torn stems. Whether it is from the cold or the fear, I am not sure. It would not be near as bad if I did not have to endure it alone.

I am unable to ponder the deviated life I have been given, for a loud call erupts from the mountain that sidetracks all focus. Descending from the slope, my eyes sight two distant pairs of wings.

"Gryphons!" Moonsight has arrived.

He makes a rough landing upon the ledge, impacting with such force I feel a slight vibration in the earth. Once he folds the majestic wings at the sides, the metallic gaze of those silver eyes scrutinizes every individual Gryphon present. I am not abruptly prepared when his voice calls loud with clarity.

"I give you all great thanks for attending this gathering. But to answer your assumption of inquiring just why you have attended," Our lead's expression now turns serious, for those eyes are concealing something that is about to surface.

"A time before now . . ." he proceeds, "one of many blessings originated upon our region. My mate bore our first kit: a daughter. Only days preceding now . . . she was taken and death followed her." Bereft is falling over the gathering. Indeed, I also grieve over this happening.

"However, this is the second occurrence of rogue Gryphons preying on our young."

That statement causes a great flow that turns every purr into a tremble. I feel that fear has reached its maximum, for I am seeing mothers strengthening their guard over their young, while many others are casting glances all around.

"Acknowledge me when I say, I do not know who these Gryphons are or where they originate from. Only that they are not of our Aquileia."

Now I see two sides dividing among us, in either relief or grief of not believing him at all. Camira and my mother are silent, but I do see a blank expression upon Hollice.

Moonsight would not lie, he is our lead Aquileia.

"We all know this is the first evil of our generation to fall upon Chromium, and I believe anyone is susceptible to harm. Vulnerability is even greater when the sky disk sleeps. Again, my daughter was not the first victim," his eyes now land upon an individual to the far end where many eyes follow the destination of his own gaze—Adelhied, "but we all are more than willing to defend our decedents."

His revelation that I am at risk does creep me out. Yet, fear is something I do not entirely understand; but, what is occupying my mind at the moment is Moonsight himself. The Gryphons who killed his daughter . . . who are they? Also, the way he had laid his eyes upon Adelhied sparks my curiosity; suggesting there has to be a connective conclusion. I must know, and to learn that, I must converse with him.

Creeping away from Hollice and Camira with cautious paws, I have sighted another ledge that will provide access to the above level. Taking a lion sprint to its base, I launch my muscles through the air, but only manage to get my forepaws over top.

"What purpose do you have of being on the same level as our leader?" The voice almost causes me to slip from the firm grip I have on the rock surface. Pulling myself up and over the stone, I turn and face Camira.

"I must consult him, please do not reveal this to my mother." The female passes a breath and takes a long gaze at our leader. I had not been giving attention to what has occurred.

"I wish that all our kits be battle trained. It is right they are given knowledge of defending themselves and each other. Because there are Gryphons entering our territory and acting to kill our young, we must all be prepared to defend." Several bows are given to ratify his proposal.

"Our leader lives among the great heights," Camira communicates in reference to the mountains, "commonly flying through them and seeing beyond the far side of Chromium. We have learned much from him, and you will as well."

"Then I have your approval?"

Exchanging a bow, she leaves me.

"Moonsight shall treat you as his own. Remember he is your lead and you must use absolute respect."

Rocks are hiding my appearance as I sprint along the

mountainside when rounding a large boulder, and finding Moonsight directly ahead; though I will not make my presence known just yet. Instead I will confront him after the gathering's completion. Settling in the shadow of the boulder, I listen as the conversations proceed.

"I presume that we engage our young in a series of competitive tasks against one another; consisting of endurance, strategy, and development of both defensive and battle tactics."

"A tournament?" states a voice from below.

"Exactly. I feel we are not properly capable of defense because we have not required it in our existing generations," from below, I hear both vocalized agreements as well as satisfied purrs.

"I ask that every kit be enrolled in this tournament and all must train. Guides apart from parents will be assigned and chosen. When the kits are ready, they will compete against one another." My ears are rising at this opportunity.

"This will also be done for our future generations. That is the reason I am promoting it for the life and future of the Aquileia." Giving one last great breath, he questions his spectators, "Finally, I ask of you all, is the holding of this tournament in your verification?"

Melodic vocals place a satisfied expression in his eyes. My generation is first in this new tradition.

Determination for consultation has not diminished, but my body heat has. Cold temperatures maintain within the earth and stone beneath my pads. Chills creep up each limb because I am still not capable of controlling my body heat; that is why I have Hollice.

It is strange she has not taken notice of my absence. My ears would have received her call, but it has not rung. I always want her around because of deep desire for closeness.

Finally deciding I am no longer comfortable in this position, I rise to my paws and quietly pad away deeper into the stones. Until Moonsight completes the converging, filling my curiosity by exploring the mountain base will suffice.

These rocks reveal many hidden shadows despite not knowing what they are hiding. This small part of the mountain is only a small grove of boulders within this great forest of stone. Each one abnormally shaped with sizes ranging from pebbles to the shaded mass of boulders.

I screech when burning pain comes to my paw's underside, sending a spasm up my leg. Lifting to examine the pad; I find it scarred and releasing a red liquid.

"Blood!" This is my first ever visual of it; a fluid of lustrous scarlet brighter than the pelt of Adelhied's daughter. Rasping my tongue over the wound, I seal it in saliva while tasting its bitter and salty metallic flavor. This was obviously caused by the small sharp edged stones lining the mountain base. Never before today have my paws left the soft forest earth.

This being the first torn flesh in my life, I instinctively pressure it by biting with my beak. Father taught me that both these actions are key to treatment of open wounds of the flesh. The best action now may be returning back, but my desire to explore is ever tempting. My leader lives high up into the summits, how is it that he does? Is his hide so strong that it rejects harm? Remembering the Rogue Aquileia, I see it may not be best to press on. Turning in attempt of retreat, I am about to comeback when shadows eclipse the light in my side vision. I have only time to sight a black figure and the beak making a grab for me.

My bloody paw bursts with talons and it swipes

across his face just as fast as he meant to snatch me in predator's grip. From the wound I have made below his eye bursts out blood as I rip the feathers away. Before my mind can even react with a plan, my body carries me away at astounding speed; fueled by both adrenaline and fear. Now I am among the Gryphon kits who have escaped the malice of the enemy Aquileia.

Scenic 10

Sable

Now I know what fear is as the shadows grow like the speed of my racing paws, carrying me deeper into the stones and up the mountain slope. Rounding another large boulder presents the ground falling away into cold darkness. My one injured paw collides with water momentarily after the decent, snapping at the ankle joint by impacting the ground beneath. This pool is no more than a puddle colder than the chilling air.

My fall has led me into a cavern, light rays down through the hole while the rest of my surroundings are mostly dark. The surface hole is the one sign of escape; but my waterlogged hide would weigh me down even if my paw was uninjured. Calling for Hollice is the logical option; she can hear and distinguish my voice over a great distance. Yet, my call will also be heard by the same Gryphon who I fled from. My instinctive reaction of escaping his clutches has led me to here; trapped underground with a scarred and numbed leg. I am now more vulnerable to any type of attack.

I intend on finding a dry surface as I limp through the water on only three paws. Finally, I do touch dry cold stone that marks the end of the pool's hypothermic temperature.

A S A P u b l i s h i n g C o r p o r a t i o n

I shake my body all throughout and rid my fur of as much water as possible; this is followed by rapidly flapping my wings in a bursting spray of droplets.

Collapsing on to the caverns floor expands the stress of my limb by returning yet another numb spasm. Holding it out before me, I inspect the pad in the available light using my night vision. The outcome the water has in soaking my fur really creates a stinging effect on the flesh beneath. Neither the sprain nor the scar are threatening, but the injury prevents function of my jumping ability. Thus my escape route is blocked.

Endurance of the cold water coat and cry of my lifeless leg would not be unbearable if I was not alone. The only comfort I have is the disc casting its rays through where I fell; revealing hope. Hope that I am not alone, hope that is diminishing.

I want sleep and I welcome it entirely as it overcomes my form and all its sensory, taking me down into slumbering shades of dark tranquility.

Hollice describes night visioning as the mind roaming free, leaving the body at rest. Night visioning is only feasible during sleep. It feels as though gravity is no longer existent while releasing the air free. My sights, nothing but blurs of warm color so bright, tears escape between the lids. When my internal warmth returns, I welcome it with great affection. But now while I am returning to consciousness, the memories immediately follow. My intended quest that brought me close to the enemy and into the deep cavern is all present in my mind, but how I am here again on the surface shows no path to this conclusion.

"No, it could not have been a night vision," I recall, rolling over on the warm stone. The sky disk blinds my eyes but I can do nothing other than greet it as well. Moonsight remains on the ledge where he continues to converse with fellow Aquileia. They have long passed from the tournament subject and now are discussing the current birth rate of us Gryphons.

"How?" I am not with Hollice, but here again awaiting my desired chat. My pelt is clean and dry, groomed not by I nor mother. But astounding most of all is that my leg produces no pain. A strong flex of my joint proves its function is as well as ever. Remembering the pad, I hold it to my eyes and find the deep scar. The dried blood locked beneath the flesh in a fresh saliva sealant, proving this was no night vision.

"It all happened," I accept, causing a burning of anxiety to ease and cool from within.

"Yes, but you endured it all!"

This feminine voice strikes me with a slight immediate rise of my heart beats; even motivating my legs to mimic the palpitations and patter away. But the style of auditory in her voice holds me back causing my form to pivot and face her directly.

She is rather large with dark leonine fur and a metallic shine creating a sort of paradox to her charcoal plumage. My dependency emerges in thirst constricting my stomach when the air carries her scent to my nostrils. Every kit is drawn to the need for milk, but she; her sweeter and richer scent is at the point of being irresistible.

"You are a mother."

"I am," she confirms with a dip of her head revealing a pair of cold blue eyes of navy. But what captures my attention in hooked talons are the red marks on the side of her beak. The same red my points had surfaced earlier.

Despite the overcoming shame, I burst out, "I am sorry, you really rose the fear in me."

"I realize that."

I think I may be beginning to know Gryphon blood too well on such violent encounters; but I approach the female and climb her shoulder to reach the scars. Licking is pleasing because I must clean away my damage. Still, I am not fond of its bitter taste.

"I appreciate your obligation," she thanks. Coughing, I gag from the taste while forcing the red substance out before mistakenly ingesting anymore.

"What you have just done for me," she breaks in, "is what I and many mothers do for our kits at birth. Think of it as a sacrifice and not a burden." I remember that kits are soaked in blood once leaving the mother's body. This requires her to clean them up by tongue, grooming each of them. But this is not what my tongue wants and my stomach most certainly does not yet want to be filled with meat. What my kit body wants is milk.

"Painful hunger?" The female invites, resulting in my giving an articulate look of guilt but also mystification.

"How?"

"I am a mother, as you know." Her eyes gleaming accompanied by a lift into her paw and drawing me close. She is nursing me despite not being her own. I thank her but remain inquisitive on just how she knew of my appetite? My mother does not know my intentions unless I inform her all on my own.

After taking in a satisfied feed, I return directly before the Aquileia and settle between her paws; just below her neck and against her breast. Moonsight forwards on as both I and this female listen. She then engulfs my form by wrapping me in her paws in a way that is all new to me.

"May I learn your name?" she requests.

"Chrome."

"Where is your mother?"

"She never pays much attention to me enjoying as

much time away from me as possible. I also heard her tell father she actually is relieved when I am absent," I acquaint, shifting to a comfortable position upon my side. Silence is the only sign of response she produces. I do not know why her grip around me increases and tightens in protective manner.

"Ohhhh!" I gasp in sudden strike as her tongue makes contact upon my exposed belly. It passes through my fur and into my down with a warm delicate touch, granting me with a grooming as I never have received. Breathing with renewed energy, I embrace by hugging her breast and kneading the feathers with the tips of my talons. Many purrs call from within her joining in my own.

"My mother has never groomed me in such a way before," I comment. "You are so soft, so warm. But why are you not with your kits?" I ask out of my wonderment. "They must have need of you."

"Chrome" she begins in a somber change of mood, "I have no kits." My ears perk up in desire to know what she means. I nursed from her mammary and she even admitted her motherhood. I am about to question her query when my mind begins to work through my past experiences.

Moonsight descended from the mountains accompanied by another Gryphon. I had not thought about who it was, but the only other Gryphon here is . . .

"You," I now conclude, "are the mate of Moonsight."

"Very perceptive, Chrome," she praises with sky disk glimmering in the reflection cast by her irises. "I am Ankara, as who you say I am. Queen of the Aquileia."

"I must apologize for bringing this up, it must be painful to remember such vexation."

"Yes, it is hard," she confirms, adding nothing more to our conversation.

I need to comfort her some way and I believe huddling close to her chest and snuggling between her paws will do. It is best that I remain silent in order to not pain her again by calling back those memories. But there is one last unanswered mystery.

"Queen, what did you name your daughter?"

"Sanora."

The gathering finally brakes up, my personal time with Moonsight is about to begin. When he turns away from the ledge; his eyes immediately fall upon me.

"Who is this?" he questions his Queen, who is right behind me pricking the tip of her talon into my flank.

"Introduce yourself," she motivates.

Approaching, I prepare to meet my leader for the first time.

"Chrome," I reveal meeting the metallic gaze possessing a rather stern expression along with a look of curiosity. Up close I see his scars more clearly than before. His body has even more than his mate, and the subject I am about to bring up, is exactly how these closed wounds came to be.

"I wish to speak to you about your daughter, Sanora," his ears lift at my request causing him to momentarily transfer to the Queen.

"It is not something we must keep concealed," she announces, "there is no harm in having him know." After a small portion of time, Moonsight ratifies and asks, "But why did you reveal it?"

"Because he asked me and it felt right to tell him." The only retort given to his mate is a bow. Then returning to me as I let loose my first question.

"Who took her, and for what reason?" He dips low to meet my desperate eyes.

"I am not at comfort to disclose to such a young kit."

"Moonsight!" Ankara interjects with the snarl I find her giving him in discipline.

"It occurred late in the night," he begins, "the attackers were in fact Gryphons. But they had no indication of being under our leadership nor in our alliance.

"We assume that they were only after Sanora," Ankara concludes; padding around me to settle at her mate's side, "it appears that they had no intention of harming us and only wished to take her life," she pauses, while her blueberry eyes hide beneath the lids before finishing, "and they succeeded." Moonsight drapes wing over her back, drawing his mate close and Ankara presses the side of her beak into his feathered breast. She is a mother in need of comfort.

"Queen," I console, resting paw over her own by practically climbing upon it with my diminutive size. It is easy to distinguish the hurt in her irises when they reopen. She brushes her feathered head with my fluffy down, attended by a gentle tongue spreading across my ears.

"Does she always treat her kit this way?" I ask myself. "She is so different from Hollice."

"Chrome," she says, her voice now filled with purrs, "do you really know how I feel? I am a mother who has lost her one kit. Sanora grew in my womb the same way you did within your own mother. I gave a part of my life to bring her to existence."

"She is an actual essence of you?"

"Our mother's gave a fragment of their life in order to form us," she exclaims into deeper detail, "I did the same, out of my love."

"Love?" Never have my ears assimilated this term.

The deep humming from within her comes to an abrupt stop. Moonsight's talons scrape the stone beneath as both he and the Queen fuse their interlocked stares.

"What is love?" I curiously request.

"Chrome . . ."

"Ankara!" Now it is Moonsight who interjects with head at a crooked angle, "no." He orders the female to silently retreat.

"Chrome," having reacquired my attention, I await for what his voice is about to carry over, "you have shown much courage young kit. Leaving your mother without consultation, passing your talons through the skin of your Queen and my soul mate," his voice grows ever angry with arise of hostile eyes, "fracturing your leg and having a near death experience. All within a cold dark cavern that you immediately accepted into your paws. Hoping for forgiveness, you cleaned away the damage you had done while taking time to recover from the mere taste of blood."

Stern seriousness remains securely upon me; how does he know all this?

"No kit has ever endured what you have in this one day. Having truly been pushed to the limits no other of your status would tolerate." No one, not even his mate could have explained all this.

"Chrome," he intervenes by cocking his head to the side in part with a playfully sarcastic expression, "it is my natural ability to hear one's mind. Specifically your own at the moment." My tail elongates in amazement as do my wings, fluttering in shivers passing through my feline body.

"You . . . hear my mentality?"

"Yes I do. But unless one's thoughts are relayed out loud as I have just done, I will not remember them. Because they are in your mind and not my own. Only when one speaks the thoughts to me, do I remember."

"Queen Ankara," I blurt out, "that is how you knew I wanted to feed. You heard my hunger."

Finally, the joy returns to her as she gives the addition of, "That is not the one reason I knew. Sure, I am able to hear one's mind as well, it is more that I just simply knew through the empowering supernatural connection with my own kit."

The sky disk now approaches the mountain by casting its shadows in a slightly different direction. The time is now expiring as the day will age into the rebirth of the night. Hollice must wonder of my location, but before departing, I raise up only a single paw. Reaching outward, I rest it upon his own. My talons are small thorns compared to his hidden predator tools. How will I ever grow to be as large and strong as Moonsight when I am the small mole hill beneath the mountain?

"I have a long path ahead before I become a true Gryphon."

"You do," my lead assures, then overlaying his opposite paw by reassuringly taking mine gently between his pads, "as your guide, Chrome. I wish to reward you for the courage and endurance you have used this day." I cannot help but brighten up like a fire hungry coal who has just been fed fresh kindling.

"Please," Ankara intercedes by springing up just as I have with obligation of, "allow me."

He grants a bow as she lifts her wing before him and I observe as he plucks a feather from her dark imbrications. It is exchanged between beaks, and now comes my turn. Her head is right before me, awaiting for my acceptance of the feather. To reach, I rise up on my hind legs with paws balancing on her beak for support. Before I take the gift, I meet the eyes of my Queen. Never have I felt such an aura of blue. Whatever its meaning, I am being drawn to her like a trusted devoted savior. It feels that we cannot part because we would lack wholeness without another. We do not break this contact even when I take the feather in my own beak.

"Chrome," her voice comes to my ears as does a fresh breeze, "take this feather as a sign of my love and promise." To know it, know who I am. "In return, give me your own promise. If you are ever alone, return and call for me. I will hear you."

I grant a low bow with allowance of letting the feather fall to where its bristles tickle my paws.
"Nourishing haven I bid you," with this final reassurance, Ankara takes to the air. I do nothing but ponder all I have been through in this one day. But before I continue on, I gaze up the mountain slope, following my leader as he and his Queen return to their mountain dwelling.

A S A P u b l i s h i n g C o r p o r a t i o n

Scenic 11

Iron Contact

"You have much to put to mind," Mother coaxes, gently resting paws on either of my shoulders.

"I am still attempting to process it all and to properly summarize it."

"That will take time," she indicates. "Learn at your own pace with most sincere devotion."

Why is it so that she cannot keep her tongue out of my life nor my mangled fur? Well, this question does not amount even nearly to what has taken place this night. I barely notice Skylar's obsessive grooming to my rough coat.

"Mother, when you were summarizing about how you hybridized your luminescent shine, you still held back the other part of you; would that not make you a tribrid?"

"It most certainly does," she clarifies, "but remember, it is meant to be withheld amongst ourselves."

"Yes, I remember. I also wonder if I share this same trait. I being your direct descendent, could I possibly have that inheritance?" She gives a small nod, meeting my expectation.

"Sleep will not be possible with all this on my mind."

"Difficult, yes," she agrees. "It may take a lifetime to absorb it all in. But please do not rush it." she advises while planting a kiss over my jaw line. "I too find it hard to sleep every night, knowing someone out there wants to take your life."

"So that is why you are so close to me?" A question I had not asked is answered.

"Yes," she declares, "even if you had not come from my womb, I'd love you just the same."

"Really? Then I would look up to you just as well." And just to prove it, I straighten up, encasing arms around her neck and return the kiss.

"I know you would," she acknowledges.

"May I go take a night hike?" My mind requires some space of freedom. But because of what I have learned tonight, Skylar has every right to concern over me.

"You may," she agrees. "However, if you are interested, I have thought of something to occupy both you and I."

"What is your idea?"

"I wondered if you would like to go into the city for a small escape as well as a smoothie."

Smoothies of fruit are one of my most favorite contraptions. Especially sweet strawberries and wild blueberries mixed with milk and yogurt to create a nutritional renewal. Yea, I had a fit serving of meat prior to now but I am an omnivore unlike other canids. Meat is just one edible pleasure of Vulpine.

"I really want to share a great time with my son," she brings out, "that being the time remaining."

"But we will both live forever," I correct. "You and I have plenty of experiences to share." My assurance to her is, "This is only one of many."

"Come," she beckons, shimmering once again with renewed gleam. I will thank her later for all this, after my stomach's anxiety deteriorates from getting its delicious fruit. I cannot even stop my mouth from salivating some drops over the corner of my lips.

We are directing to the vault. A place where Vulpine hide personal possessions guarded by the deep underground and secret only to those outside alliance. Skylar knows the way far better than I, having been long since my last visitation.

"If we are to pass as domestic," she instructs, "you must only use two legs."

"Right," I acknowledge, rearing up on my hinds to shift their muscles into biped mode.   Gauntlet is the name of the domestic dwelling I have lived outside of since birth into the wild. Of course, consisting of only domestic where the wild are not welcome. But I and my fellow Vulpine secretly live a double life. Animals of the frontier, both wild and domestic. Before entering the city, we must retrieve clothing from our vault.

"Mother, is it true you were not born and raised in the wild?"

"That is right. I lived most of my life as domestic but chose to raise you in the wild. Because my mate and your father knew it was much safer."

So Skylar is well experienced with modern life. To match her and be illusionary, all required is to control my wild habits and act exactly like the civilized creatures. Not exceptionally hard because I stay quiet and rarely open my muzzle. What is hardest overall is hiding limbs number five and six.

We have arrived at the area of the vault with its well-hidden entrance. Located along the cliff wall we have been following for a while now. Finally, mother stops before a section covered in rough stone; I recognize as the exact place we ascend upon.

"Who designed the vault?" Once surveying the surroundings and decides it's clear, she answers.

"I really do not know, it was here long before I myself was born. But I believe it was by same who dug the labyrinth. No one knows what hybrid has the capability to dig through stone so excessively." Another mystery added to my mentality of unanswered files. Peering up the vertical wall intensifies the awe of how it was all done. Yet, the climb I am not yet ready for is granting a sensation that immediately forms into an idea.

"Hey," I suddenly proclaim, "Why don't I attempt to soar up?"

Once again, my mother's internal light shines even greater, proving a definite yes by grin of approval. Spreading my chiroptera limbs, I jump high, flexing hard and attempting to catch the air. I am not rising, only seconds in do I return to the ground. My second attempt fails as well. Recreating what I had done earlier is without ascension.

"Do not tire yourself, Fox. Rushing is rarely a key to completing a goal."

"But I uplifted for the first time tonight." Her illuminating form does not dim as does hope. Mother is as bright as ever in her shining aura.

"I am not able to answer that question," she admits, "I do not think anyone knows." Her statement rather disappoints me; knowing so much but not everything.

"I had it," I growl in unbearable shame. "Now it's gone," I cry in my own humiliation. "I am sorry mother, I believed in being your gifted kit. I have proved to be nothing more than your defective kit."

I expect her to come and comfort me, no matter how vexatious I am. What I have just revealed is my cry for help and yes, she is about to console me.

"Forjah."

Forjah, she only uses my true non-condensed name occasionally. Doing so because she is consoling me both directly and deeply.

"The only true monsters in existence are those who choose to be. My only disappointment is you are putting yourself down."

"You always approach me from my most unexpected side, and you always get in." I do not know how, only that she always brakes into my psyche as easily when an army brings down a city's weakest wall.

"You may be defective for all we know," she informs, "but everything has purpose and reasoning."

"Is it possible to be monstrous and blessed at the same time?" I contradict in reference to both my natural Vulpine self and paradox of gliders flightless once again.

"I do not see why not, and I know you can make that happen."

"I will make it happen, I promise mother, I will be a miraculous freak. Even if I never get airborne again, I can still make you proud."

"I know you will ever more than you already have. But also make our allies proud, and show our enemies that we Vulpine deserve to prosper and want no control for our own." Her declaration is traumatizing to the extreme that I will never forget it. I now will live by what she has just requested. My Vulpine Instinct is strong in this to the maximum, and my devotion to becoming the freak of a miracle is official.

Skylar dispels her light just before the climb so not to attract attention like a miniature star. Domestic's senses do not match the strength of our own, yet even I don't want to take the risk.

Skylar carries me on her shoulders like a backpack and begins the climb. The vaults were strategically placed, outside a rock wall with plenty of grip holds for scaling. Directly above and awaiting is a single large tree growing out from the rock wall. I am just now remembering that this is our vault entrance and not the cliff alone.

Skylar takes hold of the roots and pulls up onto the trunk. The height is not too great but we are a good distance up.

Carefully dismounting from mother's back, I balance in the branches and peer into the hidden tree roots hiding our gateway. All left now is to carefully sneak through the roots and down the tunnel shaft.

With enhancement of my night vision, I observe the tunnel is dug exactly as the labyrinth. Just the right size for any Vulpine to crawl and mostly lined in stone rather than just earth.

"We are close," I return back to mother. "I am beginning to smell the steel."

The crawl has come to an end where we have arrived in the great chasm aligned with vault doors stretching down on both sides. Once mother climbs out from the tunnel aperture, she straightens herself up and leads me down the long corridor. I do not recollect which vault is our own, but I need to know eventually, so I will pay close attention in order to learn.

After some brief moments, we stop before a single door I am sure is ours. Its surface is designed in great detail with many bars, tracks, and knobs. Skylar turns a knob in the top left corner then slides it across the bars to the opposite side. Now she takes another and slides it diagonally to bottom left corner. Finally, she spins a third knob and slides it to the position of the first in the top left corner. For signal of approval, mother motions the tip of her tail in direction of the door. Now, I clench my forepaws in gripping the handle, turn it downward, and swing the great slab open on concealed hinges.

All is just as cold and bleak as I remember. Buried deep in stone and away from sunlight. Mainly, it appears like a large storage closet of personal possessions neatly packed away in various types of storing units. Ranging from wooden boxes, to paper folders and containers of fire proof metal.

"What is all this?" I ask Skylar. "You haven't told nor shown much."

"Yes," she verifies, "only about half of it is my own. My history and Sy's." The rare use of my father's name recalls not only his memory, but the memory of how much it hurts mother; but she ignorantly continues, "before you dive too deep in our past, I only want you to concentrate on your present."

"Conceded," I disclose in honesty.

She proceeds to the wooden wardrobe while I cannot resist my own curiosity to the many unopened packages. Diverting off to the first corner, I open the first thing I find. A rather long, slender object wrapped in a thick silk cloth. Once removing the wrapping, it is revealed to me as a long pointed object topped off by a sort of handle on one end.

Placing my paw around it, I discover it is of cold metal with a metallic scent I cannot recognize. Between this handle and the pointed end is another triangular shape of small winglets on either side. In the center between them, a jewel like object. Still, I do not know what this is.

Upon discovering leather straps wrapped around the arrow head, it draws in the points of my claws to its connective touch. It as though they are securing something.

Turning it over in my pads, I find the strands tied into a knot, which comes loose by pulling a single strand. The pointed part appears to be some type of metal dressage, sliding off easily to expose an equally pointed shape. It is made of brilliantly shining metallic steel.

"My goodness!" I huff, "it's an oversized knife."

At the sound of my pants, Skylar turns away from the oaken wardrobe. Baring selected garments in her paws

"Ah!" she smirks, "a defender's sword. Quite a bit different from your chrimsophilite. It too is a belonging of Sy."

"So is it just a large knife?"

"In a way. But most swords are a double-sided blade with a pointed tip."

"Interesting," I comment while returning it to the sheath. "But what is this, here?" My inquiry unleashes out as I take hold of long wooden stick with a string hanging from the end, baring a grip in the middle and curved at both points.

"Allow me," she offers, once selecting more clothing from the wardrobe's drawer. Placing them on top of a nearby crate, she comes to my assistance. Taking it into her own paws, she places the string end between her ankles, then bends the wood and connects the ends by the string. "It is a wooden recurve bow; much like the original tool of archery."

"So the sword and the bow were once separate tools?"

"Correct. Your chrimsophilite was once two different individual tools. Now that they are brought together into one portable item; granting one a great advantage."

"I am glad I am learning from you, because I want to learn it all." Despite the damp underground cavern, I feel so much warmer now that Skylar is lighting up again after passing on her knowledge. I feel she is about to verbalize something else, but I am flabbergasted when she gives nothing additional. Instead, mother begins to suit up in her outfit for tonight. Tying a black scarf over her breast then pulling on a pair of nylon leggings and slipping into a leather gown-like skirt.

For me, she selected a maroon sleeveless tunic and a pair of gray yellow stripe athletic shorts. I keep wings folded when pulling the tunic on, needing to tightly hold them against my back. But they remain a visible impression beneath the fabric.

"It will not work," I complain. "I have outgrown this trick."

"Now is that time," she puts in followed by a return to the wardrobe. Opening the first drawer blow the cabinet, mother draws out a folded garment of dark blue. My mind tells me it is a hooded cape.

"It is a cloak," she discloses, "wear it and conceal your personal gift." Skylar drapes it over my back, then brings the hood fold to my neck. Tying the leather straps into a secure knot, my appendages become completely concealed behind the fabric drape.

Securely locked against my back, my folds will not be able to open until much later when we are safely back in the forest and away from the domestic. My concerning hope is our dressage not doing its job to hide our identity. Most domestic's sense of smell are not near as strong as ours; so a faint scent of the deep wood should not betray us.

Indeed, our garments are nothing special because they are many cycles old and modernly outdated. Living in the wild, I find clothing all too uncomfortable and irrelevant to a coat of fur.

Mother is ready, but a diminutive impulsion spark burns a transmitting shock to tips of my claws, nose and tail. The meat from earlier regurgitates up my esophagus, a deadly sinking submerges my heart in a sable abyss, my palpitations skips a beat and paralyzes my entire form.

After this sensation subsides, my paws move to remove my belt. Setting it, along with chrimsophilite, marble pouch, and goggles upon the wooden chest beside Sy's sword and unstrung bow.

"Not taking them along?" Mother asks.

I hang my tail limp in confirmation, for everything feels functional except my jaw. I cannot move it to voice nor express emotion, what is overcoming me?

"Is the Vulpine Instinct instructing your action?" she inquires by request. "You rarely venture without your gear."

Lock-jawed, I transfer attention back to the vixen with almost my entire body clamping at the joints. I know she is looking upon me with the exact responding impression she is receiving from my own. My eyeballs are unmoved in their sockets like an owl's, ears folded low as if pressured and overstressed, never has Skylar seen me this way.

Is this how Eternity is when something makes contact with her? Does she feel sick and burdened emotionally by an unseen force? I would have noticed if Vykan ever appears this way.

Mother's shadow is now over me in the dim incandescent lamp overhead. Neither she nor I really need it with our night vision; and she still would not need it to see the foreign alien facial I now wear. Even when she passes out of eyesight, my fixation remains on the steel vault door, making me feel like . . . not wanting to exist. The vixen who is officially my mother lifts her dominant paw as it comes to rest its pad over the root of my shoulder and wing. But is it there? Is she here? Am I?

"Forjah," the familiar melody of her voice carries the breath I have known for all time. I am returning, retreating back into actuality. My physicality comes, breaks away its supernatural locks and releases my biology. Mother's tail tip brushes the space where my cheek-ruff will one day form; tickling it so, that I finally make contact with her again.

There is no method of how to translate what just took place in both my mind and body. Nothing bridges off my tongue or passed my lips; but my paws open up embrace Skylar. The cause only being that she is present now.

"Son, please," she pesters in whining worry. My head motions from side to side, please do not force that out of me again, "Fox, I think you too are adaptively fusing with the Vulpine Instinct. You are feeling something beyond the physical and even higher than your own mentality." With muzzle still over her shoulder in the embrace, I motion my tail again in agreement with her observation.

I am now ready to exit our vault and escape as far as possible from this experience; but Skylar holds back and returns to the wooden wardrobe and opening its drawer to draw out a small black box.

"What is that?"

"Something I am leaving out for you. For a purpose only my instinct is in contact with."

"I thought you had Advanced Adaptability?"

"I have both adaptability and instinct, just as you are now having a similar experience."

"You had better dispel your light," I warn her just before we step outside the vault.

"Thanks," Skylar praises in appreciation, extinguishing her shine by fading back into the harvest golden hairs. I will not visually anticipate how a domestic would react to a glittering vixen. Mother would probably be accused of dark magic and be taken from me. As great my desire is to not bring it to imagination, I am pondering on how "I" would take action. If anyone lays their claw points upon her, rage will release the wild in me. Father may no longer be present, and this is why I must assume his position. His mate has guarded me since my first beginning, now I must return the obligation to her, my mother.

But while I am preparing to actively defend her, mother brings the vault door shut and the same dreadful feeling electrifies over me like a bullet of terminal illness. The loud clanging beat produces a fresh charge so great, I fall to my knees with lungs heavy and panting. My stomach regurgitates yet again as one paw clutches upon it and my throat.

"Fox!" Skylar erupts with gentle pads grasping my collapsed self. I am struggling so hard to not black out.

Her breathing is no different from my own as she joins in with the pants.

"I have a spark of shock. One that is powerfully strong."

"We do not have to go into Gauntlet tonight. I have absolutely no intention of worsening your state." With constructive protest I convince her to not back out and that I want us to have fun and not ruin it for her as well.

"Accepted," she agrees, "let us depart."

I will fight these negative sensations I declare to myself. Not allowing them to distract from our purpose of rewarding ourselves with a brief escape from the wild. In distracting myself from this whole error, I wet my lips in preparation of the rich fruit smoothie whose berries will empower my taste buds and cloud my senses in fruity aroma.

Scenic 12

Visionary Reality

Unaware I am of my own existence. Wondering what living really is or the purpose of anything. Then how can I be thinking at all? My mind is functioning without my body, but I cannot recall or connect to my conscious life. It is as though only I exist here and now with nothing and no one.

Sleep is your body being nonexistent nor your spirituality connecting to reality; only in the mind and of night visions. They are not fragmented images out of memory, they are something entirely alien to my brain. Even when I make something up, it is produced out of knowledge my brain received from one or all of my senses.

But this place, I have never encountered nor even imagined. How is my mind producing it and just why am I here? No longer am I just visualizing, but hearing and even feeling the environments created by mentality. This particular night vision begins with a sound, pleasantly melodic and high within my ears. My recognition tells me it is a voice; indeed it must be someone attempting to gain a response and they are most definitely demanding an answer.

With this immediate understanding, I return the

calls with my own. The echoes come back with the cold, reflecting its sound off the walls of the barrier like claws prickling my side. But I am realizing they are talons.

Long black barbs of keratin are pinning me to the ground. Above, a glimmer passes through Hollice's gold eyes while mine openly return to Chromium.

"What just happened?" she demands.

Shuttering beneath the angered female like helpless prey, I plead, "Please mother, I heard a calling in my night visions, and I called back to them." It is all relieving to discover the entire duration had only been a night vision; but the true relief comes when Hollice retracts her talons, releasing her restraint over me.

Compared to sleep, time has moved on. The sky disk has gone down, veiling the whole forest in black. With the little light remaining in my eyes, Hollice appears directly above me visible only by scent and sound of breath.

"Chrome!" her voice scolds from the unseen beak. "I need you to quit burdening me. I require an exceeding amount of rest on the account of your demands." The dim gold within her gaze is hostile as it always has been.

"You wish for me to achieve more sleep and I desire it extensively. Do not wake me again!" she orders in flaring temper. Shrinking away, I gift a low bow.

"No mother, I will not."

She does not allow me to lay with her for the remainder of the evening nor to nurse my own milk or take in her warmth. But it does not matter; in order to hold in body heat, I curl up in the grass bed. Hollice is expecting my slumber to return; however, it is not coming.

Depression has overtaken me in shame of disturbing mother. Though it had all been unintentional; she is correct on the fact of wanting her to gain more rest. The claim, I only made the previous day.

The mind of a kit seems quite blank in the eyes of those mature. Truthfully, we attempt to use our minds to an equivalent of the adult's capacity; even I know I am not capable of that power. I am struggling to work my mentality so hard that I am just now taking notice of the river. For the last action I remember is leaving the barrier under the cloak of my distress.

I am watching the fresh water weave through the forest, carrying into the great body east of Chromium. I ponder how it exists as a substance liquid capable of assuming many forms. I learned from father how it rises from the bodies into vaporous mists. At times, it settles in the forest by forming droplets upon every plant, tree and grass blade. Also, it crystallizes into tiny flakes during the bitter season, then falls from the sky to rest on the land. My birth came late after the season but desire is strong to someday witness an icefall, as it is properly called.

Hollice explained how she does not particularly like the icefall, on the account of how dreadful it may be. Tiny particles of ice descend from the sky and cover the region in what appear as white grains of water. It's hard to imagine lower temperatures than that of the current. Evaron describes it as moving your own pads through what resembles sand, but what are truly transparent crystals of water.

When the cold becomes too extreme, one will experience a numb pain in their paws. I am unaware how something so cold is able to produce a burning feeling, and maybe I will one day endure it despite not classifying it as pleasant. Never am I in need of remembering Chromium's climate description.

"Never defined as warm," I echo the overused phrase, "ascended heat or descended chills." When the shivers begin, I think back to what methods of reverse there are to counteract. As part feline kit and part raptor, I am unable to control my body temperature just as eaglets are. Always requiring the heat of another that can only be given by an adult with full feathers and fur.

My stomach is feeding on its self and I assume Hollice still will not allow me nourishment till her awakening; but I have no motive to return to the barrier as hungry as I am. In spite of refusal to nourish me, it is not Mother who I long for. The other who has claimed my desire is Ankara.

The Queen, whom I only met the day before has captured my admiration. In truth, there is something beyond the dark pelted feathers shading her true nature. This caliginous Gryphon has taken my heart, cradling it within her gentle paws and holding me as her own. Nurturing me in ways Hollice never has. The moment her scent filled my nostrils I had been intoxicated by the rich sweet substance. Arousing every one of my senses, she satisfied every one of my needs. The succulent mammary gifted me new life and not even the feather was final bestowment.

Something radiates from Ankara, the same energy now burning within me. But I do not recollect the term my Queen used when sacrificing her imbricate.

"To know it, know who I am," she informed.

"Know what? She must be referring to this new feeling; the same that resulted from her kindness?" I am not able translate it, it is only a feeling from within. In addition, I also feel that it is permanent, meaning I will not lose it.

Ankara herself left me in a sort of loneliness. Voice ringing in my memory with a rise of my ears. Responding with a mournful cry, I immediately know it is pitiful; yet, if I were to be heard, she would instantly know my pain.

Alone I am, just wanting her reassurance that I am not. To know she is there grants relief, but with me is where I want her to be.

Again, her voice comes to my ears, nothing but a tiny squeak escapes my throat. My vocals would ring in purrs if only the Queen was near. But the cries continue on into the point where they are echoing through my skull.

"What do you cry for?" I whine. It is wasteful replying to a chimerical voice in my head; yet, why does it seem to be outside?

I am returned to reality by coming out from deep within my mind. It is a voice not of my imagination that summons me. My leonine eyes sight through the trees as light weaves between their branches by evaporating the moisture drops. Birds awaken into song while squirrels make their gathering routes. Mist rises from the river as the sky disk announces the new day by gifting the land with its warmth.

The sounds; the river, the birds, mammals, and insects, I ignore. Perking my ears, I listen for the voice, clearing my mind and blocking out all distractions. There, the weak call truly exists. Not Ankara's, familiar and the same voice I heard in my sleep.

"None of it had been a night vision," I declare. "This is true reality."

Through the rushing water and among calls of fellow species, these are cries of distress.

"I would have done the same," I affirm. This voice, to whom does it belong?

Only one obstacle separates me from this desperate cry: the river. On all preceding accounts, Hollice hurdled the water clamping me in her beak. Lacking flight is my disadvantage for my wings are draped in down and not yet capable of taking to the air.

"How can there be a way?" I call aloud. "I know of nothing to provide me safe passage across." A peculiar feeling is coming over while processing these many thoughts with eyes following the river's image and sound repetition.

"There is a way," a voice assuredly confirms.

It is my own.

Scenic 13

Fate's Path

Having no clarification of how I had achieved it; I scurry my paws to the unknown destination. Finding what appears to be a mass of mud and sticks providing me access to the opposing side. The moment my pads touch the grass, hectic emotion pulsed within me, sending my paws sprinting at speeds of unknown capability.

Halting when reaching a familiar environment, it is revealed as the location of the blueberry bushes. I have been here only once before when mother gave the task of seeking her out; failing from paranoia of being without her. She is not with me now; how is this any different than the event of a number of days prior?

Questioning this over and over repeatedly results in the most logical answer my mind can fashion. That passed time really awakened fear in me that was quite alien then. But here and now being in this state of rejection, Hollice is not welcoming and nor do I want her closeness now. My focus is upon responding to the call, afraid for its holder over my own personal concern. If it was Ankara, I would risk my own not only for a return thanks. Again, is this the exact expressive feeling she descriptively detailed only the previous day?

"Now is not the time to ponder the past," I decide in evasive action of forwarding to the victim's assistance. "I need pure absolute focus on the task of the present," positioning my ears to take in all frequencies, they receive a soft pulse with distinct clarity; one's heart rapid with diminishing energy, vaguely calling for renewal.

This is no difference with the blueberries considering my first experience; same tall plants emitting their sour fruitful scent. Seeing over the stem's summits is beyond my reach capability even upon my hind legs. Evaron explained Gryphons have a slow growth rate in comparison to other beasts. This means, for me to reach full maturity, my development requires a span of five times greater.

These invasive thoughts of cross-breed maturation are so intervening, I do not even acknowledge a rotting log in my path until it physically halts my venturing paws. The moment I perch upon its decomposing bark; a new scent flows into my senses from within the vegetation, as does a bright red visual creeping behind the green strands baring their navy fruit spheres.

Indeed it is a glare, becoming a blur as it springs from behind the vegetation. Making no reaction, I allow paws to impale my chest. Giving sudden force that lands me spread-eagled beneath a predator who is no more than a kit of my fellow Aquileia.

"Grounded!" the female announces. "Unable you are to match my speed nor agility," she proclaims with distinguished pride in her voice.

My now dazed mind has put me in an unresponsive state. When my conscious clears, a damp warmth soaks the fur of my back I know is crushed berries.

Sounds are returning similar to how I awakened to the day, just as the voice had brought me out of sleep. "The voice!" I announce at the moment of remembering.

Adrenaline regained, I am on my haunches in an instant. Never have I seen fire, though I believe I did only the day before.

If I caught a flickering ember, it would warm my innards as it now does for my sight. Her color is the same thermal crimson new to my eyes for only the second time. Through my teary vision, I voice out, "Did I find you?" Her tail raises to reveal its bright yellow pelt, flaunting it at her side, she correctively comments . . .

"Truthfully, I found you."

"What is your reason for attacking me?" I request with a bow, attempting to be as kind as possible, as it is my mere instinct in the presence of this dazzling Gryphon. The lids flash over her delicate iris beads, appearing so black they seem sightless. But to her, my own are no different.

"I had the assumption I was attacking my brother," the female admits.

"Such clarity," I comment.

"Huh?" she queries with risen ears and a misread expression.

"Your voice," I rephrase, "it is so melodic. Never have I heard vocals as the ones you possess."

"Is that an intentional compliment?"

"It truthfully is. As is the enrapturing sight you present in my vision," The female's heart fails a pulse and her beak instantly returns.

"Enrapturing . . . really?" she deepens in tone as bashful emotion flows from her exhale in a warm breeze. Carrying her scent of salt, berries, and even the taste the milk brings out my hunger.

"Are you revealing that I have beauty?" she rephrases dark and dazed.

"Yes," I bow. "It is my honest view." A great vibration motions through her body despite today's warmer touch.

"Never has a voice granted something such as that to my ears. You are the only kit I have met apart from my siblings," she returns with a bow of acknowledgment.

"You are the only kit I have met apart from myself."

"What name do you inherit?"

"Chrome," I divulge, "what name has your mother laid upon you?"

Now a twinkle sparks from her as she adds, "Aquila."

She and I remain silent for a time, as if neither of our minds can fall upon something to bring to a conversing level. We hold each other's line of sight as my concentration relies on studying her appearance in order to know her well and accurately. I do not even ask permission before I begin running my beak through the down of her neck.

"What is this action?" she demands, yet not in harsh tone.

"Learning your scent," I assure, "my desire is to know you, Aquila." A breath escapes her in.

"I . . . would also like to know you, Chrome." For a reason undefined, it feels amazing to hear my name in her voice.

Jolting dumbfound comes over me when her tongue makes contact against my furry shoulder.

"Do you not have a good nose?"

"Not really," she confirms between licks, "you taste of the deep forest, yet you are sweet."

"Because I am soiled after you impaled me into the blueberries."

"A proper explanation! As an apology, I will groom your pelt and also your down.

I make no protests upon the offer. Aquila will take the burden from mother today, and there is nothing I hate more than stressing her. Hoping soon I will develop my experience of grooming into a personal skill, then no longer needing reliance of others.

"I greatly accept your obligation. I am not even capable of grooming myself in the way you are." A glow flashes from her as she gifts a small bow.

"I credit my mother, my siblings and I have learned all from her; achieving so much through imitation alone."

I cannot make the same claim, for Hollice never seems content to teach me anything. From her I learn by total observation. Fortunate I am for Evaron, always taking advantage of every moment to train something new into me.

"Chrome?" Aquila interrupts reclaiming my attention like stolen prey.

"Is there a disturbance?" Holding concern at her judgment of my tone in breath still sweet with recent nourishment.

"Painful hunger?" Ankara's memory echoes. Yet, there is something the voice of my new friend lacks. The voice I am seeking.

She is a gorgeous flower among weeds and my absolute desire is nothing more than to spend time with her this day. She has just become my friend, my first. Yet she is not the original intention of why I embarked.

Startled by a distant call, Aquila provides . . .

"Mother, she would equally welcome you as I have," giving a bow and releasing a breath, I confess.

"No, I cannot at this time." Her affection grows the moment she brushes her full body length against me in a caressive manner. "I will be with you again, Aquila. I anticipate being reunited with you."

Her tongue rasps through my down with one last breath.

"As do I."

ASA Publishing Corporation

The sky disk has risen higher, warming the forest while evaporating the moisture. Still, I am in the blueberries seeking my destination. The plants have increased density since the moment I entered. Twice, a new scent came to me, but neither are anything I recognize.

"I am not ready to follow a scent trail. Yet, why have I not found a scent that may lead me on?" There have been no evidence of other Gryphons apart from Aquila.

No trees grow overhead, signifying that I have come deep into the brush.

The distant sounds of birds tell me nothing, and without scent or sight, I do not have a guide.

"I was asleep when I began hear it," I recollect, "but with my body at rest, my senses were not active. How then, had my ears received it?"

Sleeping is the one thing I did then that I currently am not. Even from when I first picked up the voice from across the river, I had been resting my body.

"Rest!" I conjure.

Lying in the cool grass, placing myself in the same position as before; covering my eyes and allowing sleep to come. The sweet berry scent continues to burn in my nostrils, colors flash from outside my eyelids, and the touch tells me this fresh grass is rough and quite different to that of my den.

"My senses, they are not used during sleep. My body is shut down during the entire regenerative process. All that remains is . . .

"My mind," this is how I know of the voice. I listened to it without the use of my physical sensory. All along, my body has been the true interference. I need to block and temporarily discontinue it.

First I willfully disconnect my ears until all sounds evaporate. Now my nose and tongue become light as air, all feeling makes my eyeballs seem to disappear. Weightlessness overcomes as my body falls away.

"Sticks!" Holding me like prickling talons and emitting their bark scent. Moving through them like a slithering snake, I am able to feel their coat of leaves, but my only desire is to rid myself of this.

Air fills my lungs upon return to my body. The sticks are nonexistent; grass is beneath me once again. Departing without my body . . .

"Fascinating," I declare. "Never have I known of this capability." This miraculous moment makes me wonder why Hollice has never explained the tactic. If I ever take this experience to a vocal level it will certainly result in failure. I do not believe it is possible for me to put this event into voice and let it descriptively pass my beak.

Still, I am not sure what direction I should make for despite my paws padding against my will, but yet, with my acceptance. Carrying my aquiline and leonine form through the blueberries in a whole new route.

The scenery has been so repetitive for the past time spans, when finally reaching the outside, I am greeted by a new vista that puts all the day's trek into the past. I had not anticipated on registering this new sight into my cranium, but how could I have prepared otherwise? It almost burns my eyes bright in appearance to be yet another new color. To recollect it in the future will be difficult to an extreme. All trees I have seen bare dark leaves, the leaf plumage of this particular tree appears to be blue, red, or a hybrid of the two together as one.

"I myself am a hybrid of feline and aquiline," relating to such unusual nature as this color mix. "Do others find it astonishingly hard to take in our image as Gryphons? In the exact way I am viewing this tree right now? I may be able to answer this question, if not for the rustling in the branches above.

Eyes returning to the leaves, a soft sound of impact lands in the thick roots. On the fact of the anticipation I prepared for this moment; I make no astounded reaction when I land my eyes on the trunk base. Lying in the roots and in my sight is a Gryphon kit.

Scenic 14

Urban Stealth

We enter Gauntlet through the forest walk way. Needing to do our best to appear as modern citizens, mother and I move slower to deceptively blend in by not creating any directive suspicion. I also refrain from looking into several directions or at civilians. If I or Skylar show any sign of our frontier life, that only brings trouble upon us. Because now I know we are not only rejected for being part wild, but because some here either want our adaptive power or us dead with it. I want to ask mother if they all are like this, I cannot observingly stare at a domestic with wild expression, but are each of them an enemy?

Skylar insists on holding my paw the whole way. Even once we are clear from the road and make our way through the streets. I really don't mind, we absolutely cannot be separated.

Right now, I am putting on what we call my 'cute act.' It is an impression of the common domestic kit; keeping my eyes wide and mouth gawked at every sight and sound. I even throw out questions to mother at a volume louder than needed.

"Why is that building so tall?" I falsely inquire.

She resounds in simplified form of, "Because it

would take up too much space if it were not."

Skylar presses on at a pace I consider slow. The urging need to drop on all fours and pick up the pace is genuinely impulsive. If she was not still grasping my paw, I might have made that exact mistake.

Mother appears official while keeping her head high and nose forward without breaking her muzzle's smile. She is acting like we come here most every day and live as everyone here does. Her domestic urban experience is an incredible tactical advantage, as familiar to the vixen as the wild is to me. But why, I wonder, did she join Sy and the skulk in the wild? Was it for security alone?

We are now nearing our favorite cafe. I feel it is time to perform an act that is convincing and a truly enjoyable pleasure. An act that should not be classified so. I break away from Skylar, approaching a lioness clothed in a dark raggedy color stained attire. A bucket of discolored water is at the large cat's paws, she is before a brick wall with a tray of paints held on one pad; the other baring a brush, neatly stroking across the stone.

"What are you painting?" I beg in my greatest impression of youthful curiosity. I am guessing just by simply glancing at her work, but still listen with wide eyes in utter fascination.

"It is Castige," she confirms. "First Vulpine to rise up in defense of the terrible things done against his race." I have only just learned of this Prince, yet is she not going into detail because of its extremity for a kit like me to hear?

Making a gentle outline of his facial fur, she takes one glance at me and temporarily abandons her mural. She is of course, an extremely large cat, more than doubling the size of mother. Male lions are even larger, meaning that I cannot imagine really how big. This female alone is larger than my mind will accept. But despite fierceness, this feline kneels before me at eye level with a most gentle voice accompanied by emotionally amber irises.

"Castige is Vulpine, just as you are. I admire him because he sacrificed all he had to defend you. If it were not for his heroic efforts, you may not even be here now."

"I know that now," I whisper back to the leonine, who is most definitely an ally.

"I admire him so greatly," she purrs back, "I even wish to be like him. A hero fighting for what is true and right. Rebelling against all evil to protect the innocent and those he loves. This is why I decorate the city with images of his influence. To inspire others to support life remaining and yet to come."

She is keeping her voice low, "I assume if we are overheard by an enemy . . . oh, I desire not to think about that."

"Maybe even when you grow up, young dog, you could be like him too." Growing up is a term used by the domestic. Back on the frontier, we always refer to it as maturation.

"Wow!" I yelp. "That would be most honorable." This is only a partial act. "I have never thought about that before now." Have others been like him, putting their own life first before even risking others? I have only just learned of him tonight from two individuals; and already he is such an empowering inspiration. His legacy lives within this lioness, and now she is passing it on through her art. Our mass extermination did not weaken her nor he, it only made them stronger just like the Vulpine's incredible adaptation to immortality. What does not take us out, empowers our life.

Skylar's is watching over closely when she lets a light bark escape her throat to signal me.

"Thank you," I appreciate to the cat, regaining focus of my act.

"Be safe little dog," she advises with warning, "use your gifts for what is truly right." Bidding the artist goodbye, I depart with renewed feeling overshadowing both my flightless guilt and the sickness that began in the vault.

"Come!" Skylar calls with a beckoning twitch of her golden tail. She takes off with a light canter through the street side. I respond by taking off as fast as my biped form allows. When finally catching up, I make a pouncing leap up her wagging tail. This is more playful kit act, I have enjoyed chasing her tail since the first moment my paws were able to support my body. We do this to an extent where the both of us get competitive in the challenge. I have learned to strike at random moments and she makes every effort to dodge.

The chase takes us around poles, up and down stairs, and into a urban playground. Finally catching her at the bottom of the metal slide, a powerful pounce upon her spine extension ends the match.

"Accepted," she admits, "I declare you the winner." Jumping down from the chute, I carefully land on four legs. Thankfully none see before I change back to biped.

Unexpectedly, Skylar tauntingly feeds my urge for action by adding, ". . . of that round." This time, I give her a start advantage, but momentarily hurl myself onward as the competition continues.

Scenic 15

Clandestine Chat

Our game continues all the way there. Just before mother even touches her paw to the door, I leap up and cling to her shoulders to be carried in as would a backpack. As usual, it is a quiet here with only a small number of inhabitance.

"You sure you have enough credits?" I whisper at her ear.

"Not much," comes her clarification, "but it will prove to be enough." The civilized have a type of bartering system in order to earn and exchange for needs. Each are electronically given so many credits in reward for tasks completed. Then these credits acquire items of need like food, shelter, and anything essential or luxurious.

I prefer our wild life, because of the simplicity and freedom.

As mother gives our order, I decide to take a personal patrol through the restaurant, looking for a good seat, as well as taking notice of all current inhabitance. Will it now be this way forever, always watching my tail ready for escape or retaliation? Thankfully, other than death dirty stares I receive from two different animals, I conclude no extreme danger here.

Selecting a booth before the window, so to feel free and not closed in; I await only moments before Skylar joins me, baring her iced tea in one paw and my smoothie in the other.

I prefer to sit back and enjoy this slowly and easily, but not so patient in giving the ice time to melt. Placing the tip of my muzzle into the glass, I lap the top portion of it with a slurp of my tongue.

"FORJAH!!" Skylar scoldingly barks in a deep, fierce growl. I get her meaning by quickly translating it. It is untamed and uncivilized in domestic culture to tongue slurp, rather to use a tactic considered appropriate and of good respectable manner. So I change to the straw and begin sucking the plastic tube, taking in the cold yogurt texture. While both my mind and will do all they can to distract me from the dull taste of the artificial stick.

"Thank you," I gift in response with strongest gratitude.

"I know it must be hard," she inputs in her most gentle touch of courtesy. "Hiding your frontier self in the attempt to appear domesticated. Before you were born, I had difficulty fitting into the wild."

"But you were brought in by Sy, where he and the skulk welcomed you," I reminded her.

"You are accepted by me," she points out, "I was raised in a place like this and only came to the wild because of my mate and that you were forming inside me. The duty of hiding and raising you safely was no longer just my own and your father's.

"Which you have done," I declare. "I love being raised under you, and I am thankful."

Though she is restraining, I see the black tips of her whiskers sparkle by her illuminating light, accompanied by a few twinkles around her bronze eyes. I suppose it must be hard to hold in so much gratitude and not expressing it by her Advanced Adaptation.

"I welcome your appreciation with my deepest thanks," Skylar accepts, "to raise you up is my obligation."

"Then I assume you are ready to hear the choice I have made this night?"

Without a comeback, she brings her paws onto the table, gripping her glass and raising it to her lips, focusing on me and awaiting my next revelation.

Before doing so, I slurp up some more smoothie to catch some yogurt coated strawberry and blueberry upon my taste buds. Satisfied with the helping, I bring out, "I have decided on traveling to Scorpula to learn which gift I have and develop my skills and maybe even become a tribrid." Her head bows with the drop of her eyelids, followed by a breath from deep within her lungs.

"I respect this option you have chosen with pride. It is most great, a sacrifice." Many negatives are floating around her brain.

In an attempt to brighten her mood, I bring up, "Maybe there, I will find and discover exactly how to fly again along with the winged Actyx Vulpine." Whether or not mother is forcing her muzzle to grin right now, I play this psychologically emotional challenge by firing up all empowered visions.

"You and also Sparrk asserted it is a great refuge for us remaining Vulpine, and that it is there in that great city we are building up our hybridized strength to rebel against our enemies." Extending my paws across the table top, I rest them upon those of my birth vixen, "I want to be a part of this mother, included in our solution to survival."

"So you will be," she confirms in a gentle reply of taking my single paw in the grip of her own. "You know, Scorpula has many vines growing from within the earth that spread all across the city. These creeping branches carry a strong electrical current that the citizens harness and use as a natural source of energy." My lips round out and my eyes widen at the same moment; her factorial is most fascinating, "that powers almost anything requiring it."

"It all sounds so beyond this demesne," I manage in to detail an answer.

"I guarantee it. The short time I spent there, really left me with an impression of wondrous awe. I know it will strike you just as well."

Does this refuge hold even more wonder than how no one around us is able to eavesdrop. Back at the labyrinth, the faintest most least definite conversation can be heard through the tunnels. It is so hard for me to believe their senses are far weaker than those of the wild. I guess they really have no need for such powerful senses in this environment. So naturally, they are adapting to a life without advanced sensory and lose them by lack of use and requirement. But I still wonder how they cannot be bothered by that annoying humming, how is it not disturbing?

"Wait . . . I did not hear it before now. That is certain fact." Skylar too is noticing this peculiar noise which has even caused her mood to alter once again. Her expression shows definite surprise, or is that fear I see? Without comment, she rises up and heads through the door to the outside.

Scenic 16

Savior

Instantly I am at her side.

"It is her," I know it. "You are the one I have been seeking. I am the one you are calling for." Her pelt is dull and matted with black down darker than my gray. Pressing my beak to her ear, I plea.

"Please give me a sign that you know I am here." My ears only intake her shallow breathing, but I feel she is showing signs of diminishing life. Resting my paw at her side, I feel a small amount of heat radiate from within her; yet, what else am I feeling appears to be emitting not energy, but life. Whatever she will lose, death will replace.

Breathing is weak and possesses an earthly scent. What I also take notice of is the lack of milk on her beak. I can only wonder how long it has been since her last nourishment.

"If she has ever drank at all." This is a time where my own mind distracts from actuality. She is in need and I am her lone provider; however, there is no capability of aiding her on my own. Painful as it is leave after just finding her, we must endure just a little longer.

"I am in great need of mother."

Diving beneath the thorn barrier with a care no longer of disturbing her, I rush in wailing.

"Mother!" her expression alone signifies my rude awakening. She attempts response with the usual tone of anger; but this is my time to vocalize without interruption. She takes in all I give and holds firm without one look of disbelief. At the time of my completion I am able to hear the disgust in her voice as I am grasped in her beak and carried outside the thorn barrier, where her wings extend out in flight preparation.

Time truly accelerates from the moment Hollice takes to the air. Wind rushes strong as the earth and forest fall away. The overall perception and aerial view is beyond my imagination as every tree, plant, and mineral are diminishing. The waters beyond are now a distant glistening field of blue while the rivers are bands weaving through the land. Should I be afraid right now, or fascinated?

But my mind reclaims back to the task at paw. For at this same moment, my eyes capture the brightly colored tree in my imagery. Standing out well like a flower among weeds.

The impact with the ground is so great, I slip out from between mother's beak and return to the earth. My adrenaline is giving new energy as I prance to the kit's location. Fear burns with my hunger; however, she is in greater need. The purpose of my expedition has been to find her; which is now complete. Now she must be saved.

"I am here," my exhale carries across her slumbering face. Black as shadows and as motionless as stone. Her body is warm yet not the proper temperature.

"You found her, Chrome?" Hollice questions the moment her figure casts its shade over the both of us. Eyes presenting the astonishment I have just put her into.

A S A P u b l i s h i n g C o r p o r a t i o n

"Did you lack faith in me? I would not deceive you."
It was not my intention to have relayed it in that fashion. Yet
these are my true feelings.

"She has limited heat within her," Hollice claims
after a brief tongue rasp along the kits spine.

"I am aware of that," I inform, "sheath your tongue.
Soaking her is of no assistance."

"Chrome, I do not feel she will live."

"Mother, I believe only you are able to save her."

"She is not my own," Hollice protests. "My motherly
devotion is only to you. A devotion that is only temporary."

"Then help me!" my demanding voice threatens.
"Help me save her. She has only begun her life as I have.
Born to live just as you and I are." Burning my determination
from within, I am in awe that Hollice has not once interfered.
She knows it is my time in raising my voice.

"She will be saved mother, under you alone by your
nourishment. Once you fill her senses, she will respond as I
do."

Holding my position, Hollice lays beside the dark
she-Gryphon. Mother is bright in both plumage and pelt of
gold; while the immature kit seems to be shrouded in her
own personal blackness. Joining her, I present beak before
Hollice's mammary.

"Please drink," I urge. "You must partake in
restoring yourself."

Hollice rests while I tend the kit. Little movement I
have felt from her, the occasional deep breath or twitch of
her tail. Her heartbeats have fallen from earlier and she has
cooled against my touch. Out of fearful instinct, cries erupt
from my throat as I call to her as she had for me.

"Chrome!" Hollice announces in her angered voice.

"She is dying mother," I remark in awful trembles
taking place of my purrs. The next moment, I am pulled away

in her beak as she drapes her wing over the one I desperately want to save.

"Chrome," my mother's clenching talons take full restraint against me.

"Mother!" every one of my protests proves no success.

"You must accept that she cannot be saved . . ." she goes silent as shock leaps through her. Reacting on instinct alone, I leave the restraining talons as she withdrawals her wing.

I am with her now as she clings to the nipple. Hugging, as it is her new life regenerating. I know these are her exact feelings.

This is the first time I am nursing with another. She does not need to feel so alone as we are now united. Living warmth radiating from Hollice's body, pulsing through me, and onto my fellow kit.

I pondered if she has ever seen with her eyes, and I may be right when the dark irises are revealed before me; pupils shining with the bright violet of the tree in particle reflections; fusing to me in mere fascination. My own communicate a kind expression of reassurance.

"Your life is now secure." To my knowledge, she has received me.

With the remainder of the daylight, the kit begins to explore her surroundings. Such an observant instinct as all is taken into her senses. This truly being the first time she is making extensive use of them. She is even learning to use her physicality as her own tail amazes her with its first motion. Hollice eventually grows agitated by the kit's continuous paces, and rises to her paws in departure.

"Mother!" I announce, "We cannot leave her!"

Reversing with an annoyed expression she retorts,

"she will obviously follow, Chrome. Any kit will out of instinct alone." Her voice reveals that typical side of hers. "However, if she does not follow, then force her." My one clarification is giving a deep bow of limited acknowledgment. I do not know her entire meaning, but I do know that Hollice is always right. To my unexpected mind, the black kit does follow without a second consideration. Trudging through the grass stems, I use my calls to keep her aware of my presence. Fascinated she is, toward my ability to speak.

"You will learn your own voice in time. That is my promise to you." The Gryphon's ears are flexing at every change of tone she picks up in my voice.

"The paces the two of you are making is unacceptable," Hollice scolds as we emerge from the grass.

"Mother, this is the first time she has ever made use of her legs. They are weak and require experience." The matured Gryphon only rolls her golden eyes.

"It will not be tolerated," she sternly conflicts by dipping her head to grasp the black kit in her beak. Without another use of voice, we proceeded on returning to our barrier.

While mother tears the scales from the fish Evaron has left her, I am left on my own to introduce the kit to our den.

"I have no doubt of this being your first sight of both shadows and darkness." She herself is a black mass against our shaded interior. Curiosity is with her at every point while shuffling her beak through our bedding, to the thorns and vines between here and outside. Allowing her continuous exploration, I return to a part of our den I have come to know well. Within these common and similar thorns, is a special dark one. Plucking the small tip and freeing it from the vines, I expose Ankara's feather.

It has become my fresh reminder and reassurance that I am being watched over. Still, I do not know who she really is to me; only that my Queen is someone special. In an instant, the kit is drawn over to me. Amusement strikes with curiosity as she passes her beak over the feather. Now she massages her tongue through the keratin strands and takes in the new scent. Goodness, even she picks up the radiant milk scent.

"This feather is a gift," I inform, "from the wing of our own Queen. I received it only the preceding day. It is a sign of her . . . love," I finally remember.

Quite an amount of time has gone by right now, and I am able to feel the loss of the kits energy. Sore legs and racing pulse are only two individual signs of her weakness. Those black sphere eyes are desperate to hide behind draping lids.

As I lay with her, we take in each other's scent in determination to never forget each other. Despite discovering her deep within the forest, her scent is mineral like. Though I am hungry and in need of nourishment, I do not rise when Hollice enters to settle in her bedding. Her milk is not tempting me, I desire another. I want Ankara.

When not keeping track of how many days the kit has been with us, Hollice makes the decision of consulting Evaron on which Gryphon can take the kit as her own to receive nurturing care. In some ways this news is pleasant, though I am not at full ratification. But to Hollice, I have no consent in this.

"Mother, it is I who found her."

A growl escapes her, "this decision is not yours to make, Chrome. You are unable to provide for her, no matter how close she has grown to you." I know this as well, she never separates from me by always following in my actions; yet, it appears she is also dearly fascinated with Hollice. My understanding of this is they are both female.

"Why does she not have a mother? I assume at least, that she has none."

"I assure you that she has a mother, Chrome. The one who bore her has left their daughter for death." Another fact that places fear within me. Why would a mother do such a thing to a kit? The kit she produced from within herself.

"You really have no recollection of your mother?" I inquire. Her ears lay back deep in thought.

"There is nothing I remember. I believe that you Chrome, are the first I ever saw. It may just be that I do not have a mother as you do."

"There is no such possibility," I contradict. "Hollice describes your mother's absence as abandoning. Yet, I am not sure of the entire meaning; she was not specific."

She has only begun to use her voice over the past few days and taking in all the knowledge she can gain. The first sound she had made was, "Hollice." Similar to how "mother" was my first. Though Hollice declared she is learning at a faster pace than I, our ages are estimated to be the same.

"Is there anything you can do for me? Helping me toward another who will mother me as Hollice does for you?" I give a bow with a somber reply.

"I am sorry. Hollice decided that she will do nothing until she consults my father." I just now might have seen a tear travel down her beak. "There is however, something else I can give you."

At the raise of her ears, she begs, "What?"

"A name, if you so allow me to do so." Prancing up,

she energetically approves.

"Yes, please do this for me, Chrome. I allow your obligation with my greatest welcome."

I have prepared for this moment. From the morning I had found her laying at my side after her day of rescue, I conversed with Hollice on the name I desired. After her advisory, I have not forgotten nor ever will.

"Kyara," my voice carries into existence as her new moniker. For this is the name of the lioness who bore the first Gryphon. Now, Kyara will carry it on through the Aquileia.

A S A P u b l i s h i n g C o r p o r a t i o n

Scenic 17

Raining Ember

I now focus my glance out the window, shifting my view from down to up in the dark clouds. There are flashes in the sky; lights of aircraft I assume. Easily seen despite Gauntlet's light pollution. However, I have not seen them before; nor this horizontal formation spreading across the cloud cover.

Now a number of spotlights ray down upon the fields, shining through the forests and now mixing in with the city lights. All I can do is ponder what is occurring.

"Those aircraft are awfully low," a panda points out one table over.

"They must be looking for Vulpine," states a hare from the other direction. I take the chance and look right at the sow. As predicted, she is staring right at me. Even Skylar receives her projectile voice right through the glass. Returning inside; holding open the door and reaching her paw out to me, I abandon my treat and come.

My purrs are reforming into only the slightest vibrations on the disturbing cause of how mother is in absolute silence.

Even though I lack the knowledge, my impression is

Skylar knowing specifically what she is doing. I cannot help but watch these spotlights descending from the clouds by creeping closer to us every occurring moment.

Mother is in a tranquil unresponsive nature I have not seen her in before now.

"Mother, I wish you would penetrate your silence," experiencing her claws prickle the back of my neck, a definite fear pulses from her. "What is happening?" I plead, "Something feels so wrong." My whimpers are coming out in cries. For this is that same terrible feeling I first received back in the vault.

"Forjah, I . . ." she is cut off by what I think is screaming. Truthfully, it is a high pitched siren of some sort. Even over all this noise, I hear the vixen's strong heart within her breast skipping beats as her fear becomes my own.

The sirens die out; the entire city goes black as all lighting and machinery die, followed by a most dreadful quietness over Gauntlet. Instantly the aircraft reclaim attention of my ears as well as my eyes. Hovering beneath the shallow cloud cover and directly overhead the skyscrapers. The only light is their own.

I so wish Skylar she would light up, pierce this darkness using her internal star. But her aura is only a glare at my side. Reaching out my paws, I take hold of her long golden tail to bury my maw into its pelt, hiding eyes and inhaling her scent. Attempting to forget what is happening and ultimately reassuring myself that she is here and I am not alone. Now, I know that I am feeling true fear. Instinct influences me to run against my will to remain here.

"Stay with her," I decide, "there has never been a moment she has not been near. From the first moment within her womb, we have never been separated." When hugging her tail ever tighter, I experience tears shed from my eyes. Pouring out so greatly, it soaks my facial hairs and her tail. She snorts with many whines of her own. Settling on to one knee to take me into her arms and touches her nose to mine.

"You understand what is happening?" she exclaims in her astonished mood.

I respond weakly, "I feel it is eventfully bad." In even greater comfort, she wraps her golden tail around me as she did when I was newborn; managing to light the tip and swipe away my tears.

As her claws massage and prickle the sides of my jaw, I focus on her ignited tip. Again, she only lights up when in a good mood. But even with our somber combined, those few hairs remain lit upon her tail as hope's smallest shimmer.

"Come now!" she orders, sprinting north down the street-side and away from the aircraft. Skylar has summoned all strength within her, running at a speed I cannot match. These strides of her's are far greater, but I know I can match this speed on four. With senses on full alert, I leap into the air, immediately shifting beneath my clothes and taking off toward mother in quadruped.

Why are there so few in the streets? Every animal appears paralyzed with his or her eyes on the sky. No one seems to care that two Vulpine are maneuvering through the streets at intense speed—Not to mention that I am on all fours. We are not allowing anything to slow us down.

Mother is now just a gold shimmer ahead of me. "I desire to have her inheritance within me," I declare unto myself through every panting breath, "It is said the dog is usually stronger than the vixen. Meaning that someday I may be stronger." But she has the advantage of maturity; as I am still a kit with much development ahead of me.

I could attempt to fly again. Maybe it is feasible with

all this adrenaline; yet, I need to strip down to even expose my nicely kept wings beneath the tunic and clothing. Running with the cloak dragging behind is somewhat of a challenge. Being that it is thick and heavy and interfering with my tail's balance.

"Positive thoughts!" I remember. Never unlatch your clinging to hope. My mind's only intention is to not lose mother. No distractions can be let in. She is leading me further down the street, not showing the slightest sign of decreasing speed.

Now the road and walk are leading onto an overpass of a bridge. Curving to the far off left onto the highway and out of Gauntlet.

"Is this her idea of an escape?" There is absolutely no time for answering questions and my only option is to continue following. My pads already hurt against the stone, for I am galloping as hard as possible. But as the ground gives away from concrete into asphalt, I am finding it littered with ruminants of rock salt for dissolving ice. Hard it is to ignore the taring of my skin against the two of them combined, but I must at all cost not allow bloody pads to halt me.

Vehicles are going in several directions; attempting at U-turns and anything else to reverse direction. My ears flare back as a chorus of screeches echo off the still towers. Accompanied by explosive eruptions, the ground beneath me jerks with such force, my bones snap at their joints. Bringing me down upon the now cracked bridge surface.

"MOTHER!" I wail the moment I impact the stone, feeling stupid for calling like the helpless kit I am. She cannot possibly turn around and help me, that's an endangering risk to herself. She is strong for me and I should be for her. But in only an instant she is here with the overwhelming scent of adrenaline. Who else could double back at incredible speed?

My lower skeleton aches from the fall, but exactly what violent terror has shaken the ground at such a devastating level? Exchanging nothing, Skylar heaves me upon her back.

Gripping her shoulders, I bury my muzzle into her furry neck as she takes off. Her running speed is increased again as she pants hard without rest. Now I am beginning to notice a most peculiar heat traveling from my tail tip and up along my spine; accompanied by a great ember like flash from behind.

From on her back, I now see that this overpass is winding between the building structures. She is not intent on heading any further down the road. Coming to a halt, Skylar makes a 180 turn to face where we had just been moments earlier. My sore leg joints are going numb along with the rest of my physical and emotional self. The emptiness of fear inducing events are now coming together as a chaotic collaboration. Now I know the reason for the warmth, the terrible earth quake, and the eerie glow. Towers of stone and steel and are now pillars of fire.

Scenic 18

Night of Inferno

Imagine these air craft are large birds producing black droppings silhouetted against the inferno glow; raining down to explode on impact. Before having the chance to collide with anything, Skylar carries us prancing into the air. Timing it just right by uplifting from the quake spasms beneath.

Crackling, crumbling follows the bursts of these explosions. Returning repetitively like a pattern of drop, detonate, drop, detonate. Does she know this, having guessed, or perceptively realizing it ahead of now?

"Mother?" I bellow from my windpipe before catching on to her evasive directory. Right in our path is an overpass light pole with a base atop a building below.

Force of wind throws my ears back, my claws pierce into her delicate shoulders, doing all I can to ready for this beastly escape. As if Lola has passed on a contagious feeling, my stomach goes into colic. She grasps both arms and legs around the smooth cylinder; now we slide down to the roof below. Breaking into yet another run, Skylar hurdles over to the next rooftop.

"My son, we must remain above the ground as much as possible." I love her voice, however right now there are no purrs in the panting breaths. Her rapid heart is no more than a hum on its own.

The vixen halts before leaping to the next roof with intent on being airborne at every quake. This must be why they are in horizontal formations. One line attacks after the other in a pattern to scourge every point of the city. Will these aircraft run out of weaponry, or will Skylar be reduced to fatigue?

"We caused this," I erupt, "we attracted them."

"NO!!" Mother rejects, just before our next leap. Once safely on the next landing, she adds, "They choose to come regardless."

The air is plagued in smoke. It's dreaded aroma drifts into my nostrils, now reeking in my mangled fur. What began as a cool evening has become a night of inferno. For Gauntlet is becoming a city of flames. The aches in my legs subsided, but mother continues to stress with each bound. Always landing with a stumble, I of course, am the reason. My excessive weight is holding her back.

On the next leap, I immediately see her bounding thrust is under powered. Gravity is taking us over, falling short of our intended landing. Roaring with every amount of energy sapped from my adrenals, I open my leathery drapes, ripping through the fabric of both the tunic and cloak, flapping hard in desperation of completing our leap.

But no uplift.

A deep cry escapes Mother as her outstretched nails manage only to scrape the stone brick wall; where gravity now takes us over entirely. This is something I have no preparation for. I feel weightless as my stomach turns and shifts within my abdomen. Colliding with an awning, I break away from Skylar's shoulders on impact.

Though I rarely ever come to Gauntlet, I always

know the streets to be cold. However, this stone is unusually warm just like the waves of air coming from the south. Now the adrenaline is as strong as my fear, increasing with each new earth tremor approaching from behind. As equally disturbing as the cries of citizens they are associated with.

"I feel more nauseous every moment I hear the wails of the innocent," pulling myself on all fours, I gaze up from where I had fallen. "Mother!" I call as strong as I can possibly manage. A relief like no other overcomes me as she peeks over the awning's edge. In the midst of all the devastation, I see that loving shine sparkle on the tips of her whiskers.

"Here," even as I bring forth the reassurance, there is a threatening sensation overcoming the atmosphere in the absolute opposite way she just has. Skylar's ears flare back in my same realization. Raising up to the sky, she reacts with parting her lips and letting out a growl.

Her siren like call rings out in alert too fast for my reaction. Dim against the smog and haze, I sight the dropping with eyes flared open. Upon impact I am unsure if the white flash or deafening sound comes first. The force of the explosion launches me back and parts my lips to inhale the flames. Traveling down my windpipe, into my lungs, and entering my skull through the eye sockets.

Scenic 19

Fission

No longer do I feel my body as my consciousness and memory burn away; evaporated by the heat. Even the scalding pain vanishes to the point where I am not even here to hurt. My mind and senses remain. I see the warm colored flames fade from orange, to red, to blue, and finally violet. I take in the scent of the fumes through my senses to inhale smoky earth odor. This flickering taste of the flares tickle my tongue while the rest passes over my fur and softly massages the skin beneath.

I still have my mentality and sensory, but I cannot have those without a body. Does this mean it is not cremated? Because my Vulpine form feels no more, as though fire has assumed its long held position.

"My life must be beginning, and not ending," I conclude. "I do not know where it originates, but must be bringing me to life." This birth is soothing, so warm and cozy engulfed in this intense furnace. But to whom does this womb belong?

Smoke and iron are at my senses, accompanied by an awful ringing in my ears and a throbbing pain in my cranium that brings me to consciousness. I have lost him in

A S A P u b l i s h i n g C o r p o r a t i o n

the explosion but know he was thrown back in the fiery ring spreading out from the bomb. Structural walls all around me crumbled from the force; turning the buildings to heaps of debris. The awning fell away the moment the explosion made contact, taking me down with it. Flames surround me like a flowing river burning both me and striping down to my fur. The ground that had once been cold is now eerily warm as my nose presses to its surface. Rising up, I manage to bring myself onto my knees and attempt to recollect what has occurred. Peering into the smoky haze, all strikingly returns like the bomb itself. To navigate through this smog is proving to be a challenge; however, Forjah is all that clouds my mind.

Climbing over the remains of the awning, I locate him in the wreckage using my nose alone. With bare paws, I dig through wood and stone; throwing and tossing away everything that separates he and I.

Exposing his Vulpine head is the most soothing moment. Eyes are sealed shut behind their lids and his fur soiled gray in ash.

The pain of bringing him forth from the rubble is much like the intensity of when he was first ready to leave my womb. I cried to my mate to please remove the kit as his gentle assisted the birth of our son. It seems now I am freeing him from in utero once again.

Delivery is almost complete. One last thrust, summoning all adrenaline to heave with ultimate strength. Screaming with vocals not that of a Vulpine, I bring the kit into existence and into my arms. Gripping him at my breast I collapse in gratitude, lungs pantingly inhaling as they did when I first bore him. A dog, my son.

He arrives, golden hairs powdered in ash, paw pads seeping blood from their scars, body burning with inferno fever. Most certainly this is a wacky sensation of de-ja-vu.

Freeing him from the rubble as I had done from my womb. Coated in the same black fur, eyes sealed behind their lids, he really does resemble the newborn that he once was. Why has this supernatural feeling come to me, it is as though I am giving birth to him once again.

Tears flow down my muzzle out of impulse and relief that I have found my kit. I have never felt someone so warm; yes, for some reason his body is extremely feverish. Licking him, I clean the soot from around his eyes, then close the scars of his paws with a nice coat of saliva. Pressing my ear against his chest, I join my purrs with his strengthening heartbeat. Even giving off just a bit of shine for his life remaining. Yet it is not his heart alone that brings new emotion. This emotion is fear because I hear them coming.

Without a second thoughtful consideration, I leave Fox after concealing him in the debris to camouflage his location. The Vulpine Instinct is overpowering me, telling me to hide him, as well as the identity of who is coming for us. Crawling on my belly, I abandon him to pull myself out into what is left of the street; drawing attention away.

"Take her," one orders the moment they come into my view. Claws gash into my muscles as I am gripped between two of the beasts. These thugs know I am a Vulpine, so why not sterilize me here and now? Why are there no blades drawn to carve out my torso?

No matter what this reason may be, I feel it is my burden to bare. A sacrifice for the kit I bore and love. Being a mother, I gave part of my own life-force in order to create life. All the pain from conception to the time I gave birth; I see as a sacrifice. To the dog I fell in love with and to the dog I bore from within me. My obligation as his mother is not complete, it never will be. This is what I hope he will know one day. For he will forever be my son, Forjah.

Scenic 20

Transition

Feeling energetic after my nourishment from Hollice, both Kyara and I are ready to leave the barrier. Leading her under the bramble wall, she follows close behind. Hollice then joins us by coming over it in a gracious leap.

"Kyara," the young female beams at my mother's voice, "I must confer with Evaron. We are to meet him this morning." Granting an acknowledging bow, she angles her head up to give a question the moment their eyes lock on.

"Hollice, are you able to find a mother?" Kyara remains curious as the adult's eyes roll within their sockets.

"That is obviously the reason I am speaking with Evaron. He can help you." This sneer in her tone is possibly a form of dislike. But mother turns her tail to claim the lead, passing over the gentle ridge rising up near our den, without any additional advice or info.

"She has such a beautiful golden pelt," Kyara compliments. "I love how her feathers blend into her fur."

"Well observed," I comment with interjectory. "Evaron has made similar comments toward her."

"Who is he?" she inquires, "can he really help me find a mother?" With a touch of my tongue, she goes calm.

"He is my father and mate of Hollice."

A hint of doubt shows in her monologue, how can she not have faith in my father? Resting my wing over her shoulders, I guide Kyara up and over the rise.

"I am able to promise you will be with your mother this day."

After a time, I begin sprinting in order to reach mother, but realize I am leaving Kyara behind. Slowing my paw's pace; I retreat to her assistance.

"You move so slowly," the claim brings her head up, showing eyes filled with fatigue.

"My legs continue to pain me. Do you know of when it will cease? In answer, I give a small nod.

"I know what pain you go through, Kyara. It was upon me only for a time as it's now upon you.

"You are inquiring that it is only temporary?"

"Yes," I reassure with a bow. "Would it help if my mother carried you?"

"No," Kyara hisses between throes, "I must bare this burden and earn the strength of a Gryphon." I cannot help but be astounded by her courage.

"Then I shall proceed at your side, if you allow me?" I offer. She approves with a weak but pleasing welcome.

It is a long while before we catch up with Hollice. Yet, I am on edge now that Chrome and I are approaching. For at his mother's side is an even larger Gryphon. This one bares a brown pelt with a taint of white on his feathers. Eyes so stern they seem unnatural.

"Hello Father," Chrome calls the moment we halt before the Gryphon who returns the greeting with a deep purr.

"Such a deep voice," I observe. I have grown accustom to being small but the site of Chrome's father is immensely beyond my brain's acceptance. Only when he asks for my name, do I make a response.

"I am Kyara, are you here in order to find a mother for me?" Giving a bow, he avows.

"That is my current purpose. I believe you will accept my assistance?" He is not conveying any different from his mate or his son; meaning my own communication will be well met.

Evaron's body takes a deep bow in order to meet my eye level. The leonine eyes are set firmly behind his raptor's beak baring irises of deep green. Will Chrome bare such eyes one day? Will I myself develop a beautiful pair?

"There is no need to emit your fear of me, Kyara. I assure that you are in complete safety."

"I also hope she will not fear her to-be mother," Hollice cuts in.

"I doubt such a happening will occur," Evaron specifies. I have not thought of what my mother will be like at all. Will she like me, will I get along with her?

The one retort I give Evaron is the same small customary nod Chrome uses. Returning to his full height, he takes the lead to a destination I do not know. Hollice follows, but I turn to Chrome.

"I wish my confidence was at equal strength of your own," flexing his small talons so they knead the earth, he hesitantly enlightens.

"I have not emitted fear much at all. The first time, it made no sense at all because I was in no true danger. The last time, was genuine fright. When your life almost expired."

He and Hollice are the only to have experienced my close call separation from life. I was only partially there; but here is where I would not be if I was to remain undiscovered.

"I will always be thankful for your heroism, Chrome. Even when I am with my future mother, you will always be my first friend." From these relayed linguistics, I receive an embrace within his wings.

"Thank you, Kyara," he appreciates, creating a moment filling with purrs from deep within he and I.

Ignoring all pain she had complained about before. Kyara is now running at my side undisturbed by her sore legs.

"She must be toughing it out," I conclude. Never did I think a small Gryphon could be capable of such strength. She is impressing me yet again.

The forest is almost completely rid of the moisture as it is now a mist overhead. In time, the scents begin mixing with the fresh aromas of the surrounding water. The hard ground transfers into the slick grains of sand. The bay now before us.

Kyara reacts with an instant alarm by throwing herself into the soft earth, leisurely crawling past my parents with intent to reach the water.

"This is terrific!" she calls out, "never could my mind create a chimerical comparison image to this. It can only be visualized from reality."

Blinking my eyes, I glow at her exuberance. Now my own adrenaline is coming in; sprinting ahead to join her the moment she sets her paws in the water.

"It is so cold," calling out the moment she flops down with the waves falling over. Pouncing upon her, she and I roll together in the continuous water washing upon the land. The early morning is chilling to the both of us, transferring our warm purrs into trembling shivers.

"The two of you are endangering yourselves,"

Hollice scolds, "the cold will claim your lives." Just like that, mother is spoiling our fun.

"Is that true?" Kyara sputters, regurgitating water. With an inferring retort, I take her down in a playful manner adding.

"She knows best," after tiring of the cold, we return to Hollice. Huddling against her flanks as Evaron proceeds to the cliff side.

"He is going to bring our friend, Adelhied. She and her kits live here within the rock." Mother is just as agitated as usual; yet, I am unable to recall when she was ever joyful.

"Is Adelhied to be my mother?" Kyara questions. I am wondering the same.

"I do not know," she indicates, "right now the two of you need to stay warm. Meaning you need to stay close to me," she then mumbles, "how unfortunate." Hollice's temper is radiating much welcoming warmth; however, another thing is occupying my mind. If Adelhied lives here, does this mean I will see Aquila?"

Throughout our time here, I am keeping track of the climate changes. As the sky disc rises higher, the day grows warmer. Life is beginning its awakening yet again. Surprising that we ourselves awakened long before now.

"The birds are so sweet," Kyara comments, welcoming the new day. A chilling breeze continues to come in from the water, but it is not taking long to realize it is my mother's shadow preventing the light from beaming down. Taking a number of jumps through the sand, I now give myself entirely to the solar rays, allowing fur and down to take in their intense heat. This has to be the warmest I have experienced yet, being how rare it is for Chromium to have a day of warmth. My entire outside temperature is arising at the same moment as my internal. There, advancing toward me, bounding in the sand sprints a red Gryphon kit.

"Chrome!" she announces.

"Aquila!" I proclaim. Without giving any reaction, I welcome the frenzied pounce similar to how I had first met her only a number of days ago.

"You are here," she cries as I am pinned in the sand under her weight once again, "I knew it was you the moment your father announced arrival."

"I am the only Chrome there is," I assure, "and I have not seen such hyper activity apart from your own," I inform, pulling myself closer to her, "this energy bursting from you is most strong." Without giving her a single warning, I throw all my strength into my hind legs to bring great force upon her as I launch myself from the sand to take her to the ground with tremendous momentum. Interlocking our eyes, I clearly see the shock in her expression.

She palpitates with a dazed look, "You really got the advantage of me." I know her meaning, for not knowing that much strength was within me. Resulting in surprising both she and myself.

"I intended not to harm you," I plead. My friend bares a gleeful grin while extending her neck to swipe her tongue below my eye.

"I take no offense, Chrome."

Afterward, completing our pouncing attacks. Aquila introduces me to her mother, Adelhied, a leopard Gryphon who bares brown feathers and a white spotted pelt. It is peculiar how this mother and daughter do not appear related; however, Avalon, Aquila's sister; sports a similar appearance. The same brown fur while wings and head are draped in down

She then introduces Tauro, her brother. He has the kindest glare with a mixture of black and blue furs within his hide. The shape of his ears and the nicely rounded beak are much like his mother's. These introductions are brief yet significant. Then it is Evaron who brings forth a new subject.

"Adelhied," he directs, "I must converse with Hollice upon Kyara's matter. Are you willing to care for both she and Chrome until my mate and I resolve an agreement?"

"I am," she confirms, "take what time you require. Your kits will be safe along with my own."

Without giving a goodbye to my parents, I watch as my father leads Hollice away and into the woods.

"They must be heading out and will then bring your mother here," I whisper to Kyara, "That is my assumption." A breath of relief escapes her. I promised she would be with her mother this day.

While Kyara further acquaints with Tauro, I remain somewhat antisocial toward everyone. I cannot remove my mind from the current subject that causes my worry for her. If a mother is found for her, she will be taken away from me this day. Still, I wonder the same question Hollice brought up. Is Kyara to join Aquila's kin? To be raised as Adelhied's daughter?

"Chrome?" Aquila interrupts. My mind now departs directive attention to her but my heart is not doing the same.

"You appear depressed," she observes.

"No denial," I admit. It is not until she convinces me to explain my troubled thoughts that I make any enlightenment.

"I have grown close to Kyara; she is as much my friend as you are. I stress over the fact that she will be taken away from me this day." Aquila remains silently attentive, so I continue.

"Sharing my den and my life with her has been a great enjoyment. At times, I lose the thought that she is not my kin." Aquila takes in my entire meaning.

"You wish to have a part in who Kyara is taken in by," she describes, "so that you and she will never break the bond."

I dip my beak in response.

"I know your hurt, Chrome. I admit that it was hard to separate from you after our first meeting. I was hopeful we would reunite, and now we have."

I cannot help but brighten up with satisfaction. How thankful I am to be here at this moment when all feels as it should be. Apart from my gripping pain of being separated from yet another close friend.

"When my mother and father return," I voice in declaration, "I will voice my concern. Neither she nor I ratify our separation." Aquila massages herself against the down of my chest. Pressing her beak to my ear, I take in . . .

"You are committed to the will of your strong heart and mind. I so admire that Chrome." Admiration? Being praised by another is new to me. I would only expect such an action from Evaron, as Hollice never congratulates me on anything.

"To have you all at my side . . . I welcome it to the full extent," the moment her tongue meets my neck, my ears receive her.

"I am committed to you."

A S A P u b l i s h i n g C o r p o r a t i o n

Scenic 21

Kin

Evaron is leading me to an unknown destination. I cannot help but be curious, and yet, confused.

"This will do," he rules after giving a halt. Stopping in my tracks, I express.

"What is your meaning? I assumed you would present Kyara to Adelhied?" he grants a bow and continues. "That was a consideration from the moment you suggested I help her." His voice raises up my ears. I am not sure if I should give him any answer, for I have nothing to add. But when forcefully managing a response, I bring up.

"Then . . . how do you intend to help her?" My mate's wings gave a shrug by shifting at their roots upon his shoulders while he mentally prepares his dialog.

"Hollice, I will be proud to accept Kyara as our daughter," these divulging words have such force, I come close to losing my balance and settle on my haunches. Tail curling around my paws, I seek the effort to contradict.

"Daughter . . .? I cannot. Chrome is enough."

"In the beginning you revealed that you desired to have many kits," he breaks in, recollecting my thoughts from the past.

"Chrome is biologically ours," he presses on. "If we

take Kyara, he will have a sibling."

This entire idea of his causes every part of me to tremble. I am in no way approving this.

"Evaron, I am hardly capable of dealing with our own. He causes me such an amount of stress that I am failing in health. I need you to be strong Hollice as I am further committing myself as your equal and as Chrome's father. As we take Kyara in, our son will live a healthier youth." It is a great amount of information to take in a short time. Enduring every bit of it, I allow him to further detail.

"Now that Chrome has further matured, he will tolerate being away from you for a time. He and Kyara will remain with either myself or Adelheid, giving you a day to yourself. Pulling this off by alternating who attends to them."

I am beginning to like this idea.

"Because of the recent attacks upon the Aquiliea; no kit will be left alone. Please Hollice, let us take Kyara as our own. For both her sake and our son's."

I feel paralyzed from my mate's request. Relaying so much while all I have done is take it in. He is not giving any sort of order, only asking for my obligation to be a foster mother.

Clawing my talons through the grass and into the soil, I utter, "I wish to appease you Evaron. I will consent to be Kyara's mother." In thanks, I receive his wing embrace accompanied by a tongue massage against the side of my jaw.

The sky disc has risen high over the period of Evaron and Hollice's absence. During this time, I am becoming well acquainted with Tauro. Being the only male of a litter of three, he has a distinct personality. But it is his sister who is now claiming the attention of us all.

"My awe is expanding," she voices. "Chrome is sort of your heroine," Aquila brightens up, setting her focus on me, "I understand that you are the reason for our brief introduction that day." I give her no avow cause I do not understand what she means; until Chrome begins to detail do I even begin to.

"In truth, you have configured the event accurately Aquila. That morning is when I heard Kyara's distant calls. Making every effort to reach her, I triumphed in my task." The red kit joyfully jumps from her sitting position. Eyes so fixed on him, they refuse to move in their sockets. However, Aquila's dark spheres have not left the Gryphon who had saved my life at all today.

"I wish I had hearing that advanced," Tauro calls over from he and Avalon taking in a mid-day nourishment from Adelhied. She offered to nurse both Chrome and I, but I declined with perfect content with the nourishment I acquire from Hollice.

"Will I feel the same toward my new mother?" Another thought to add in my tumult of a mind.

"Your hearing will develop strongly," Adelhied assures her son, "the time will come."

"I also desire strong senses," Aquila breaks in, "when will I mother?"

"When it is meant to happen," she reassures, "development will bring it."

I am hesitant to an extreme that prevents myself from joining into the conversion. It is just my bashful nature with preference to listen along in constant flow of thoughts.

Somehow, I know they are more mature than Chrome. Upon another relative thought, I was born after him. So this entire mental outcome is why he seems more advanced than Adelhied's kits? Their maturity level is greater by their time of birth but it is Chrome who has advanced sensory.

"Kyara," he interjects in a soft assault, "you have shown severe tranquility for quite a time," now feeling I should communicate, I mumble through my beak.

"I am showing my bashfulness, aren't I?"

"Yes you are," he clarifies.

I really do not enjoy socialism, rather thinking to myself than use my voice. But interruptions attack my mind, plaguing it with visuals.

Chrome sports gray down in place of where his fledgling feathers will one day sprout, and later, his true flight feathers. Fur of gold much like his mother's, the gradual curve of his skull and beak are similar to Evaron's. In comparison, I bare night black plumage. My fur is of a glossier shade with various silver strands. Most noticeably of all, I am the smallest here.

"Kyara?" this time it is Adelhied's voice. Inhaling a fearful breath, I straightened up and face her with many vibrating trembles that are no longer purrs, but shivers.

"You have been in an unresponsive state since your arrival here. Is there anything I can do for you?" With a deep sulk, I shake my head while resting upon my belly, desiring to further force myself into the sand and sink deep beneath the grains. Yet, my eyes stop me as I begin to focus my vision on Adelhied's wings; dressed in gorgeous white and brown feathers. Instinctively, I begin to flex my own. Oh do I wish these gray fuzzy limbs could make me airborne. I could ascend up past the cliffs where the disc had first peeked over a time ago; maybe even into the regions a distance past the forest. To be myself and to not have others hovering over me. A place I would not need to be afraid.

My quiet nature is appearing contagious. For Adelhied's family is now in an unresponsive state. Chrome remains close to me as Aquila keeps toward him. Now I feel ashamed of how I have caused this tranquil environment.

"I have caused this among us, so maybe I can counteract it," summoning forth energy from an unknown force of will, I take in a desperate inhale and bring up my voice.

"Adelhied," I began. Not only do I grab her attention, I also captured the focus of Chrome, Aquila, Tauro, and Avalon. This is what I should expect from finally breaking my silence.

"I . . . I want to see you fly." Almost faltering to retreat behind my eye lids. Unable to imagine their expressions, I wonder what responsive action I am about to receive?

"A most interesting request," she comments. "As you asked, I will perform it."

The five of us watch as this Gryphon makes distance between us. Adelhied's six limbs flex in preparation to spring as the sky disc glimmers upon their imbrications. In an instant she charges into the air wings spread, forcing downward in strength filled muscles to form a crater in the grains. Legs locked close to her belly, she rises high over the water, gaining altitude with momentum building speed. She displays countless feats; flying so high to appear diminished in size reduction, sharp banking with tight angles for increased thrust by catching thermals, gliding dangerously low over the waves to strike the surface with open talons, and spiraling in deep descents as would a lightning bolt.

For a finale, Adelhied lands atop the cliff side high overhead. Without moment of hesitation, she leaps down the wall beak first. Gravity claims her entirely on this downward charge; does she mean to penetrate the earth? Like the swipe of a squamata's tongue, her wings unfurl in midair, transferring the Gryphon into a glide, sailing overhead by eclipsing a spread eagled silhouette against the daylight.

We all gaze in awe from beginning to end. In completion, Adelhied lands upon the sand, folds her her raptor's limbs, and gives a deep bow. Oh do I wish to be like her one day.

Easily recalling the day I had seen Moonsight and his Queen descend from the mountains, I am easily able to compare Gryphon's flight patterns from each other. Experiencing it on my own however, gave me a different perspective. When Hollice carried me through the air, it had all been sudden and shocking to be so high traveling at great speeds. Adelhied has done it with great ease. Appearing to not be out of breath and still burning with energy.

"This has been an enrapturing experience," Kyara outbursts so we all hear. "My body feels so light and fluttery from the excitement. Adelhied, you have really made this a most enjoyable day. Thank you."

"My pleasure."

Kyara now turns to me, "what did you think of her aerial display, Chrome?"

"Most amusing and inspirational," I infer. My mind tells me that I will learn the flight strength when the time comes. When that arrives, I will also be ready.

Time has now entered past midday. The disc may no longer be at its highest, but the great light sphere continues producing its ardent rays. I am now basking on a rock with my eyes in deep focus into the forest; still awaiting Evaron and Hollice's return. I expect a third will accompany them, the female who is to take Kyara, to take her away from me. Aquila lays at my side, distinctively aware of my worry.

"I long for a way to help you through this," she offers. "You are so stressed over what you cannot change," my friend is now sharing my depression. Kyara has gone off with Tauro. In a way I feel she has done so in attempt to hide from her new mother. Hollice would not allow me to have any inclusion. She claimed it is meant that she and Evaron make this decision. Now I feel we will be apart for life."

"This does not seem right in any way," she points out. "You and she will not be the same after this day. Will this mean your depression will reoccur and continue?" Without giving her question any thought, I predict.

"That seems so."

Tauro had now given a tour of his territory; their barrier, hidden in the ground and burrowing beneath the stone cliffs. He explains that every awakening is accompanied by the water's waves which hold such gentle maneuvers flowing from each rock to grain of shoreline. Allowing Chrome and Aquileia to remain together, I allow Tauro to easily grab my attention. He and I are frolicking further along the cliff wall to where our pathway narrow in point where the sand dips sharply into the water. The cliff wall expands far out along Chromium's shoreline, winding around the island and out of sight.

"I wonder if I will ever see anything taller than these walls of stone," calling back, Tauro indicates.

"My mother claims the mountains are even larger," I turn my head in attempt to compare but the cliffs shield my view.

"I really enjoy coming here," Tauro opens up, "it is quiet for having time to myself. Away from my sisters and my continuously hovering mother."

Unaware if I understand his meaning, my one comparison is Hollice, never scrutinizing anything Chrome does while always allowing him to do as he pleases. It must be normal for a mother to be either observant or careless. But as Adelhied has this difference, Hollice has her own with agitated temper.

"How does your father treat you?" I question when halting before a large rock. The revelation to follow attacks my unprepared mind. Working against what I can relate to, but prevents me from accepting as genuine fact.

"I do not have a father," my heart gives a jump from this communicated message now recorded within me. It echoes from every nerve to vain.

"I do not have a mother or a father. Do you relate to that in any way?" I utter in the calmest voice I can manage. He nods.

"I have asked why we do not have a father. Mother only infers it is not for her to explain, then stating that we will learn in time." Instinctively, I flex my wing and drape it over his back and give this consoling dialog.

"It is strange for me to not have parents of my own. You are in a better position than I am, Tauro. You and your sisters are blessed to have Adelhied; I can only hope my new mother will be a blessing for me."

"Even if your mother is not beneficial, know that you have me as your ally. I would even accept you into my family."

His statement sparks joy within me. Though it would be away from Chrome, I would still be near.

"It is off topic," he breaks in, "but I would like to ask. Are you participating in the tournament?" Before opportunity is granted to input, he leaps from the sand, hurtling over the water where the rock face receives his landing. Willfully, I follow with my own leap. Falling somewhat short to dangle from the edge by my claws, tips of my hind paws and tail soaked.

"What are you referring to?" the moment I bring myself up and lay at his side.

"The tournament Moonsight is holding for every kit

in the Aquileia. It is a series of competitions we partake for purpose of building our strength of defense. Are you interested in participating?"

"Yes, I am," I openly declare with a flutter of my eyelashes. "How will I qualify?"

"You must have the approval of Moonsight, as well as another to train you, who must be an adult apart from your biological parents."

"That should not be a problem for me," I specify in obvious recollection of being parentless. "Who is training you?" I now put out.

"Evaron, I have also been tripled with my sisters, so he is guiding the three of us in preparation of our defensive skills."

Now I need the guidance of an elder Gryphon apart from a parent; however, I do not even have a mother to begin with where I began. So seeking an inspirational figure is irrelevant at the moment.

"Optimistically, I know that I am not alone as I feel." Now realizing that I am not as uniquely exclusive as I once believed. Tauro having no father, and I not having any parents. But I am still alone in such a way that it deeply stresses me. But Chrome's prophetic is echoing in my thoughts again and their return is building confidence.

"I promise that you will be with your mother this day."

Scenic 22

Crimson Strands

How long has it been? Am I even awake? All is so warm as though within a furnace. The heat seems to be internal, originating from within me. I intend for Skylar to hear and come to my aid, but it only takes some brief moments before recollecting what previously happened.

Once finding I am able to move, I begin crawling with my remaining energy. What feels like wood and bricks brushes against my belly, proving that at least my sense of touch is working. My head is throbbing in unrecognizable pain as I now understand I am blind and deaf once again. Even though I vaguely remember, I had first found mother by scent alone; but it and my taste are nonexistent. I can only feel what my physicality is telling my mind, but my spirit does not want to believe it.

I am so frightened because of this isolation, alone in this tranquil darkness as only my body is alive. Is my once Vulpine vessel emptied of soul and senses? Is it the last part of me still living?

"Get it over with!" I demand, "Why am I still here?" Yet, here I remain only partially alive. "Wait . . ." I conclude, "I'm . . . living?" This can only mean one thing. "My body is clinging to life, rejecting whatever form of death came upon me. My blessing of immortality is overcoming these fatalities by building and strengthening my body's immunity.

"What does not perish me, strengthens me." Now remembering how we hybridize and fuse through infection. "I am not withering, I am only regenerating my return. This is it, my entire form desires life above all else. Not giving up satisfying its demanding urge to prosper and carry on. Neither am I.

There is an intense burning present inside me as though my lungs are cooking. Breaths are short, coming out in wheezes touching my throat. Each exhale is painful as air passes through my sinuses like boiling steam.

Through rock and wood, I navigate with only what I can feel in my path. As much as I want to open both my eyes, to take in and receive the aftermath, I am completely unable. They are sealed tightly shut, not even opening when I attempt prying them free.

After crawling through the debris for a time, the temperature changes beneath me to the extreme. Almost as though I am creeping over hot coals.

My first shimmer of hope arises in the reawakening of scents and sounds. My nose locks upon the smell of burnt ash, my ringing ears pick up   the faint crawling; both are a sign of recovery leading on into my relief of rising hope. I have summoned my instinct to guide me, the Vulpine Instinct.

My body desires water, but what I really want is mother. I can only hope she will be at the river because this is where my instinct is leading me. I feel like a Joey on its way to mother's pouch. Navigating through a city's wreckage like a thick pelt of fur. Our purpose is the same: to reach mother.

From memory alone, I find the river still flowing cold at the touch. Letting myself go, the water submerges me into its mineral tasting depths. The chilled liquid has every part of me consumed in refreshment that has never come over before. I am the fire, the river is ice, we create a dueling paradox of infinite contradiction. It will not extinguish me; I will not melt it.

When the claw points of my hind paws penetrate the surface of river bed. I kick off the mud and open my wings to paddle to the surface. Breaking with ascension like marine mammal, I let out a howling roar in triumphant cleansing, expressing the most powerful relief against all this devastation. I feel like the single candle flame penetrating perpetual darkness.

Bringing my head and paws close. I wet my sealed lids to scrub the soot away. Sure enough, feeling returns with a soreness in the sockets. Without hesitation, I expose my vision sensory organs.

At first, my visuals is blurry then progressively improve with adjustment to the light. Here I am in the river now running brown from all the dirt. White steam evaporates over head.

"So I really am steaming, from a fever most likely," obviously explaining my high temperature. The air is still hazy over the remains of Gauntlet while the only life I see are the last of the burning flames.

"It is so quiet, all feels dead," I observe, then remembering, "but I am alive." Thankful I am, that my home lies outside the city. But unlike me, the domestic citizens have no close refuge. Now that I think about it, I am not even sure there is anyone left; for there is only silence to be heard; which further expands my feeling that Gauntlet truly is lifeless.

"I have survived," I declare. "I cannot be the alone."

Deciding to further clean myself, I begin scrubbing the soot away beginning with my pelt. I really expected to see someone else doing the same, but all I pick out along the shoreline is scattered debris. There should be survivors, because the city was not bombed in entirety.

Finally, my gold inherited fur is reappearing beneath the black ash. The same as Skylar's pelt that I am proud to have.

"Please be at labyrinth," I pray, "waiting for me." When the majority of the cinder is washed away, I decide that it may be time to leave Gauntlet and return home. There is nothing left here other than myself.

I am about to leave the river when something catches my eye. Something small and red mixed within the gold hairs of my wrist. Dipping my arm back into the water, I scrub the crimson spot vigorously. Raising it to the surface, I find it remains. Upon even closer inspection I find that it is a single red hair mixed in with my golden furs.

Taking it between my thumb and index claw, I tug on it to prove it is definitely my own. Why is a deep red hair forming among all my gold?

"Goodness!" Immediately finding even more sprouting up everywhere else. Along my arms, legs, and abdomen. Once bringing my tail around, I find it too has many red hairs spreading up my spine extension. Something is in error, fur cannot change colors in that short amount of time being unconscious.

"Wait!" I shudder, "how long have I been out?" There is no way to answer that, but was it really that long?" No, it could not be. The city is still freshly smoldering with fire and smoke.

Taking in a strong breath, I attempt to ignore how painful it is to my airways. Obviously there are some biological difficulties here accompanying my fever. Though all the destruction produces many odors, a new one has come to my nose on the gentle breeze of the wasteland. My sense of smell has returned and it is taking in a pungent one that reeks of decay.

Taking one brief glance to my left, I touch down focus upon a motionless figure. Black as I just now was, hidden amongst the burnt wreckage, attracting both hungry fish and insects

The charred carcass sends me into a feint much like the one I came out of. Water submerges me beneath and into its peaceful depths. The river's current delivers as I embrace my knees in the fetal position. Visualizing I am still in mother's womb awaiting my time instead of floating here expecting death.

Scenic 23

Out of Ashes

The moment I can no longer hold my breath, I surface to the wood of the river to be greeted by bodies limply floating and caught in the fallen trees.

With impulse like the prick of a blade, I regain footing onto the river bed, then charge to the dry bank in relief it remains green and not charcoaled. My body aches beyond what adrenaline I have left, and I cannot even voice it. But with these inflamed lungs, body soaked in water tainted with smoke and decaying flesh; all of me gives way to collapsing into the root of a maple, to where I unleash every burden in a stream of tears.

"Mother?" I manage to call in what little voice I have left as desperately when I was first born. There is not a breath nor drop of reserved energy in me by the time I reach the labyrinth. To quite an unexpected astonishment, the area is much more tranquil than I have ever known it to be. It is disturbing that my wild home appears equally as dead compared to the urban city.

"Could animals have really fled the entire territory from the air raid?" That is a definite theory. Managing to land on my knees before the entrance, I again call for Skylar in every motive to work against the wheezing.

The whimpers of my voice echo through the deep stone tunnels as I enter my domain. My den's entrance is up ahead to the left. Once entering, I am deeply disappointed she is not here. Unsure if I expected this or not, I proceed to our item pile of bundled keepsakes at the far side of the den. Mainly there are essentials when we need them, such as thick blankets for the cold nights and bottles for transporting water.

Desiring something cold, I pry open the lid and gulp the cylinder empty. Letting it fall from my pad, I take the second to drink it dry as well. I am left with a refreshment as a slight counteraction attacks my fever. I wish I could cool down my wind pipe and lungs; yet, nothing is stopping me. Grasping mother's canteen, I unscrew the lid and touch my lips to the rim. Instead of swallowing, I inhale the liquid past my uvula into my cardiovascular system. Immediately I am forcing it back up and onto the soil of my den. Friction in my throat builds up from the coughs, giving me an inflammatory feeling.

Breathing water is indeed a bad choice, but now my mind seems to be returning into sanity. Doing my best to clearly process my thoughts, a personal favorite item here is the leather pouch of marbles Skylar granted me. These colorful spheres fascinate me just as fire does.

The thought of it brings a warm and fiery ember into my being; yet, fire right now does not belong in my mind. It has always been a pleasure, and has now become a devastation.

Taking the marble pouch into my paw, I crawl over to the bedding, withdraw the thick blanket back and revealing the bed of straw and domestic sheets. This is where her scent strongly remains in her memory. Contacting me from here to her past there.

Descending into the bundle, I snuggle beneath the warm covers. Protectively gripping them in my claws, inhaling mother's aroma by bringing them close. Tears follow my shivers the instant of taking in that I am alone as never before.

As these liquids leave my eyes; her lingering scent enters my nostrils to fill my mind with her visions.

Her pelt glows in the morning light as she focuses those copper eyes on me; yet her muzzle is motionless.

"I am alive and you cannot die any more than I can," I now refer as her scent clouds my night visions in her image.

My sleep is plagued with Gauntlet's attack, shaping into even greater traumatizing terrors of cold darkness, black as the ash remains in the city. The same soot I had rose from once I awakened.

Rising from my sleep within the den I have known my whole life, the emptiness proves I am still alone. Only my heartbeat rhythm is heard within these hollow tunnels.

Judging by the faint glow my nocturnal eyes see outside the den, I assume it is twilight. Before now, I had frequently awoke to excruciating pains occurring throughout my body. Most of them triggered from my abdomen to expand into every limb and tail. Plus, my brain is again throbbing within my skull.

I heard that certain bombs emit radiation to eradicate their victims. Could I be suffering such a thing as radioactive poisoning?

Sparrk may have been right.

"We Vulpine are immune to death, that is why I have survived," I indicate. This does not answer why I am experiencing these ailments, nor why the great Prince Castige eventually died leaving only the theory that our immortality is limited.

After some brief moments of waking myself up, I make the decision that I should leave. The other Vulpine obviously fled once the bombing began. I do not blame them for doing so, if our enemies knew we were hiding and raising Vulpine in this area, they would seek to destroy us all. They'd begin by killing off those in Gauntlet.

"Well, I am one you have not taken." Whether or not they care that the less Vulpine remain, the more immortal we are. They will do everything possible to sterilize us.

Despite my feverish temperature, a slight chill comes over me at the thought of a new suspicion.

"What if that is what these bombs were meant for? To destroy our fertility?" Inspecting myself, I find no visible change. Being not yet reproductively mature, I should be concerned for the future. Now I may not develop as I am meant to.

In a hurry, I organize what I feel to bring along. Opening mother's pack, I find something both remarkable and familiar. This moment is so heart sinking that my mind blackens to this impossibility.

Sliding the black case out and into my paws, I recognize the same box Skylar had extracted in vault. The same one she had left on the wooden chest that night. To add to it, I left my chrimsophilite, goggles, and the marble pouch in the vault as well. Here they are.

"How . . .?" I am at an even greater blank than before. Passing my nose over each of them to pick up an identity of a scent I do not recognize, and only a faint scent of mother.

"She did not place these here. Who?" To make it the first time, I open the clamshell lid revealing a silver arrowhead with a transparent diamond at its center. It has two winglets curving out from the top, and is entirely suspended from a silver chain.

"I have no time to study this," I decide. Closing the case and returning it to the pack, then adding the remainder of my needs. Securing my gear, I slip the pack onto my shoulders and lock my folds protectively over it.

Outside the labyrinth, the day is coming to an end as night prepares to fall. Thankfully, life is returning with crickets and frogs chirping along with the last of the day's bird song.

"I am grateful to not be alone in this survival."

Taking one glance back at labyrinth's entrance, I tell myself that this period of life has ended for me. Now, a new cycle is beginning.

Scenic 24

Out of Ruin

I am now on the first hill out beyond the woods. The first in the meadow, and the moment I come down over its opposite side, my past home will be gone. No more glances, not at the woods or the remains of the city structures beyond.

"The Vulpine Instinct reveals that I must go on. Where, I do not know. The only knowledge my spirit is giving, is that I am required to keep moving. I have been this way from the start of my life, always roaming from location to location and event to event. So many Vulpine remain in a single place for life, but not I, never staying in one place too long. I am independently unique and enjoy roaming like a mustang.

In what I classify as destined fate, this very moment when I move a single paw forward, a familiar sound returns to my ears. One I know so well and doubted to hear again. Those galloping beats and warmth now build up inside me to an overwhelming level. A name most special comes upon my tongue.

"Lola!" I call out. Here she is, the bay mare running to me as though nothing has changed. Why she is still here is currently a mystery, but here we are touching muzzles, both ecstatic we are not going forward without each other.

"Thank you Lola," planting a kiss upon the bridge of her nose. In her own communication, she lets out a breath from the great lungs and forcefully rubs her head against me.

I protest gleefully. If this is her affectionate side, practically using me as a scratching post. I personally pay no concern to this habit of hers.

She dips down on her fore legs, allowing me access to mount her back. Passing paw over her star and down through her mane, a moment of interruption causes me to retrace the tips of my nails again through hairs, coming back in contact with her white star. There is an impression beneath the flesh in the form of a bump.

"Did you bruise your head in that exact spot?" She only draws her equine head away from my paw to stomp one of her hind legs. Maybe it is better not to ask questions now. We need to get to safety . . . wherever that may be.

Lola starts off without me giving a single demand. After all, I do not know where to go, but she obviously has some idea.

The night falls further to where my night vision sets in. Grooming my friend's mane has occupied me, diverting the plaguing loss and pain. The mane comb from my pack is clenched between my digits as what is balancing my sanity. Claiming all focus and attention is the exact goal, to ease and neutralize this painful flocking from the one place we knew and into the unknown beyond and out of ruin.

Scorpula was the departing destination, is it now coming sooner than expected?

"Is this our departure?" I project out in the Vulpine tongue equine cannot understand, "Are you delivering us to Scorpula?"

Long into our trek, does the sickness return yet

again. Gripping Lola's sides with every intent to stay awake, I hope she does not mind when I need to vomit. Nutritional nourishment had not been able to overlap nor cross my lonesome isolation. The unfinished smoothie was last to fill my belly; now it is empty just as the rest of my form. The end, is who I essentially am, with no longer a beginning nor a following. My origin past is dead; there is no vivacity in the future.

"Fox, you really need your sleep. You yourself know it is a physiological need. Plus, you need the rest in order to fuse into the dog you are meant to be."

"I am still a kit," I argue. "That bomb did not kill me, the one theory is it was meant to sterilize me."

"You don't know that."

"So, it may be just a delusion?"

"I believe so."

"Well, here is to hope that you are right . . . wait, who are you?"

There is a truly strange sensation when you first realize you have awakened. You do not always remember where you were only moments ago, only knowing that you were somewhere in your sleep. Because now, the memories are flooding back into my mind as the rest of me wakes up. I'm finding it a miracle of managing to both fall asleep and maintain balance upon Lola.

At first, only my eyes break open, finding it is still late in the night with dawn distantly away. The mare is proceeding on a steady trot through the grass lands. All sense of direction is lost, but when the sky disk rises in the west, the compass will return.

With outstretched arms, my pads gently stroke either side of her neck to inform her of my awakening. Sitting up, I take a great spine stretch followed by a most sickening shock waving its way through me. All stomach contents may have been brought up if my belly was not running on empty.

"I must hunt," urging my herbivore companion, commanding atop her back. My scent is masked by her from any animals down below. This concealment must be used to its full advantage, for not only is my belly hungry, but the rest of me as well. It is a new, supernatural hunger burning through all parts of me; body, mind, and soul.

This drawing consumption devours in a way I have not experienced before. It is surfacing a part of me that is like an infectious contagion. This young sensation builds up making my head hurt and body ache in famished emptiness . . . a hunger equally as demanding.

"Uhh," I groaningly growl, "the fever is enough," yes, I still have this same high temperature. The mare almost feels cold against my pads, unnaturally meaning I am much hotter than she.

But this is only a beginning of new symptoms rising up in the biological rebellion: cramping pains throughout my muscle structure, eerie burning in my abdominal organs and a throbbing migraine in my skull. All are a raging war enemy working against my biology. Oh, am I ill.

An available option is to continue resting; but mysteriously, my hunger is expanding beyond stomach cravings. Naturally, I alert all my senses. Ears high, motioning in all directions to receive the faintest sound of those worthy. Eyes wide to capture any visual, nose held high to take on any aroma. I am the hunter, still as stone but internal self raging on, waiting for just the right moment to be released.

Deep into my concentration, my senses are rewarded. Lola takes just a few more trots, and there it is: A single doe, grazing there either feeding late into the night.

The deer pays little attention to Lola as she crosses paths with this opposing hoofed mammal. Her time is now.

As soon as Lola trots forward and the deer's back is to me, I lunge off the mare's hindquarters. First to reach the deer are my opened jaws; latching them around the back of her neck, locked under the grip of my arms. She puts all effort into escape by frolicking away and attempting to shake me off. She is strong, and all this action is only adding to my migraine. But I hold on, sustaining myself by further biting my way onto her spine to sever the cord.

In only moments, she begins to slow, then limply, brings the both of us down. Having claimed her life, it proves a feat not known possible by a Vulpine. Lola however, reversed that.

Without a moment's hesitation, I begin my meal. Ripping open the flesh of the belly using my teeth and paws to dig into the organs, taking the warm internals in my jaws, devouring the freshly caught prey is a pleasurable dining. It is as though I am tasting every nutrient upon my buds, coated in the refreshing blood. But this prey is satisfying a frenzied spark now igniting within me. Flowing from my stomach into my limbs like oxygen feeding an immature campfire.

A newly born intoxicating feeling arises from within as it takes in supernatural energy converted from the physical food source. My body is revived with new vitality with the meat's nourishment not only restoring my energy, but another side entirely. Adrenaline floods my body with levels of unstable power. An overload so immense I begin unstably trembling out of my control. Like boiling water left over coals; panting hard to meet the fever's return and climaxing anxiety.

Moments into quadruped shift, every drop of adrenaline fires through my system. Unleashing a bellowing howl as strong as a sound bomb, I charge forward into the woods on four paws like the raged mutt I am.

This internal burning is unbearable, so much, the one motive is beating it out of my body. Power, this burning power is making my body a factory of pain, boiling and bursting from within like a timed bomb in detonation. Fighting pain with pain, I crash into tree trunks, snap through branches, tear dampening any visual sense of direction. Inside me, whatever it may be, desires to break free of this physical form: pulsing beneath the flesh in attempt to gain freedom. I will continue torturing it to surface outward.

Tearing myself through thick undergrowth, I keep my legs moving without allowing the interaction of any obstacle. Thorns catch my legs, their points penetrating flesh to the pulsing muscles beneath.

Next, I lunge myself into a large mud puddle, burrowing the nose point of my muzzle beneath the moist earth, its nightly cold temperature so refreshing to my overheated self. Rolling over onto my back and unfurling wings, I too soak them in the black forest mud. Yet, these fresh chills are only lasting momentarily.

Splashing and spraying mud water in many directions results in throes spreading into my extra limbs, fueling energy to an even greater level of power. Does this mean it will not stop until I am completely burned out?

"I must keep rampaging!" I growl, insanely banging my balled up paws against the bark of a nearby tree. The pain production of my torn flesh is much more bearable than the hot stinging shots now claiming the tips of my limbs as destination.

Already a muddy, bloody mess, I hurdle over a fallen log and shift back into quadruped. Limply throwing myself down a steep hill, colliding and surpassing every tree, plant, stone, and rock. Delivering a counteracting force against this heat.

Tumbling to the mountain's cliff like edge, I keel over in completion of my rolling hilly descent. Downward and directly below me, is yet another earthly forest floor awaiting my landing; but it is the air I am landing upon.

For my sails flex open again to embrace the air as a long lost friend. Carried over the ground and beneath the tree branches silently as an owl. Despite the access weight of the pack and mud soiling, this glide is normal as any winged animal. But why I cannot attain actual flight as I did earlier is still a great mystery.

Unsure of how to discontinue airborne, retracting my limb folds presents as the one option. Doing so causes immediate gravity dominance, bringing me a gulping belly landing upon a boulder.

Creeping to return to up, fore paws meet the moist earth below and shift my form back into quadruped. Breaking into yet another sprint, all physical existence demands more.

Charging deeper into the unknown, crashing through branches and brush with not one care of wound or bruise; tripping over rocks and running into solid objects do not stop me either. I psychotically continue beating my body against anything and everything. Exhausting myself to defeat this fiery pain is failing.

Finally in the darkness of my senses; colliding with a stone wall brings me down upon my back. Body a blood-gored, bruised figure now lying hurtfully on the ground. The inferno remains within me, burning like surging, deadly venom; touching every part of my inside by induced contact.

"Cannot fight this," I enunciate, slightly coming back to sanity. "Resistance is unsuccessful and I cannot refuse it.

Whatever is taking over me."

Passing into unconsciousness may have happened, if not for Lola's return. In all this mental penalization, I only know she is here by scent as she rubs her soft nose over me.

"I have lost the battle with this force," I infer to my friend, unsure if that was even voiced because I am now feeling just as when awakening back in Gauntlet's rubble. Losing all feeling in my body but even when that falls away, here I remain. Just me and the pain.

"I did not know it was possible to feel pain without a body," but here it exists despite how little is left of me. Withdrawing eyelids I find that my physical self indeed remains, six limbs as always, from tip of nose to point of tail. As weightless as the air, free as gravity.

"But where in existence am I?"

Are my paws in water, air, or sky? They are most definitely not on ground. Everything spreads out in endless values of blue and violet with no beginning, end, or depth of perception.

Maneuvering around requires no effort; I just need to feel to soar ahead light as the air.

Alone, I am not, in this dimensional expansion of cold blue and purple auroras. My instinct informs me so, even before she enters my visual. The closer the approach, the warmer everything becomes.

There, crouched in a defensive position, is a golden vixen. I do not know her, but how she is supported on four legs distinctively reveals her frontier wild side just as my own.

Shifting into quadruped as well, I threaten by snarling with exposed teeth and a battle ready stance. She hisses back with wide eyes and flattened ears. Hairs rise up along our spines, she and I begin cycling in a circular motion with eyes fixed on each other.

Battle ready, we leap into the air, colliding with teeth and claws. Remaining locked in combat without separation. For every bite and scar I give her, she returns with some of her own. The pain she is dealing to me will not cease unless I put her to an end. Battle I must, to defeat the pain.

We go on until thrusted apart vigorously: A tuft of her fur on my lips and a torn piece of my neck flesh in her own. Spitting out the keratin strands, I take notice just how gored the both of us are. There is not a limb without a blood flowing scar. She and I are so battered we collapse at the same moment   alongside together.

She still wants to deal me pain and is not backing down or submitting defeat. As long as she battles me, I will not quit either.

"Why won't you conclude?" I angrily growl through clenched jaws.

"Because you won't!" she sneers. "I want to live and you are in my way."

Exactly . . . that is exactly what I want.

"We have the same purpose to live on? But are in the way of each other's goals. If we continue, neither you or I can become the victor."

With consoling expression and understanding me as I do her, she suggests, "If we cannot defeat each other, maybe you and I should unify." During a night vision, I do not think as normally when awake. But in the visionary world of the mind, the most meaningless of events have great purpose. Yes, this is a strange action, but I must embrace this supernatural vixen. Not only the obvious choice, but the one right choice.

My blood pools into streams as it pulses from my body. The vixen's scarlet liquid also flows from her own wounds, trickling together with my own.

It is time.

With remaining energy, I outstretch my forearm to her. Rippling through the blood puddle to where our sights meet just before our paws do. Gripping it hard, I let her pain consume to absorb me. Combining with whom I thought was the enemy, but is truly a friend.

In one instant, the ember feeling succumbs me all entirely. Like an internal explosion, I roar and flare out of night vision. Awakening to my howling muzzle in a voice I cannot recognize. Inversely returning, only to depart back into the same blackness I entered in Gauntlet. Into warm sleep inducing blackness.

"I have not heard a sound like that before now," I declare to Kyara, who trembles her figure at my side. I comfortingly drape my wing over she and hold close.

"Can this roaring and howling possibly be from the same source? The same creature?" As it continues, she buries her head into my neck down. "I am afraid this thing is coming for us."

"Likely, yes." Hollice breaks in, answering her daughter from over in the grass bed. After all, I am sure she does know best.

"I bet this thing is coming for us, Kyara. But I know we can defend ourselves against it. I will protect both you and I."

She is showing only the slightest sign of ease.

"Also, mother is here to guard us as well."

"Hmm . . . the little female finally purrs in reassurance. From inside our den I hear Hollice let out a scoffing breath, but I am not sure why. Whomever we are hearing bellowing its voice, I cannot help but hear it as suffering. Who is this creature, and why does it keep changing its call?

"I agree with you," I tell my mate, "for the intent of these cries are of pain and I feel no different as I was the same night of Sanora's capture."

"I do not need to hear your thoughts to understand that," my queen acknowledges.

Giving Ankara a gentle nudge, I lead her outside our mountain den. Leaping off the ledge, we take to the air; flying over the summits while gradually descending to Chromium's forest.

"Moonsight, where do you believe the location is?"

"Close enough to echo through the mountains, but not too far within the woods."

My calculation is correct, these howling wails are close by and it is not hard for feline-raptor hybrids to detect its origins. I only know someone needs our help.

Scenic 25

Cat Raptors

Picking up an even fainter roar, this animal is seeming to be calming down. I must be sure not to lose train of detection. Once over the last mountains, we circle over an area between the cliff side and tree line.

"Here!" I announce to Ankara, "I see something; or rather, someone." I am picking up an animal far down below. Whatever the identity of this species, it is laying there spread eagled, covered with brightly colored fur and patches of mud. Additionally, I both see and smell patches of blood. There is however an even larger creature closely hovering near.

We land a safe distance for security. But once grounded, we take in this sight.

A heavily beaten and scarred animal lies motionless on the cold grass, but alive at the view of his chest rising and falling. The beastly four legged animal sets view over us, but not in aggression.

"Can you help him? Will you help him?" she begs pleadingly with her thoughts ringing into my mind. Repeating her pleads so not to forget them, I answer.

"Yes," I assure the hoofed, long nosed mammal.

"We can, and we will."

"Thank you, mighty Gryphons. My one last request is to please inform my companion that our friendship is eternal." With this final request, she gallops off into the deep woods in series of thundering beats, leaving Ankara and I with her ally.

"My one last request is to please inform my companion that our friendship is eternal," my mate repeats to properly document. Hurrying to the beast's partner, I begin taking note of the injuries while my Queen prepares to clean away the mud blots.

"I don't detect anything that won't heal," I convey, "just a large amount of bruises and penetrations." After successfully swiping away much from his body, Ankara proceeds to mend his wounds by sealing them in saliva. I decide it is time to rule out the species of this newcomer.

Is he a feline or canine behind those pointed ears and muzzle? Arms and legs lean as the beast who was with him. A thick pelt like none I have seen before, patterned in warm colors. To add to this one's abnormally striking features, he also bares a pair of large flat leather limbs attached at the shoulders. Are those sails?

"We must transport him to the den."

"Yes," Ankara agrees.

Gently taking the creature into my fore paws, I securely hold him to my chest in preparation for flying him to our region. Surprisingly, he is much warmer than any mammal I have ever felt. Is a strong fever the cause?

"Strange," Ankara points out before we take off. I catch her eyes the moment the mental transition communicates into my own. On her beak and ringing over my brain is . . .

"This animal's beast ally is an Equine. I have seen them before, but this one doesn't have a long horn protruding from its forehead."

The pain, it is gone. But the cause remains clung to me, latching on as a warm and gentle attachment. We are not attacking each other, we are one and the same.

"We have triumphed together," I tell my new friend, "because we are allies and not enemies." Just as I am presenting this, my mouth actually motions, physically speaking again. "I am returning!" I declare in remembrance of everything, "Lola! I am awake." She is the last I remember of the physical world. The soft ground from before is absent with cold stone now its substitute. Light coming into my blurred vision is closely followed by my natural sight adjustment. Finally, the familiar feel of my body returns.

I am in a cave with a good sized entrance leading out with light raying in. To the left of the opening sits my pack, untouched. There is a slight chill in me now, why was I much warmer only moments ago?

Raising up fast proves challenging to my fatigued body, stumbling backward to collide against the warm side of another animal, startling it awake.

"Oh, you have awakened," It acclaims, obviously female. She is a large animal, quadrupling a full grown Vulpine. Finally, after getting a good look at her, the need of bringing forth a series of questionnaires proves to be irrelevant.

"I am a Gryphon," she confirms, "Queen of the Aquileia. We are hybrid descendants of the breeding of raptors and felines."

Is she hearing my . . .

"Yes, hearing your mind is exactly the truth. "but I will forget everything in your head cause they are yours. If however, you would like to tell me about yourself, that would be nice. In return, I will be self-informative as well."

"You are a cat-raptor!" The enemy predator of my race, the entire reason Vulpine began social lives.

"Is that right," she brings out. Immense, having Skylar know my emotions was enough. But here is a Gryphon female hearing ever one of my thoughts like picking up a coherent radio frequency.

"Remember, I will not remember your thoughts later on, because they are not of my own mind. So it would be appreciative to tell me about yourself."

Turning my own expression into something between fear and disbelief, the Vulpine instinct informs me that this cat-raptor Gryphon is nothing but a female who is so sweet I can even pick it up in scent. If it is milk I'm detecting, then where are her kits?

Scenic 26

Predator and Prey

I instantly agree. It will be great to voice all that has happened for the first time. It's hard when not having anyone to chat with, but a Gryphon never even crossed into the territory of my mind as this particular one is. Yet before diving into introduction, another enters my mind.

"Lola!"

Not awaiting explanation, into the daylight by charging out into open is where I am taken. But stop immediately cause of what the surroundings have become. Mountain peaks in all directions, producing plant life and rock barren. The same mountain peaks I gazed at afar from back on the labyrinth's ledge.

Now I am high upon this ledge, before a devastating slant angling downward to create a steep slide of rough stone. Could Lola really come to a place such as this?

"You are referring to your Equine friend," the Gryphon brings up as she comes to my side. "She asked that we would help you and left one last message." I give her a look of confused paralysis, but allow her to give it.

"Our friendship is eternal."

"She spoke to you," I scoff. "Why has she never vocalized to me?"

"You do not understand, we only heard what she was thinking. Her thought process is indeed different, only capable of concentrating on one subject at a time. But her one subject was you and she asked us to help.

"She is gone then?"

"I am afraid so. But by what she had me pass on, assures the two of you will reunite. She is quite easy to recognize on fact she has no horn."

"Horn?"

"The only other Equine to have crossed my path all had a single long horn growing from their forehead. Unlike your companion, Lola."

"I have not seen such a horse like that before."

"Horse, so that is your classification term," she acknowledges. "By the way, my name is Ankara, Queen of the Aquileia."

In the light, I give her a good look over. A body much like a lion with the head of an eagle topped off with feline whiskers and ears well set behind her ink blue irises. Jet black feathers form at the root and tip of her tail, and of course, her majestically large wings beautifully imbricated against her third pair of limbs.

"You are really pretty," I comment, wondering if all Gryphons are just as nice?

"You are a handsome creature as well, with that coat and leathery drapes."

"It is nice to receive that from a first encounter. Most reject me because of them."

Expecting her to proceed with an inquiry, I find the cat-raptor angling her head on its feathery neck, much like Lola when in a shift of mood. Meeting the expectation of this Queen is now my one concern. Ankara intently listens without an interruption.

"You see, many see them a deformity. A defect that

came upon me in conception, carrying on into birth to now through life. Even when learning how we hybridize and fuse in order to develop and mature, I was crushed down ever more by failing my next attempts at flying. My hybridizing proves to be absolutely pointless."

"Not sure that is true," the Queen consoles. "I see you as something different, an individual who must prove himself a blessing and not a curse. Because this Queen knows this little creature with her now has a beautiful future and purpose even for his flightless wings."

That is exactly how Skylar feels and has always voiced to me. But she, Ankara, could not have taken it from my thoughts. Mother was absent from my random access memory until a moment after. Another of an enemy race treating me like her own kit is it just weird, or maybe . . . miraculous.

Unsure if to believe her or not, she is making me feel greatly improved with her verbal remedy. Becoming so relieved that purrs are arising in my voice box.

"The title my mother passed on to me is Forjah. But condensed to Fox, if that is easier to recollect." I take advantage of this time to groom; really not liking all the dried blood beneath the fur making it coppery.

"Something wrong?" she breaks in while I attempt to clean away the mess.

"I am trying to get the dried blood out, but the difficulty is extreme.

"Forjah, I thoroughly cleaned you the moment we found you. That coppery tint is your fur color."

While resting here in the den, all I can think about is my new likeness. My fur has changed, but the alternate coloration is not the lone difference. Back against the stone walls of the Gryphon's barrier, paws rested over knee caps and tail laying out between my feet. Raising it up between them to take in the imaged transformation, the furry tip has become bright golden yellow; fading out from the red and copper hairs just before leading into the point. Almost resembles a candle flame.

By seeing the new fur coat of unusual coloring, I cannot help but ponder if my facial looks are any different. Ankara describes my features as warm, with the thermal secondary colors of yellow and red.

"But your eyes," she detailed, "are of icy blue-violet." I suppose she means they are now a mix of blue and purple.

Finally, she observed and described another strikingly unusual feature. The area of my scalp between my ears is sprouting crimson red, but these velvety scarlet hairs are continuing on down the back of my head, through my upper spine, and all the way into the tip of my tail. The Aquileia Queen theorizes that eventually, the red hairs will form a great stripe from scalp all the way down my spine to gradually disappear into the extension.

This evening, Ankara's mate returns with freshly caught fish for both she and I. Bashfulness deteriorates by those glistening rings of silver, revealing immediately I will like him.

"Judging by those teeth," he points out offering a fish by sliding it before me. "I assume that you are a consumer of meat."

"Clarified," I confirm, "but an omnivore, so I eat almost everything within the diets of both herbivore and carnivore."

"Most interesting, a species of both meat and vegetation. Not sure to have met any other."

"Oh, we Vulpine are not the only ones."

"Vulpine?" Ankara repeats.

"Is that what you are?" her mate adds.

"We are by far the most unusual of the canids. Not only is our diet different, but our physicality and spirituality as well."

"When we first found you a number of days ago, I wondered if you may be feline, but you are indeed a dog?"

"Yep," I initiate taking another bite of the meat beneath the fish scales. The taste must be mineral-like because it is taken from a nearby lake. So this explains the waves I had been hearing and fresh outdoor air.

"Thank you for this," I comment, "the meat is rich in health. All that could improve is smoking and seasoning it," but the response I receive from the couple are lost focus of concentration.

"Oh," immediately understanding. Being purely wild they lack knowledge of domestication. It is best to keep my description simple. "Do you know what fire is?"

"Yes," they establish.

"Well in my origin, we use fire to partially burn meat to tender and juicy. Topping it off with what we call spices, which resemble a soil or mineral to add an even better taste."

"So cleverly unique and advanced."

"Most definitely," Ankara additionally inputs. "You are from a world far different from our own."

"I am indeed," now deciding to enlighten them even further. "There are now two statuses in this demesne; Wild and domestic. Wild being the way your race lives. Now domestic, is the modern way of life. It is however, a challenge to explain and gain a full understanding."

"Then let both your dialogue and mind speak to us. That way, we will take it through your brain's translation."

The BOTH of them are capable of that?

"Yes we are," Moonsight emphasizes. They have definitely fused beyond the cross of bird and cat, but I can also accept they have adaptively developed into a fair and peaceful species.

"I give you my willful acceptance to the challenge."

"The main thing about domestic life is the use of an element known as technology. It is the manipulation of lightning or electricity, using it as an energy source. Mainly for simplifying tasks that prove challenging. They also wear garments on their bodies, called clothing."

While I bark out, I think up my most detailed and informational thoughts, offering images of electric lights, vehicles, and machines. Even going into description of how these things work, from digital imagery to sound recording and reproduction. But all these thoughts are bringing back my memories of Gauntlet's devastation. For it is there I learned close to everything about domestication. "That is what I know and experienced there. But it is always changing; as their technology continues to improve through developmental advancement." Doing my best to hold back the devastating memories, I conclude, "I am a frontier animal. Living and raised partly in both the wild and domestic."

All this overwhelming past makes me realize now it is all just memory, nothing more. Mother is coming back to me draped in these past recollections. I cannot help but let her memory burn like the everlasting fire. As telling her I visualized the night before. These records are now draining from my eye sockets in hot tears. Both Moonsight and Ankara are taking in my every emotion, every thought.

"I cannot secretly hold theses traumatizing things in, the psychological scar is much too deep."

According to Queen Ankara, they only remember what I put forth, not my thoughts; because they are not of their own minds.

"Will they think I made up this sad story myself?" For that I am hopeful, I decide. Making a bow, I attempt to hide all tears, being unable to stop them from reaching the stone floor of the den.

"Forjah," comes my name in the Queen's breath. The female Gryphon brushes her side against my own to curl around to my back; now perching protectively before resting her head atop my shoulder.

"I know these thoughts of yours are not fictional. They are most definitely past happenings. Your emotions are far too in tune, imagery too clear and definite to be products of the imagination."

Paralyzed, I do not know what to do. A Gryphon I have just met, probing my mind and acting like a mother."

"Oh," she somberly purrs, "in fact, I am a mother; but have lost my only kit. Just as tragically as you have lost your mother."

"In absolute truth?"

"Yes," she consoles with the most soothing swipe of her tongue just below my eye and above my ruff. "Our daughter, Sanora was taken from us. By Gryphons not of our Aquleia."

"For what reason?" desperate for the answer.

"Where is your mother? Why has she disappeared?"

"Do not know," exhaling in deep realization of her meaning.

"Exactly, I know no reason for Sanora's bounty either. They are both a dark mystery."

Empowered by their motivation and my own decision, I begin to further detail about myself and my experiences. Including our race's history, our bestowals, the ongoing genocide, and our adaptation to immortality.

"Immunity to death, you Vulpine surly are gifted," comments Moonsight, "for a race as threatened as your own, it is a necessity."

"We are more endangered than threatened," I add, "yet we believe our immortality has its limits. Because Vulpine have died despite their mortal immunity."

"So, that could expire?"

"Yes," I admit, "and if they cannot kill, they sterilize. I even think that bomb did just that. Not killing me, but my fertility. I also theorize my sudden exterior changes are because of the bomb. What I am going through is radiation poisoning. Still sick with a fever and even went insane back there in the woods by mad self-infliction."

"But you do not know that you are barren for sure, do you?" The Queen has that mother like twinkle in her eyes again. As though to console and comfort me as she would her own.

"No, it is only a theory," I confirm. She brings those large but gentle paws forward to then drape her wing around my back in partial embrace. The size, soft texture, and thermal warmth bring return to my early days burrowing behind the drape of Skylar's tail to block anything from entering my eyes, nose, or ears.

The Queen's wing is presenting a new shield, one that I accept by curling within to dry my eyes and secure me safe. I am here with cat-raptors, whom were my enemy before now. But destiny has made it so to arrive in Chromium as guest of the Leader and Queen. Whom have gained my trust, having earned my own.

Scenic 27

Mending the Unbreakable

My parents had long returned from the forest, alone. At this moment, I assume we leave Kyara with Adelhied. We come out, and she accompanies our departure. Bidding Aquila yet another goodbye proves difficult in spite of promising each other it will not be long.

Evaron separates, leaving Kyara and I with Hollice. She leads in silence where my ears receive sound indicating approach to the river. Rushing water informs me in auditory before it does in imagery.

Mother arches over the trench to take a long drink before even noticing my and Kyara's worry. Who is to be her mother?

"Kyara," she begins, "I am to be your mother, you will remain in our kin." I give no intake, Kyara is also voiceless.

I look at my ally in a whole new way. Somewhat more than a friend, a companion who will continue at my side, the one who will counteract my lone birth. All is now clear with the realization now echoing in my mind, venturing out with...

"We are kin."

A S A P u b l i s h i n g C o r p o r a t i o n

Never thought once I would have a brother. Even though he and I will never be true siblings, we now are in accordance to Hollice. Mother, I mean.

"Wonderful to not feel alone anymore. It has been a joy to share this den with you even before now, sister." Brightening a return to his declaration, I follow with.

"Never felt so welcomed before, brother."

Our first morning as siblings, first dawn with my mother, first day as her daughter.

"Kyara, my body requires extensive rest," Chrome informs. "There is much on my mind that has prevented so." I dip from my neck and leave him to slumber. Now is my time to converse with mother

Deciding to crawl out from beneath her wing, the morning air welcomes my arrival. "Goodness," these chills are moon cold compared to her thermal sky disk. Hollice's great aquiline head rests over her leonine paws. Each revealing the points of retractable talons, much like the curve of her tainted yellow beak. Someday I will become equally as powerful; but now is the moment to concentrate upon time's present.

Approaching, I caress my side against her ear. Awakening with cracked eyelids, she exasperates,

"I am here, Kyara. What is it you need?"

"I wanted to ask, mother; about the tournament. May I?" an aggravated sigh escapes her.

"You are greatly inexperienced," she argues. "However, the entire purpose of this competition is to reverse that entirely. I have nothing against your participation."

"Thank you," I exclaim in gratitude. "Who is to be my inspirer?" Upon granting the question, her talons flex into the earth of the den. I feel she is holding back anger.

"I will ask my sister if she will oblige to train you. Let

us hope she approves."

"What about Chrome?" I add. "Will he want to be a part of it?"

"Answer your own question," Hollice orders, "you are more than capable."

Personally, I do agree and will consult him later. At the time we are all awake and fresh for this new day.

"Are you interested?" Kyara pleads.

"I have had an interest since I first heard Moonsight bring it forth. Though, I have not given it more thought beyond that."

"But you have interest," she bursts out. I confide.

"Yes, Kyara, "I am just in need of a trainer and must find one before the evening tomorrow." That is when the gathering comes, when each kit and guide must present to our leader.

"Do you have a Gryphon in mind?" Kyara is showing both curiosity and worry.

"No, I am unable to take one into mind. But the desire for a guide who will devote themselves to me as I do to them would suit me." My sister shakes her head.

"I have no suggestions, sorry."

"It is for me to work out. I have faith I will find an inspirer." Kyara pulls us unto a wing embrace, holding me tight within her lock while pressing beak against the side of my neck.

"You are strong, Chrome. Therefore, I know your will is true to your faith."

Kyara is quite anxious toward meeting Camira. I personally have no worry of a refusal to be her inspirer. My entire concern is upon myself, having not prepared for the event at all. Training alongside my sister under Camira's eye does present an option, but what is summoning sharp talons from deep inside me, calling this out as a wrong motion?

Mother allows us to accompany on a hunt for the first time, provided we remain the quiet kits we are. Residing in the concealing roots of a great oak serves as our cover. Despite the river rushing in the distance, I know Holice is near without a sound.

Kyara's dark feathered wings blanket her back to create excellent camouflage. Adding to concealment, her eyes are no more than black beads against the dark down of her head. Having inherited this bright pelt from Mother, my gold fur shines out against our entire perimeter. It has unique beauty even in my eyes, but is showing disadvantage at the current moment. But Kyara is catching on.

"We must remain undetected," she hushes while draping a single wing over my revealing gold fur. "Remain motionless, my brother."

I have no desire in admitting the risk she took by movement as well as sound. I am however, grateful for the concern. Fear of what? Even I am not sure. We Gryphons have few enemies, yet being born so small does make us vulnerable. But to who or what, I do not know.

Unable to further any energy to continue thinking, Kyara now emits a strong purr from deep within causing mini tremors in her breathing. Would such a pleasant sound lead me to her? Can Mother alone detect our presence here at the tree's base?

"The two of you would have much better concealment if you burrowed beneath the leaves!" her disgusted sneer is fierce as always, but we catch onto the fact we are laying in the leaf shed.

"She is right, we should have hid ourselves beneath them," my sister bows in ratification, drawing back her downy wing to turn away in shame for making the mistake, one that enshrouded us in fatal risk.

"I am not waiting for the two of you to come out of hiding. There will be no transportation over the river, you both may remain in the den."

"Coming mother!" I announce with a spring from the leaves.

"Do not leave us behind," Kyara pleads right before arising. Within instancy, we are matching Hollice's speed with canters. Today is the tournament's beginning for all kits, maybe all apart from myself.

"Chrome, do you wish to be trained alongside Kyara?" Surprised, I am; this being the first direct contact she has used toward me today.

"I do not know," I concede in my own hesitation. "I would really like a personal inspirer."

"You must act today, bring your final decision to Moonsight and his mate." This very moment, a spark ignites within, servicing a new idea to my mind.

"Ankara!" I announce aloud. "I will ask her to be my guide, she highly inspires me already." Both Kyara and mother stop to transfer focus upon me, as I have alternated into this new reality.

"Seriously?" Hollice responds in disgust, "The Queen?"

"Why not?" I contradict, Kyara shares the approval by the raise of her tail. When a deep breath is taken in and released, mother responds.

"Do as you desire."

This is only my second gathering, while being first for Kyara. Her bashfulness does not require its own presentation, for her anxiety is most noticeable. Not far from the mountain base, I am already able to hear voices of the attending Gryphons. Ears having become stronger than ever.

Hollice treks on without a care of acknowledging that my sister and I are falling behind.

"I recollect my first experience of attending a gathering," I recall to Kyara, knowing that socializing will indeed increase confidence, "making a judgment according to the many voices I hear ahead, many have attended and are forming a bulky group."

"You know I am not accustomed to large groups," she stammers, "I am already out of my comfort zone."

"But I am also part of that comfort zone," I remind her. "With me around, you do just fine."

"Because you are the first Gryphon I knew, trusting you from the beginning as well as becoming my brother. Upon that topic, how are we to pass as siblings in all this converge? We look nothing alike."

I follow with response of, "It is a risk we must take."

Every Aquileia falls silent almost as fast as when we arrived. Moonsight, as well as Ankara are perched upon the high ledge. Our leader's call to order is a strong announcement, but it is not sidetracking my mind from what I view settled beneath the stone ledge.

Before giving it a second look, I give a questioning glare to my sister to see the same mark of astonishment. Her shock is of fear while my own is of curiosity. While continuing to hold focus, my observation begins taking in the details.

The size of this creature is rather in between; with thick and untidy monochromatic fur. Its slim body is four lean limbs topped with a head featuring a pointed set of ears; striking violet eyes positioned behind the long furred muzzle. Each limb has a paw, but the fore limbs feature what appear to be long flexible digits. Quite eerie looking, my talons are not near that level of flexibility. The same gleaming gold fur spreads over the facials. The hairs down its neck to the lower belly are white while the strands traveling from the back of his head expand out long and wavy. This bright red pattern passes down his spine to fade into the yellow tip of his long tail.

In an instant, something rises up on either side of his shoulders, which appear to be black leathery folds flexing out on joints in a fan-like motion.

"Are those wings?" Kyara spits out, directly seeking my advice.

"OH! I believe you are right." She has to be, because this animal obviously has a third set of limbs just as we do. But they are completely bare, while our own are feathered.

"Those fans of his are certainly ugly and he is no better looking." My sister's feisty attitude is most definitely produced by her bashfulness. Evaron explained anger is produced by fear.

"Chrome!" she blurts out all frantically. "He heard me." While my pretend sibling conceals beneath her own wing, I decide to investigate the claim on my own.

By returning to the mystery animal, I find that his iris eyes are indeed focused upon us, but cannot pick out his emotion. The expression is quite unchanged, however, I believe he did pick up Kyara's insult. That pointed nose of his dips down, revealing the negative effect produced by the criticism he took in just now.

He is receiving many stares apart from my own. I know for a fact that if I were in his position, I would be terrified by the multiple eyes of a foreign race upon me. As shy and unresponsive to a dead calm extent.

"I am filled with delight that so many have attended this gathering," Moonsight begins with a cheerful ring in his voice, "apart from the beginning of the tournament for our kits; I wish to introduce a new friend from an outside region." It is obvious that he is referring to this same creature. Withdrawing from his perch in a single stride, Moonsight takes a new position at the side of the animal. Though its fur is mangled, it gives off a silky shine as he acknowledges with a bow; then rises up upon his rear legs. Holding that position for a brief moment, then taking a step forward into the light. All around astonished by his ability to move on only two legs.

"This is Fox," our leader introduces, "he has traveled from outside our territory." Fox, as he is called, draws back the sides of his muzzle. Lips parting to reveal a healthy strong set of carnivorous jaws expressing positivity and unthreatening nature. "He is of the Vulpine race and is our guest." Returning his attention, Moonsight instructs Fox to now verbalize on his own.

"As your leader reveals," he starts out, "I am only a visitor here because I have nowhere else. My hope is to learn all I can from you Aquileia in order to gain the knowledge and skills required to survive and live on." The foreigner's voice is rather different and unlike any I have heard. Though he seems respectively good and is by far the strangest looking creature.

Moonsight goes deeper into detail about his stay; asking all Aquileia to welcome our guest. This great need of how to live in the wild as we do, requires methods of study, skill gain, and observation. My best will be put forward welcoming him, pondering if even I could teach him something.

Now comes the time many have anticipated. Gryphons come forward mainly in pairs, baring gratitude in the inspirers and frenzy in the kits. Kyara pads away as Camira motions for her to come, Aquila with both her brother and sister attend my father as he urges them forward.

They are blessed and do not believe they could have a better guide. Just as I claim there is no better father, in thought of not having one of their own.

While Moonsight approves the teams, I know now the chance of opportunity. Not even informing Hollice of departure, I make this evermore repetitive by meeting again with the Queen.

There she is, black and settled proudly watching her mate approve the guides. This time, I do not look upon Ankara with fright. I gaze past her ferocious features to familiarize my instincts that she is a friend.

"Chrome!" she announces with a prideful dip of her head.

Returning the greeting with a bow of my own, I address, "I am honored to see you again, my Queen."

Giving a gentle nudge of her beak, she urges, "You may call me Ankara, Chrome. You have this Queen's permission."

"Ankara," I correct myself, "there is something I wish to ask." Her ears raise, ready to receive this request. Instinctively, not veering off subject, blocking any laming hesitation, I bring forth, "Will you be my inspirer?" Her great lioness tail gives a vertical wave of uprisen joy.

"I am honored Chrome. Yes!" In my frantic joy, I leap forward to hug her paw.

"Thank you," the dimming light of day reflects off her; as certain as it will return, I for sure have my one choice of inspirer.

"We shall begin tomorrow," she decides. "Let it take place right here at the foot of the mountain. When the sky disc is at its brightest."

"I will most surly be here to learn much more from you."

"Your expectations will be satisfied. I promise to make you a true warrior." Again comes a term that cannot be grasped in understanding. The mind of my new inspirer exceeds my cranium's capability; yet, it grasps hope to soon have a psychology rivaling a Queen's.

"I like the sound of that!" I put out in emotional response, dueling as way of hiding my misunderstanding.

"Such embolden devotion! My race and I highly admire warriors. To learn this hidden side of you is an utmost blessing." A voice comments in my Queen's direction. The holder is unseen, yet unmistakable. Transferring attention from Ankara, I expectedly land on Fox the moment a whole new idea forms in my brain.

"Ankara, could he . . . train with us?" she too is tuning in.

"What do you think, Fox?" he lets out a great bark of a breath, which causes me to jump back. Ankara garnishes her lost air in a deep pant; For at the same moment Fox opened his maw, an eerie glow appeared in his throat; accompanied by his violet eyes practically flaring up with a shine. Who can explain exactly what my Queen and I saw just now? Maybe only him.

"Yes, please," he roars out in delight to spread his arms, hugging Ankara's side."This makes us partners," he addresses before our guide. "I am Forjah," the vulpine introduces. "Yet, also Fox."

"I am Chrome. You have two names?"

"Technically one with two forms. As you are two hybrids and one creature. Is your actual name Chromium?"

"Mother did not name me so, as yours did I suppose." By bringing it up, the canid seems to diminish into a darkened color. Literally shadowing Ankara. But as the shock he induced over me just moments ago, it has left me with bodily instinct taking over in returning painful hunger.

"Ankara, may I . . . "

"Yes," she allows, "you really are that hungry, aren't you?"

Yes, I am. Pressing myself against her mammary, I suckle the milk that was originally meant for Sanora; continuing to feel guilty by taking it. Though my hunger has never been this severe and Hollice does not have milk near as satisfying. I am not sure why, but it is of my own personal fact.

Complete relief comes over as the gathering breaks up. All anxiety is diminishing. Upon meeting with Moonsight for the first time, I observe he appears kind but find horrid the number of scars spread throughout his body. His voice, however, is pleasant along with a majestic shine in those silver eyes. Concluding chat with Camira, we take a glance at each other, but only make brief contact before breaking away.

"I acknowledge your fear, young kit. I Hope in time you will learn to trust me," my one response is a shrug of my wings.

So many Aquileia in my entire surroundings cause me to feel smaller than previously before. My black down paired with the dark fur appears shadowed among all others. Just about every Gryphon here is open and bright toward each other, the exact opposite of myself.

"Where and how do I want to be? Having so little of a beginning and such a vague future; a future not sure will happen. Who am I?"

Chrome is my true beginning, having saved me, but is that as far as we are going? My brother has socialized with many in this short evening. Engaging now with that little red Gryphon, Aquila. The way she watches him with those lovely eyes is an action I still do not entirely understand. From across the distance that separates us, I observe the fellow female coming directly in contact with him. Nuzzling quite vigorously with her touch, passing both her tongue and body over him. Even from this far away, I am able to see the enticing reaction my brother is receiving. His gleaming eyes continue revealing wonder with each individual moment.

Now back into my own present self, forcing my mind not only away from Chrome, but from the entire gathering. Padding away from all commotion turns into a breaking run. Traveling deep into Chromium's forest undergrowth is where I vent the depression and allow my mind loose from its own stress, "I may just want to sleep here for the night. Concealed and safe before returning to the barrier in the morning." Ignoring the distant voices from the breakup proves so grand to be alone, separated from burdens clouding my mind.

"Kyara?" A voice instantly returns me to reality in a jolt, by both surprise of the moment and recognition of the host. Approaching paws shuffle through the plants. My preparation for this unexpected pursuer is not working out, regardless; I give a startled jump the moment Tauro emerges.

"This location is awfully isolated," he greets before resting himself beside me; passing exposed tongue over my ears. "How are you?"

"Do not know," I shortly admit. "Just desired some time alone for head clearance. I am under much social pressure." Able to see his every assisted attempt, he avows with a gentle spread of his wing over my back.

"I assume there is much on your mind and unsure just how to handle it?" deciding to agree, I give him a dip of my head. "Would you prefer I leave you to yourself?"

Considering his offer, I emphasize. "Denied, I like having you near. To be with you is cozy and exceedingly warmer."

"Have you entered into the tournament?"

"Yes," I answer, delighted of this topic shift. "My mentor is Camira, the sister of my mother."

"Then may I inquire why you are so negative?"

"To begin with, Moonsight is frightening to an extent. Plus, my confidence is not on the same level as my desire of participation. Simplified, I want to be a part of it but my courage is quite limited." Tauro now pulls himself closer to me and voices, "In attempt to change your perspective," he directs. "look at the whole tournament as a personal challenge. View it all as a game you must triumph over."

"Nice perspective," I comment. "How did you come up with it?"

"I didn't," he corrects. "It is the lifestyle and culture of the Snorkblade race. According to mother, they see life as series of challenges they must complete one at a time. To them, life is one big game."

"A most interesting cultural view, but I am unsure I could ever adapt to it."

"I will make you a promise," he vows while tightening his wing over my back. "When and if you and I compete with each other, we spar fairly."

"Thank you, then I will make every attempt to turn this into a fun experience. A game, just like these Snorkblades."

After a time, we both leave our hiding spot and return to our mothers. My hollow belly is roaring within me and the rest of my body is in need of nursing. So by instinct, I seek out Hollice and feed from her mammary. Because of Tauro, my psychological side has greatly improved. Relieved I am to carry on.

Scenic 28

Into the Negative

"How soon before we leave?" Chrome begs with complete impatience while mother takes a morning groom before being escorted to our inspirers. I closely imitate by following her tongue strokes with precise duplicative action. This is how I am learning to neatly touch up my fur coat, and my future feathers. It is from Hollice, I will learn almost everything in becoming a full-fledged Gryphon.

"Are the both of you prepared for the first day of training?" It is about time she includes herself in the present. Chrome immediately brightens up and avows.

"Yes, Mother."

"As am I," I add. Hollice scrutinizes the both of us where I see a sort of expectation in her eyes.

"The both of you may lead," she entreats. "We shall first head to the mountain's base to leave Chrome with the Queen. Afterward, I will carry Kyara to my sister in the westurn forest." Chrome and I give a bow in understanding, "You must understand, Kyara," she indicates with a somber change of mood, "Because it will only be you, the transport to Camira will be by flight." This info my ears are accepting; can I possibly have received it right? Turning to Chrome, he sees my form of expression pleading for advice.

A S A P u b l i s h i n g C o r p o r a t i o n

"It is eventful the first time," he recalls.

"And what experience did you undertake?"

"Oh," he pauses briefly before continuing, "sheer fright, but transferred my entire focus back to saving you, Kyara. Not allowing fear to cloud or interrupt intent on your rescue."

For a reason unknown, my drapes close while the cardiovascular side of me takes a relieving breath. Hope arises from the depths of my mind that I can continue following Chrome's exact paw printed influence.

Despite limited info collected, I cannot help but wonder why Chrome selected our Queen. I find it impossible to see past her dark features.

"It may be that he sees her with a total different perspective," which does not provide any additional comfort. The final choice is to stay back, hidden away from Ankara behind Hollice's wing. At the Queen's side is that strange creature whom only presented himself the previous day. Fox, as I remember his name. Knowing not to have ever seen a creature of such uniqueness, he frightens me to the same extent Ankara does. That multi disk colored hide is as striking as lighting. Beastly breaths purr with thunder, while the blue of his eyes spread into violet with gentle asunder.

"We Gryphons are hybrids," I remember, "but what explanation is there to define the canine? He is the ugliest creature to ever pass my visuals, having no absolute idea what he is. Wondering whose womb concocted this creature, I certainly refuse bringing up if 'being born' is exactly how he came to be. What mother could possibly generate him inside her?"

"I assure you, Kyara. He is born of his mother." I am unsure if I should be in disbelief that he was indeed born, or that somehow Queen Ankara knows exactly what I am thinking right now. But I dare not remove myself from beneath the protective side of my own mother, not to face the two most frightening creatures I know. Again, Ankara is proving equally as scary as Fox.

"Just do not give attention to the either of them," I decide. "I am not required to socialize." Yes, I am whimpering to myself. Becoming so bashfully scared, I am trembling beyond control.

"I will return your son myself at the eve of the day, if you will allow it," Ankara confides to Hollice.

"I approve," she consents. "Return him when you see fit." Without another exchange, Hollice takes me in her beak and pads away. Wings extended, she prepares for flight. The ground falls away beyond my time perception. Wind rings in my ears that had not been there before.

"I want the both of you to jump beyond the length of your body," she directs. "Put maximum strength into the spring of your legs. Visualize pouncing upon prey as you would during a hunt." Fox truly does impress by the agile movements synced with maximum speed.

My body has strength not previously known. Along with the spring in my legs, I unfurl every limb at every leap for additional thrust. For the next test, she requests, we bring forth our ability of jump height. Suspending paw overhead, she instructs to leap straight up and grasp in my own, twice my body length above. "You are making the same jump," Fox advises. "Only this time, the change of challenge is doing it vertically. Use the same techniques and propel straight up." He then reassuringly rests a flexible paw upon my shoulder. Possibly a sympathetic gesture of his race, proving most comforting.

"Do just as he instructed," Ankara urges.

Pairing their advisory with instinct, I hurl high with

paws outstretched; having them wrapped around Ankara's digits instantly.

"Excellent!" she praises. Without a warning, I slip from the target in a violent beat to the earth.

"I have used what remains of my energy," conveying in breaths and a thundering pulse. This lack of strength has burned me to fatigue.

"Chrome?" Ankara claims my weary attention with a strong concerning tone. "Did you not nurse this morning?"

"Did so," I assure, "with my sister right before departure." My stomach gives a growl that both Fox and Ankara pick up in a raise of ears. I am now so weak, that it has surfaced out. "On absolute promise, my mother suckled me."

"Then you should have plenty of energy," Fox cuts in by looking to the Queen, additionally questioning, "am I right?"

"Absolutely," she clarifies. "Chrome, you did not take in enough milk. Possibly from your impatience of our buildup beginning."

Drawing me close to her belly with the point of beak, guilt of accepting Sanora's milk has all disappeared. Because my desperation is more than just for nourishment, it is for my life. My instinct of survival overwhelms my hunger. Wanting to live requires her milk.

"Fox, it is now your turn to vertical leap," she extends the range with a raise of her paw, giving my companion a slightly higher target for grasping. Assuming because he is slightly larger than myself, I await his acceptance of the challenge. The Vulpine clears the ascension with no trouble, causing Ankara having to find an even higher target.

Satisfied with a low hanging branch of a nearby tree, she instructs my partner yet again. Fox impresses the both of us with wrapping both paws overtop the branch. To excite the experience ever more, he pulls the rest of himself up to suspend down inverted by the joints of his knees.

"By the memories you are feeding me," Ankara rings out, "your mother trained you in multiple physical and tactical advancements. All from the first moment you made use of your legs."

"Correct," he verifies with definite somber emotion of toned expression. Taking in my own inconclusive mentality, our inspirer enlightens with a change of emotion.

"He had an experience that opposes my own. You see, Chrome, he lost his mother."

I bring nothing forth from my beak, but not because I am feeding from her nipple, because relating to Fox's past proves no easier than visualizing Ankara's. To the extent of savoring her milk over my mother's, the mystery remains why I feel weaker than ever today. I will suckle from Hollice more frequently as my Queen instructed.

This is my first time in this part of Chromium. Here, the trees are larger and greater in number. The eerie quietness grants impression that something is concealing itself from sight. My instinct reveals its presence, and there is a scent in my nostrils that was not there a moment ago; though it is one I do not recognize.

Camira runs me through what she refers to as basics. Having me do a variety of physical movements that range from sprint runs to leaping upon tree trunks to climbing to the height of my capability.

"You are quite strong, Kyara," she observes. "You indeed have powerful physicality; but now, I wish to test your mentality." As she has challenged, I open and expand my senses to the entire surroundings: accepting any new sight, sound, taste, or smell. My spiritual side takes in the same eerie supernatural detection it picked up in the beginning; communicating with the rest of my form by putting all of me into uneasiness. The sensation stimulates something here beyond Camira and I. This something, totally out of what I know to be ordinary. As though the entity strays from time itself; its only connection to this reality being . . . me.

"What have you observed in this period of contemplation?" my guide breaks in, taking notice of my change in mood.

Replying with a bow, I detail, "This land is far different from any I have previously visited. It has the most peculiar aura."

The golden Gryphon gives an eye so familiar, I immediately see her likeness to my mother. But Camira is far more joyful in comparison.

"A most interesting observation by one so immature," at the conclusion of the phrase, she continues, "every Aquileia feels edgy in this part of the region. Describing it in ways totally similar to your own."

"I do not find that hard to believe," instead of questioning myself, I take it into an inquiring level and grant this question. "Why is this so?"

She gives a shake of her head, "There is not a single Aquileia who understands it or its purpose. Not even Moonsight has a theory; but he wishes to expose an outsider to this area. Hoping that he or she can diagnose what is called . . . the aura."

I blurt out, "Fox?"

"I assume so, yes. He may be of great help if he understands the condition of this region. If so, he is a most precious gift," astonishingly, a breath of relief escapes my beak. Fox may be a frightening creature, but this bizarre entity is even more frightening. I hope Camira is right, that he is our blessing.

"What is next for my training?" I ponder, departing from subject.

"I believe it is time for some combat," she decides. "I will do my best to oppose you today. Tomorrow, I will pair you with another kit in order to train you in battle.

"Who?" I pester in my overwhelming curiosity.

"I will chat with the Queen in order to collaborate a combat training along with your brother. For the time, train with him this evening. Use your virtue of instinct in order to defeat each other. Remember, no beaks or claws."

"Absolutely," I clarify. "I promise to impress you." Presenting a glowing expression of gratitude, I can only long for mother to act this way toward me. The two sisters have such a similar visual likeness, yet, entirely different overall.

This night, Chrome and I train together for the first time; putting every strength of our own into it all by even accessing the adrenals. "I will not allow you to keep me down!" I protest at his first attempt to restrain me. "You have the advantage of size, but I will not let you win." Chrome's only reaction is a deep purring vibration in his throat.

"Now is time to show strength not even he can expect," readying my hind legs, I give a tremendous kick against his belly to force him off. Springing into immediate action, I leap from the barrier's floor and bring Chrome down before gravity has the chance. The exact moment I set myself upon him, he brings forth a great breath.

"Did I knock the wind out of you?" I banter from above. My black figure upon his golden body gives me shadowy sensations. Still, I am amazed we pass as siblings.

"You have indeed astounded me," he indicates with

delight. Heaving myself off, I give him a chance to straighten up, but at the moment of dropping defense, my brother takes his chance and unexpectedly knocks my hind legs out from under me with a single paw; rolling me over back down to restrain with his weight. "I believe we have a draw," he teases, giving a gentle lick on the side of my beak.

"For now," I agree. We spend the remainder of the night grooming each other. Hollice arrives soon after to allows us to nurse. She is not thrilled, which I see in her glare.

"My night vision has improved," I announce to her, "I am even able to see the light through the forest. It is not long till dawn."

"Good to know," she fumes with not a hint of interest. With intent of pleasing her, Chrome and I nurse without any more conversation nor interruption. Requiring our energy for the upcoming day, sleep and milk are the only way. When having taken my fill, I huddle close to mother's belly and proceed into sleep. My brother however, nurses for a longer period. His suckling continues on even while I doze out of consciousness.

"There is something returning to my mind," Ankara pronounces with misty breath in this chilling night.

"Will you present it?" I remark with great interest. Drawing all her attention to focus upon me, she continues.

"Do you remember what Kyara recalled to her brother this day? The moment we arrived at their barrier?" Thinking back to earlier today, I divulge what I do recall.

"Telling him about the presence of rather strange aura's in the north west forest?" Gifting a bow, the queen confirms, "Exactly that."

"Do you know what it is she experienced?" I prompt.

"In belief alone, it is caused by a presence that we Gryphons are unable to detect with our physical senses. We only feel sensational energy touch our emotions." Having no absolution to why I am part of this, the queen immediately picks up my misunderstanding.

"I believe you, Fox, are able to detect these creatures in a capability beyond our own. A difference of you being Vulpine compared to us Gryphons, means you have a special something we lack." I desire to deny all that she just relayed but there is a spark igniting deep within my spirit. Knowing something I do not.

"You are not sure entirely of this? As though your body is withholding something from your mind?"

"You are an excellent thought listener," I comment, "but why include me in on these unexplained energy auras?" Though it is night, a flash passes across her eyes from what little lunar ray there is. "Because you, Fox, emit the same aura as these mysterious impulses."

I feel like a particle of history with a future concealed by incurable blindness. The Aquileia have given me a home, an opportunity to start fresh. But not only has the environment changed, I myself have alternated. Born with these flightless bat limbs validates only my first beginning. Black furred like any Vulpine kit, which changed into the same gold pelt of mother's. After my survival from Gauntlet's destruction, black again coated my pelage in ash. Concluding my cleansing, Skylar's inherited coat of gold changed into the values of a dawn.

"I have lost your image, mother. My visual and physical inheritance is no more; for I am now something totally different. I am wondering even, if I am still Vulpine." Every assumption that these physical changes are radioactive remains a strong theory. Apart from the black of my paws, my pelt is of copper red. Yet, the fur creating a long stripe down my back is most striking. Beginning at the brow, it extends down between my wings, continuously traveling to my tail and fading into the yellow tip. I have not been in front of a mirror in a great while, but Ankara and Moonsight also granted me my facial description. I understand my cheek ruffs are coming in because every Vulpine dog develops those, significantly in the colder climates. But these hairs are becoming the same warm values that grow in my spine stripe.

Additionally, they also describe the stripe fur of my head and neck growing out noticeably longer than the rest of my hairs. Adding that it is resembling a type of mane also intensifies my freakish self. The once blue irises of my eyes form a violet ring around the outer edges, as though red fire mixed with my blue pupil muscles, burning them purple.

Accepting I am strikingly ill is no longer challenging. Fever only rises, both my mind and body are far different than recently before, changing into a heavily deformed freak of nature. "No longer can I consider myself natural."

Tomorrow will bring the future. The one true knowing is when Ankara will lead Chrome and I into this mysterious region. There I will encounter whatever awaits. "To the best of my capability learning something to teach my allies."

"Hey Chrome," I voice gleefully as the Queen leads us onward into the territory of Camira, "you seem tired, brother."

"I am," he admits. "Just not energetic as I usually am." Without mention, I too have a dreadful feeling coming over as my limbs tremble into numbness. To add to it all, my stomach is drained empty, my mind is struggling for focus, and cannot help but feel small and powerful twitches of fear.

"Reentering your existence! Announces a voice

both foreign and distinctly of my brother's partner. As done previously, I acknowledge him as I refused Ankara. If not for Chrome, coming here would have left me absent.

"Ready for a sensational trek?" he greets as the two touched wingtips. It presents itself rather peculiar that I saw Fox on two legs yesterday, and now four. Summoning out some courage, I give my voice to him for the first time.

"Do you have two or four legs?"

Barking in hysteria, he enlightens, "At the moment, four," The next happening causes my head to straighten up for better view. The creature gives his legs a snap as bone and muscle shift beneath his hide. Forepaws leave the ground, spine straitens up, now supporting his body upon only his two hinds.

"My answer for you, Kyara. Is that I have six limbs just as you, but most of my race only have four."

"You are the only one?" I question his declaration.

His head bows with confirming glare from a flash of those violet eyes. I cannot ever imagine having such iris color.

"The only Vulpine with a pair of wings; I suppose that would be like the one Gryphon without wings."

Time is close to midday when the forest gives way to the northwest. Immediately, those creepy energies ripple throughout.

"Never before have I felt this way," Chrome becomes first to announce. "It all feels so alien to the rest of Chromium." Fox throws his eyes in every direction as though he is not sure where to look.

"Are you as afraid as I am?" he pants, directing to us all.

"Unsure, this electrical energy is most powerful," my brother observes. "It is much like your own, Fox." His tone is both fascinated and afraid as he concludes . . . "There is not one presence; rather there are many."

"Are you afraid?" I ask my inspirer once joining her side, attempting to draw the anxiety away from Chrome and Kyara.

"I really do not know," she indicates. "The aura here is more powerful than any I have ever experienced. Because you share it, is why I have brought you here." Taking a breath, the Queen turns back to check on the kits who are moving faster than before, hurrying to keep close.

"Do you understand anything about this, Fox? I remain abstruse while viewing nothing more than thick forest." Her statement takes me into an outpouring paralysis as the shock passes between us. Whimpering . . . growling . . .

"You do not see them, Queen Ankara?"

Why does so much of this seem so familiar? These creatures do not feel any different to me, yet I know I have not seen them before. Mother would understand, that I am sure of. Too many questions are asked by both myself and the Gryphons. When I make contact with the red gaze of these chrome like beings, I find they are closely watching in a way similar to how a predator watches prey.

"Your fear is as strong as mine was during Sanora's capture," Ankara breaks in, taking notice of my anxiety.

"I am uncomfortable, and something feels terribly wrong," If I voice over, they will hear. So instead, I allow Ankara to hear my mentality. Not sure if she is able to understand the advanced sensory of the Vulpine Instinct, I do pray she understands these mortal fears of mine.

The desire to battle train today has left my spirit as these dreadful sensations of the area build into my emotions. Without bothering any of the Gryphons if I may temporarily depart, I leave them without so much as a glance of my depressed expression. Chrome and his sister are strictly focusing concentration upon their battling skills while both Camira and my guide are determined to build them up to the full extent. At this same time, I notice neither of them will remove sight from either of the kits—A most definite sign of being on guard without straying or dropping their defense.

I remember learning that through combined will and Vulpine Instinct can be so strong, it overcomes deep personal fear. The fear within me is paralyzing; however, I tread deeper into the forest even the native Aquileia forbid to explore. How do I even know that it is my instinct leading me onward?

"I thought I was developing into the Wild Inheritance?" Because I do happen to be walking on four's right now, but is it the Vulpine Instinct guiding me? "Prince Sparrk did inform us that every member of our species is born with all three gifts, and usually develops into one; from what I remember."

At the rise of a new thought, I force myself to halt in my trod from a mental shock of realization. Analyzing the memory of exact information Sparrk had given us, I unearth.

"We 'usually' develop into one of the blessings." That simple term details the difference, completely bringing the rarity to light. Yes, it is possible to have the Vulpine Instinct, just as Tia and Vykan. But partially infused with the Wild Inheritance additionally.

When mind and body hold me back because I cannot see the right nor the purpose, I sense with my spirit, guided by faith alone. Still immature, I am only beginning to understand this.

I feel like purring from bringing back the past

A S A P u b l i s h i n g C o r p o r a t i o n

memories but cannot with so many unwanted watchers. If they do not know I am aware of them, will they keep their distance. I long for the times when I was able to purr almost every day around my fellow Vulpine and Lola. The only pain was the intolerance some had toward my deformity, before amounting by my love of being part quadruped.

But I had overcome all that where some even learned to accept me as the freak I am. But now, every burden is a risk of life, not just my own anymore. Instead of critical views, I am plagued by the bloody gazes of these intentionally evil presences.

"Who and what are you?" I want to roar out in disgust of these silvery chrome like creatures, "why are you visible only to my eyes?" These beings are officially documented as my enemy. They only continue gawking with their menacing stares from the tree branches and vegetation. My whole desire is to hurl myself forward, howling with release of adrenaline charged fury. Instead, I collapse in soil without grass. Every tree and plant is deadly silent, not the weakest breeze rattles the branches, no familiar animal scent fills my nostrils and only one sound arrives in my ears.

It is quite possibly the first sound I ever translated. Remembering it from my earliest days as the pleasurable sound mother made to pass on into my own body. The ability to purr. . . but I'm far too depressed to contribute. This near identical humming, is of these disturbingly watchful creatures.

It is not until we leave Kyara's inspirer, do I begin conversation.

"Nothing will ever motivate a return there; it is more unwelcoming than the domestic."

Breathing in relief, Ankara coveys, "Experiencing it this once is the extent of my request. You have done just that, I thank you." Trekking further away and into the territory my companions and I know, satisfactory begins setting in. But I am unable to dismiss the desire to take a glance behind my tail.

"I know I will see them," clarifying out of instinct. They are there, maliciously watching in disturbing view. Skylar taught me to turn my fear around and make my enemies afraid. Having not adapted so, I pray strongly, pleading to learn soon.

"You appear distant, Fox," the queen breaks in, whether hearing my mind or not. "What is on your mind?" Oh how I hate to generate the negative energy. Taking in a breath, the oxygen fills my lungs to expand.

"The Vulpine Instinct assures me that these creatures are extensively threatening." That kind of just came out on its own, but it is my honest factorial thought. These creatures selfishly desire something of major wrong. Amazing it is, how a phrase alone brings forth mortal fear. A simple energy of sound, pitched at different frequencies and melodies. Our minds then process the energy into communicated messages to which we respond with emotions. Just it alone causes a major change in life, time, and outcome. With attention transferred to Chrome and Kyara, I think how the two will become larger than I. But at the current time, neither are half my size, "They are so vulnerable."

Ankara agrees, "Kits are Aquileia's most precious treasure. They have been a target of destruction for a great while. My daughter had that exact fate."

At the first mention of her, Chrome blurts out, "You mean these creatures only Fox can see, are the ones who took Sanora?"

Now Kyara jumps in, "Sanora?"

"My deceased daughter," the Queen details,

following the beginning of a momentary pause. She is taking in a load of thought by what Chrome has just placed in her mind.

"I . . . have never thought before, that these creatures may hold responsibility for the predation of our young. Could it really be possible?" Neither Chrome, Kyara, nor myself are able to answer.

"But the captors," she continues, "were indeed Gryphons not of our Aquileia. Not these silvery creatures you describe, Forjah." My friend's rushed accusation does not bring the two occurrences together. It further bathes the silver beings and the kit predation in total separate mysteries.

Learning that not only my race is endangered, the Gryphons have a personal genocide of their own. But why are kits exclusively targeted? It does no good to wonder, only another question added to the bulk of mystery.

Ankara nurses my two friends who are both pressing hard against her nipples. Cautiously watching over them, I worriedly wonder what they are to do. How can they at least attain survival against both murderous rogue Gryphons and vengeful hungry creatures their eyes cannot visually process?

Looking up into the sky, past the treetops to where the stars appear as the sky disk fades, my mind wonders into the unknown, seeking a reassuring answer.

"What can I do?"

Memories fill my mind, flowing like salmon returning to their location of birth. For that is where my mind is traveling. My first home . . .

Relaxing my muscles, I crouch and squat in my quadruped form. Comfortably moving my tail, tuning it to the rhythm of my thoughts.

"Fox, come. Fuse your eyes on your first sight of day. Do you not want to be the first kit to see this?" she urges.

"You are taunting me," I smirk. She gives the common glare I always receive from her.

"Perceptive, I am impressed you know me so well; but I know you even better. You desire this over your fear." She is right, but I do want to please and make her proud. Closing eyelids, I pad from the cave entrance. The light remains a burning red casting its warm touch to my unexposed pupils. Just like being engulfed in mother's fur, guarded from the dark labyrinth's chills.

"Not too far," comes Skylar's voice, stopping me before advancing. "I will not have you plummet down." She is always positioning herself between me and harm. I know this is the natural action of a mother. So huddling close, I fear both the light and vertical drop.

"Fox, I know you trust me. See, you will not be blinded." Having complete trust in her more than anyone, I bow my head before opening up before the wilderness. This is what I am visualizing.

I see what Skylar describes as our forest, mighty trees of green growing high just below the cliff tops. To the north, I see the great steel towers of Gauntlet, the domestic city. To the south, an expanding meadow with more forest and mountains beyond.

With mother's permission, I gently poke nose over the side, cautiously peeking over the edge. This height is intense and if not for Skylar, I would not feel secure right now.

"Why does everything seem so small?" I ask in observation of seeing adult Vulpine come and go between the labyrinth and outside.

"From a distance, everything appears smaller than up close," she explains. "Even the buildings you see in the

distant city are much larger than their distant appearance."
I will accept her confirmation, because her claim makes
sense and she is raising me by passing on her knowledge and
skill. As I am now taking in the distance from here to the
ground, a new feeling comes over me apart from the slight
acrophobia. It is a growing sensational desire in my third pair
of limbs.

Now I ease my paws over the edge for a reassuring
grip, instinctively opening into the air's breeze for the first
time.

"Do not carry away," Skylar warns, picking up my
craving for flight I cannot deny. But now is time to use will
over bodily desire. Retreating back by returning to Skylar's
side, I shake off the shivers before diverting attention to her.

Momentarily my scrutiny meets her own as is the
realization of seeing her for the first time. Never knowing
before what beauty she has of shining strands. But bringing
forth mother's appearance most, are the copper irises.

"You seem dazzled Fox, never before having seen
me in the light." I bow in clarification.

"No mother, I never knew of your beauty. How can
my dark fur compare to your shining pelt?"

Tongue rasping over my ears, she explains, "You and
I are extremely different. But in time, a bright shining pelt of
your own will replace the black. I promise."

"I am seeing you in your full glory," not able to help
but be visually fascinated that she illuminates with the
internal star even in daylight. Now I am beginning to wonder
if I really am her son. How can I be?

"Indeed, I am in my full glory," she enlightens,
lovingly wrapping tail around me.

"I hope to be like you," I pray, looking up to her with
my most serious an expression. "Do I not have inheritance
of either of you or father?" She bites the tip of my ear to

silence me.

"I did not bare you to be that way. You are your own dog." She pulls me tighter against her chest in conclusion of, "I once believed I was born for a different purpose. In time, it became clear truth when revealing itself. I fell in love, conceived, and I bore you, Forjah. From your first moments, I knew why I had come to the Vulpine."

Came to the Vulpine? I wonder from where.

Our muzzles touch as she completes by reassuring, "I am still serving my purpose this day. My devotion is to you, my son. I became your mother and will be forever."

What is the assumed purpose she had before baring me? How had Skylar come to the Vulpine, and from where? She raised many questions in the short time I knew her. Most I believe to never be answered. "Supposedly, I must focus on my own existence. Not her lost history," I decide. "After all, dwelling upon what I can do for Chromium is becoming top priority. How I can help protect the Aquileia?"

High Prince Sparrk explained the three Vulpine gifts in such detail, it will always be easy to remember. The Wild Inheritance is surely my skill, but now I have Vulpine Instinct. Advanced sensory to supernatural forces, just like Tia and Vykan. Oh do I hope they found safety and to meet again.

Based off what I mentally developed after experiencing the auras of these silver creatures, I feel they are determined to fulfill their evil needs. Still not knowing specifically what these intentions are; there is new theory.

Because foreign Gryphons are plotting to kill Aquileia, how do I know they are not the same ones who began the genocide against my race?

"There must still be cat-raptors who prey on us apart from the Aquileia. Could they have domesticated and dropped those bombs on Gauntlet? Now preying on all

Vulpine and wild Gryphon kits?" The more my mind loads up with these developing questions, the more anxiety and depression cling to me. Only theoretical thoughts, could any of them be true. Could all be true?

"Tomorrow is a whole new day," I remind myself as I do every night. "Tomorrow will bring something entirely different, no matter how similar." But the Vulpine Instinct is directing me toward something far from good. I supernaturally sense a dreadful distress.

"The tournaments begin tomorrow," Ankara brings up. "The subject is defensive combat. Something I know you value, Fox. Are you ready to show off that talent?" I prepared and have my answer for the Queen.

"I am ready."

A S A P u b l i s h i n g C o r p o r a t i o n

Scenic 29

Third Coat

As the day comes to a close I find myself climbing Moonsight's ledge for a slightly different perspective. The chilled stone is lifeless in equivalent to Gauntlet, where all that thrives are embers.

The endless water mass charges its trembling nightly breeze. Moonsight informed us that this water expanding from Chromium's shoreline is completely fresh. Explaining of another form called saltwater.

"Your mate is so full of knowledge," I praise to Ankara from above, "he is much like mother, always having something new to pass on."

"He acts as father to the inexperienced," she carries out. "I attempt to portray a mother in that same way. As it is my instinctive desire."

Ankara now eases our conversation deeper into this topic; so I tag along with participation. "I never knew my father, he only vowed to remain until my eyes opened. He even delivered me when the time came."

Having repositioned onto my belly, my muzzle slightly dips over the ledge while resting head over my folded arms. Ankara joins me, and to my unprepared reaction, brings her head low proceeding to massage her tongue over my mane, neatly combing the tangle the strands.

"I want you looking your best tomorrow," she indicates, treating me like her own. Denying such affection is a no dare, for I adore it extensively. Not yet a professional at grooming myself, my thickening hairs are increasing that challenge. Ankara's tongue is most welcome as its barbs grip the strands of my spine stripe to lay it neatly. When making her way down my spine, I open and spread the roots of my shoulders, allowing her to continue.

This new feature I recently developed continues its growth, changing into warm colors of crimson gold and copper; all the while multiplying in an outbreak accordance. Indeed, I am maturing into a dog just as I am meant to. I grow in size, mentality changing and strengthening overall. So I should expect these changes along with hormonal reactions of my mind and body? But adding to the formation of an abnormal fur stripe from scalp to tail tip, my cheek ruffs are altering in the exact same color; described my companions.

As kits, our fur is coal black before gradually fading into a warm valued coat of the traditional Vulpine. My fur became more of a gold, inherited from Skylar.

"This is my third coat," realizing with a shiver. Never heard of a Vulpine's fur changing twice, just as mine has done.

"You are cold?" The Queen notices. Before connecting with response, a sudden flash of heat flares up in my lungs proceeding to fill my abdomen. Then, slithering and raging to the tips of my limbs and tail. I would have collapsed if not already down, for this hotness overtakes my entire interior to an overwhelming level.

"I . . . am so feverish," but for the first beginning, not of illness. This internal warmth is intensely comforting.

"Forjah, I think you just manipulated your body temperature," I can only agree with her, but what is this peculiar ability?

"You are well over your average," she clarifies after pressing a paw to my side.

"I am cozy as a wood fire," I purr with warm delight to Ankara, granting her a mental image of our fire we had outside the labyrinth. Wrapping arms around my torso as the pleasuring heat builds inside, I rage like an organic furnace. Each moment, inhaling a gulp of fresh air, the heat of my abdomen builds and feeds my lungs.

"Ohhhh!" I moan and howl while prickling my claws up and down my rib cage, "I feel like just evaporating out of my own body."

"You are saying that, it is inside you?" Validating with a grinning bow, she orders, "Come," leaping from the ledge, I follow her lead into the darkened forest, thankful we are both blessed with night vision.

The Aquileia Queen stops once we are deep into the thicket. Many insects chirp in the night, the clicks of bats overhead chase their prey with their own miraculous gift of echolocation.

"Do something for me," Ankara pleadingly requests, "put your nose below the undergrowth. Take in every scent that comes." Without a challenge, I do as she instructs. In quadruped form, I keep the tip of my nose below the plants to sniff thoroughly; sure to not pass over any unscented.

In moments, I have a sniffle. Raising up to let out a discharge, something extremely hot travels up my sinuses. Once reopening my eyes, they rest upon what is now before me.

"Ankara . . .?" she knows I am whimpering for guidance. In exact location of where I let loose, the brush is now inflamed. I am not sure if to be afraid or just in totally fascination, "That fire . . . came out of ME!" I announce. "I discharged fire." The Queen lingers near with equivalent awe.

"I have only ever seen fire in your memory. Now to have it physically before me is a new experience entirely." The mother raises forearm at elbow joint to extend it to the flares, retracting it by a flick of restraint when making contact. Wetting the pad by her tongue, Ankara divulges, "I just needed to feel the danger opposing the beauty."

This little action risk of hers fuels my inspiration like oil to a match. If these flames are living alongside me, does this mean . . . Unexpectedly, my instinct kicks in on choice of action. My wings unlock, withdrawing out to drape their tips overhead. Lower, lower, until directly in over the flares. The fire hurts to a parch against the leather, but absolutely no burns form.

Now I extend my fore paws and physically grasp it. The touch of fire is so intense, I almost draw my limbs back; but the thrill empowers further contact. Ankara comes to hither, peering in for a closer more detailed observation.

"I am touching fire," I detail. "It really hurts, but furs are not perishing nor is my flesh parching."

"I assumed so," she admits. "This answers so many things we have pondered. Your body must have adapted to the fires of the explosion, meaning that you have fused." She is right, I have advanced from a hybrid and into a tribird.

I sigh, "Time is just getting so much more extreme and complicated. And it all seems to be happening around me. But I must slow down and focus on the present.

Shifting into biped, I proceed to further come in contact with the smoldering brush. The keratin barbs of my feet heat up and expand into the nail root of their digits. Remembering to only do and not think, I charge both feet into the fresh embers. Straddling the flares, my frantic tail flares on its own escape. But with discipline to my reflexes, I rest my spine extension to relaxingly hang, gasping as the flames begin traveling up to catch and enflame the tip. My legs are strips of oiled kindling as they fall victim to the arising fire. Both hips and abdomen accept and feed it like a fresh dose of oxygen; rippling through my fur above radiated skin.

The hairs of my stripe stick up as they too flare up in glorious newborn phlogiston. Ankara keeps back to a safe distance when the bare leather of my chiroptera appendages turns to a bright pink. Embers rage behind my pupils and spark behind the irises.

"This is what it is to be fire."

In a short instant, every flame absorbs into my body by instinctive will. As though the water of my body has both extinguished and preserved it. Darkness of the forest returns and I find myself smoking in a black crater of ash. Ankara reproaches while I cool myself. Meeting the Queen jaw restrained, she brings forth, "You have become the everlasting fire, Forjah."

I have made the decision to remain nocturnal at the moment, here outside the high ledge of Moonsight and his Queen. All around is nothing but darkness and walls of stone slanting up into their peaks and summits. The same tectonics I viewed distantly from my first home in Gauntlet's region. "Now I am here," I announce. Taking a peek over into the north west results in failure of seeing my birth home. All visual is shielded by another mountain peak. If I were able to fly on my wings, could I rise above all this earth? I am now a tribrid, so why not? Seeing the city ruins in the distance, the cliffs concealing the labyrinth. Both locations even more lifeless than where I am.

Rock is not alive but I cannot shake the awful

sensation of everything around me being so . . . dead. As though the only living within the area is myself and the two slumbering Gryphons. I never asked why they choose to live here, I really should.

My reason for feeling so queer may be because this ledge is the exact location of Sanora's capture, and her death following shortly after. Both her mother and father have scars remaining from that fateful night. "What if Chrome is right, that those creatures I encountered today are truly responsible for claiming lives of Gryphon kits. Possibly even to blame for the Vulpine genocide. But Ankara and Moonsight witnessed the captors as rogue Gryphons. These chrome like beings only visible to my eyes are clearly are not."

Falling upon my knees and flat onto my stomach, I crush my head between my paws. So much emotional pain, excruciating to take into my brain that I may explode out of my own thought train. The lack of maturity limits me against what I must learn in the future. Physically, psychologically, and spiritually, I raise my head and roar in breaking the silence. So strong, it reaches the stars overhead, echoing off the stony mountains and out over the water.

"If only I could arise again," I wish in desperation, "travel so far and escape all this depression to start a new life. I attempted by coming here," I recollect, "but that hardly changed. This new life is full of new troubles, proving to not be the escape I anticipated. But I have attained survival," though it is hardly a life to be lived.

Yet, I am not alone here. The Aquileia suffer just as much, willingly desiring to live on as well.

"Living to fight for your life." That is the current purpose and motive, here and now. Sanora, as well as others have become victims of death. Surly, the enemy wishes to continue on and claim more.

The only kits I know are Chrome and Kyara. Based entirely on my theoretical outcome; they may have become targets just by being in the territory of those creatures this passed day. But that makes two hunters, added to the already hostile rouge Gryphons?

Leaping to my paws, I shift into biped. Focusing on a great distance while drowning completely into mental reality. But my mind is now so overwhelmed, that I once again faint. Hoping this time to fall out of consciousness completely. My brain has become more fatigued than my body, every one of my thoughts consuming each individual calorie. Resting my mentality as well as my physicality is a must.

This chilled ledge of stone does not bother because my insides are a raging inferno. Goodness, with my new level of body temp, I can keep anyone warm.

As I pass into that sleep cycle between alpha and beta, I sense another nearing me. The scent reveals Ankara, who is somehow hoisting me up to carry into the barrier. When she lays me at her side, I inhale the milk scent that brings pleasant night visions into my conscious.

I am with Skylar again, mesmerizing when I fed from her breast. Enjoying her fresh caught muskrat as first meat. So tender, so delicious. Now I run at her side from the forest and into the meadow. Lola joins, I leap upon her back to then hurl from the hill and into the sky; flying with only one pair of wings between us, somersaulting in the wind at speeds beyond time.

"Our friendship is eternal," we reassure each other.

A S A P u b l i s h i n g C o r p o r a t i o n

Scenic 30

Combat Circle

I do wish we could have had something such as this tournament in my Vulpine home; yet, now that could never happen.

I am carried by Moonsight high over the mountain peaks, trailing Ankara leading us on through the flight. The two keep their wings open, catching every thermal possible. My riding on his back surly demands more energy.

"Fox, what were you going to ask me?" I am more afraid of how high we are than the fact that both these Gryphons are hearing my thoughts like a psychological hack. Only when one speaks of it to their ears, do they process and remember what is picked up. So the determination is strong in not allowing this.

"I wonder why the both of you choose your dwelling in the mountains?"

Unsure of why, Moonsight ascends higher, practically approaching the clouds before adding, "we choose to live here because we are miraculous Gryphons. Neither Ankara nor I fully understand the extent of being blessed with supernatural abilities. If something were to happen, it would be away from harming others."

"Would you prefer I stayed here as well? For the

exact same reason?"

"I do. Because you have just learned of your own blessing."

"I would like to be like you," I imagine. "Keep my distance in order not to hurt anyone, but close enough to be social." The moment the two give approval upon my decision, Moonsight does the unexpected.

In one brief moment, he makes a quick spiral causing me slip and fall; all is now inverted. Just ahead, the sky disk falls out of the earth. The rocky mountain side approaches closer every moment of decent.

Summoned by instinct, I immediately unlock and open every limb. Managing to flip, I catch many thermals that each result in flight failure. Next tactic is to flap; doing harder than ever before, summoning every amount of strength and adrenaline. Still, nothing . . .

Well before reaching the hard landing, Ankara swoops down, locking in her paws to grip me against her underbelly. Resuming flight by directly gliding above her mate, I am released on returning to his back. When securely comfortable again, my cardio is heaving so hard that sparks and smoke escape on my breath.

"It did not work," I infer, "despite doing everything possible." This is all I fume before covering my gasping mouth to catch the tingling sparks on the pad of my paw. "I must be sure not to mistakenly fire breath at today."

"Agreed," Moonsight ratifies. "Just be patient and concentrate on going airborne later on. You have much maturity ahead of you."

"Do either of you believe I will again?" I ask in a faltering tone. The two mates have their minds intertwined, answering at the same moment . . .

"Yes."

Once the sky disk touches and warms the mountain

side, the tournament will all begin. I believe both Kyara and I are rested plenty. The next sleep I hope to have will be after today.

"I wish to prove to Ankara the strength she has granted me. Use every bit of knowledge she has given and apply it all to my physical and mental ability." Perched here at the entrance of our barrier, I patiently watch the disk evaporate the morning dew, then comes our time of departure to the mountain's base.

"I wish it was time," my sister groans coming to my side, greeting me in the morning's arrival. We huddle close, providing each other a warm snuggling body.

"I know you are not my true brother, Chrome. But you are dearly close, and cannot choose anyone over you." Truly, I only saw her as a sister once in the beginning. We are indeed close, but not like siblings anymore; more so as inseparable friends.

"Before you came to be, I desired to have a companion," recalling those lonesome days by draping a downy wing over her back. "now you are here."

"Hmhmmm," she purrs in delight, "I will not be an easy opponent today. That I promise."

"Excellent!" I appreciate. "Challenge is what I welcome." Picking up a deep growling from within her, I join rhythmic purrs by invitation of . . .

"We need to nurse. This day requires it most of all." Revealing my ratification requires no response. Giving a quick bow, we retreat back inside. Hollice has remained in the grass bed, resting silently with head over paws. Funny, but she almost seems depressed.

"Mother?" I begin. Her eyes shift unto my location without moving any of her golden body. The fact that I may grow larger than she one day is an exceptional wonder. Still able to be carried in her beak, learning we hybrid animals develop slower; It is reassuring I will not remain small forever.

Clearly seeing Hollice has no interest in chit chat, she is also totally ignorant of my worry. Whether that is her intention or mistake, I do not know. So out of respect that she is my mother, I leave her in this depressed state, joining Kyara as we both take in our nourishment.

The milk is not near as rich or satisfying as Ankara's. I drink only from mother because I need it now, but the Queen's mammary brings forth the fuel for my life. Without the nourishment and love she grants, I am utterly devastated.

"I keep all of this in," I analyze, "never exposing my feelings to anyone. But I certainly cannot withhold them much longer."

Today is granting a slightly warmer atmosphere than usual. I welcome all of this but feel down for my sister. Camira has not showed as promised. We suspect an error because this does not seem right. My parents are discussing it over with Moonsight and Ankara. I decide to deviate from the group and accompany Fox over at the ledge.

"Chrome," my partner greets in a tone softer than usual. The Vulpine appears almost paralyzed with hind legs hunched and forepaws over knees. His ears positioning in a variety of ways and direction.

"What are you listening to?"

"I am tuning my ears to every voice of each Gryphon arriving now. Additionally, to any-'thing' else."

I bet he is referring to those silver beings he described yesterday. Chrome-like, just as my name means. One of his paws transfers onto my back to gently stroking down between my wings,

"Please do not go off on your own, Chrome. None

of us want you ending up missing."

"Camira?"

He confirms with a bow, "I now believe we are all susceptible to becoming victims. There has been a bounty on my race since before either of our births," my friend relays, taking in a deep breath to pungently exhale as soft as possible, "By coming here and learning from your own. The Aquileia's life are not so different."

"But why, Fox?"

"I do not mean to scare you, my fellow ally. But I do not know exactly who our enemies are, and even less about their purpose of extermination."

"Are you sure it is not those chrome-like beings?"

How miraculous and astonishing the mind of a youth is. Its simplicity prevents the mistake of over thinking and keeps topics as basic as they can be. Chrome's simplistic figuring of the silver-like creatures being responsible for my race's genocide, feels both irrelevant and ingenious.

"But that still does not solve the mystery of the killing rampage of rogue Gryphons."

Fox and I both know more about fighting than before; having advanced by Ankara's training. Today is only the first of our challenges in using these new skills, and we are entirely aware there is much remaining to learn. As much I have already from our Queen, I am still not quite confident in my own self-defense. There is a single description for the exact answer to accompany my squirrel sized body and limited strength.

"Immaturity."

As a kit, it is natural for me to have fear and desire a personal shelter to shield me from harm. The one place I flee to for safety, is the one whom I desire at my side right now.

Simply putting my desires into mental command, I project out, "Please come."

Ankara's head turns slightly away from the group, transferring upon hearing my call. When she is here, it takes a moment before I gather both my thoughts and courage to begin conversation.

"Ankara," I plead, "since I first met you, I see you as a most wonderful Queen and inspirer. Not just to me, but all others." She could imply something right now, if unaware that I have yet to finish.

"I love Hollice, I really do, because she is my origin. But the two of you are so different, I feel divided." Now is the time to break down and simplify this revelation, "I see you as my mother, Ankara. You have shown your love to me in a way like no other. At times, I feel more your son than Hollice's." Rhythmic purrs now ring out from her as she brings herself down to my eye level, meeting iris to iris and beak to beak.

"I feel the same toward you Chrome. Meaning I experience you as my own. What I am doing with and for you, I would have done regardless."

A role of second mother is somewhat new to me. Ankara not only treats me as a son, but Chrome as well. Does this make him my brother? Skylar never detailed the kits she had preceding my birth, my true biological siblings. Yet the more I remember her, the more I see the connection of similarities of she to Ankara. The care, love, and guidance is that of motherhood, and I am a son to her despite diversity.

"You cannot take Skylar's position, however, you are most certainly carrying on her duty."

The Queen raises her enormous paw to strokes my companion's spine, causing those downy wings to spring up out of ticklish reaction.

"If Sanora was never taken, I would treat the both of you no different. As my sons," she appoints. "Chrome, there is no wrong experiencing me as your second mother. And Forjah," she adds once claiming my attention, "I am succeeding directly where Skylar meant to carry on. Not by replacing her, but by continuing her goal of advancing you into the dog you are becoming."

Out of my delightful praise, Chrome hugs her paw hard. I leap by wrapping forepaws around her neck. Whether or not she has any idea or knowledge of a kiss, I give her one directly below the eye to praise her for being far more than a Queen. After a moment of honorable silence, she asks both Chrome and I, "Are the both of you ready for the tournament's beginning?"

We both tremble tri paired limbs to declare, "Into battle!"

"Ankara, I know both you and I are afraid, but it is my promise to not open my muzzle. When needing a moment of recovery, I will remove myself from the battle entirely," she observes me with most proud eyes; much like Skylar.

"You are most trustworthy, Fox. I know you will do well."

"So I have permission from my inspirer? Despite my dangerous new self?"

"Absolutely," she again confirms.

Chrome and I perch side by side with Ankara settled directly behind. We have taken our place in the great circle formed by fellow Gryphon participants. I see every kit cautiously eyeing each other. Whether looking for a worthy opponent; strongest, or weakest, I do not know. Some are granting me expressions I am unable to translate, but no kit nor adult questions my involvement with their Queen representing my partner and I.

"Our rules have important significance," Moonsight's announces perched upon the ledge. Looking upon us all, he begins, "this battle will be fought without the use of claws, beaks, or any method of flesh penetration. Use only what your inspirers have put into your mentality and physicality. Instinct of defense most pure is tactical advantage. Think of this as your own survival, as well as the life of those you love. Each of you are about to become locked in combat with determination to carry on and live. Make enemies fall to your power." While catching his breath, I gander to the far left. Meeting eyes with a kit perched directly below Evaron.

Aquila.

The red female appears to have been watching me for a time, for she has locked her sight with lids touching their pupils in a most beautiful way. She brings her tail around to slowly trail down her side to which I track the tip's movement; passing over her figure to grant me its warm valued features. From maroon down to nicely curved hips.

"She is by far the greatest definition of beauty." Momentarily into this trance, the shadows shift from overhead, casting down to where Ankara's beak meets my leonine ear.

"Now is not time to focus on her fascination inducing figure. Chrome, you must scrutinize the instruction my mate presents." As she took on the duty of inspirer, continued following of her training is most prudent. As a steady transition, I give a bow to the maroon kit just before returning attention to my leader. The time of our first battle is arriving.

"Battle to your limit. Remove yourself when you can do no more," Moonsight advises. "The last kit within the combat circle will be our victor."

"Are we afraid or excited?" I challenge Fox.

Drawing back his lips in that pleasant toothy grin, he assures, "Afraid and excited."

Once in position, Fox shifts into quadruped, everyone advances forward thirsty for fresh action. It is as though life has completely silenced and put out my existence. This paralyzing moment instantly breaks when Moonsight projects out.

"Commence combat."

Chrome and I split off, each encountering an immediate opponent. Quietly planning my strategy, my first quarrel is a flaxen female. The two of us lunge at each other, locking our paws in the attempt of a takedown. She pushes hard, intent on breaking balance and putting forth all strength into resistance.

Now comes to me the answer of tactical advantage. Propelling upward by bursting with wings and hind legs, I take her up in my grasp and into the air, instantly allowing gravity to direct my weight down upon her. Voices from around flare up as I impact the female into the earth. She forfeits, leading into satisfied triumph.

"I must use the full strength of Vulpine Instinct. It may just be key advantage."

The way it is, everyone is one on one. I am alert when my chance presents itself. A small female has broken away, leaving her larger chestnut opponent alone on the combat circle.

Rushing forward, I lion leap to bring her to the ground. A vigorously slap by her wing proves just enough to gain her freedom. She is on her paws in only a moment before taking me down in a powerful tackle. My head takes the greatest impact to where I now feel dazed. The chestnut female leaves momentarily satisfied with my downfall.

I cannot shake my wonder of how Fox and Kyara are doing, but in a number of moments following the return to my paws, who waits for me is none other than she herself.

My sister and I exchange a bow, signifying we are both ready for an official battle. We end up rolling around; but neither she nor I stand down. Strange, my mind premeditated a greater retaliation.

She lunges again once returning to stance. Thrusting herself to strike me down with adrenal induced force. From above, she cries.

"I can do no more, brother. No remaining energy."

Unable to give a testament, I release Kyara with a much weaker departure than desired. Removing myself and granting her leave, she exits from the field with no concern for defeat.

"She said she would be tough on me, but is tuckered out from one brief encounter?" Yet these pondering thoughts of mine last momentarily before I am impaled again.

"Hi Chrome," Aquila greets from above my defense. The red Gryphon has her hold on me, while lovingly kneading talon tips into my shoulder. In returning fashion, I expose my tongue to swipe it under her eye, giving ultimate opportunity of deception. Pressing hind paws against the underside, I begin to tickle her belly with the points of my nails, thus distracting her ever more into her sweet bubbling purrs. Now, forcing her off with a most empowering thrust of my feet proves ingeniously effective. She grunts in frustration to realize.

"You really had me under your subterfuge," her hairs and gorgeous red down are on end, flashing that admirable beauty once again. But it is not stopping me from my next attempt at knocking my friend off balance.

Diving between her legs, I give myself enough time to lift her onto my back from beneath. Then roll Aquila belly up, pinned under my weight.

"Deceived you, I did indeed," I reveal from above. "But I meant every romantic moment of it."

"Hmmm . . ."she purrs.

"But I do wish you were a worthy opponent," I tease.

"At your request," she tauntingly validates.

I then confirm, "Yes please," Aquila and I wrestle with every amount of strength we have. Putting it into both physic and strategy, I am about to make my next move when something overcomes me. Aquila is there, now . . . nothing.

"Chrome?" I call out to my companion, lying on the ground yet absolutely unresponsive.

Abandoning my opponent, I rush to his fallen form. Calling out his name as does the red Gryphon he was sparring with.

"Chrome?" we call together. I touch my paw pad to his body and I find a strong pulse despite his being completely unconscious.

Now is time to abandon the battle. What is happening to my companion exactly, I believe is fainting. Changing into biped, I take the Gryphon into my arms, carrying him off the combat circle. To my astonishment, his leonine body proves extraordinarily light. To the adults, many give a startle as a casualty was most unexpected in this tournament.

Setting his sleeping form in the soft brush, I ask the red Gryphon.

"I am Aquila," she greets. "Chrome is my friend, and I am pupil to his father. We were battling just before he collapsed." Stroking a paw over him, I run my pad over his side and then stop.

"What," Aquila desperately partakes in my shift of mood.

"There is no fat between his ribs and skin," I declare. "He is dangerously thin as though he has had nothing . . .

"Forjah," Ankara's call interrupts with both Moonsight and Evaron trailing her lead.

"How can he be this way?" she quickly files away my thoughts by closer inspecting Chrome herself. Feeling the muscles beneath his hide, finding only the smallest amount of fat.

"He is wasting," Evaron says upon seeing his son. "He passed out?"

"Aquila testifies, "just fell asleep."

"There has to be a biological cause," Moonsight brings forth. I know he is right. In an instant, Kyara joins us with fear for her brother clearly visible. After seeing him carried off the battle field in my arms, the kit is deeply ruptured with trembles.

My brother described my small unconscious form when first finding me in the forest. Now I am hovering over him in the exact same circumstance; in desperation of saving him. Time has made it so our roles have reversed.

"Do you know what caused him to black out?" I am about to answer, but my own thoughts interrupt at a sight both new and born familiar. I had seen Kyara leave the field before her brother. Last I knew, she had been resting herself under the trees. Now finding Chrome in this state, it is too easy to notice the similarities in his sister. Kyara is just equally anorexic with a load of visual fatigue. Additionally, I hear a deep growl from Chrome that I know to be the sound as ones' craving stomach.

"I do not," I finally manage to respond. "Chrome's

fainting is a mystery." A term I am beginning to hate. First Mother, Sanora, the chrome-like creatures, now Chrome himself.

Without another exchange, Ankara makes her move. She takes Chrome into a paw, and places him between her haunches. In an instant, he begins stirring. His dark eyes weakly open and upon realizing where he is, magnetically latches to Ankara's tit.

Kyara gets the message, and she too begins nursing from the Queen.

"It is like they haven't had anything in their bellies," Evaron brings out. "My kits are dangerously thin as they were not before." Their father's declaration is true, the reason for this all is unknown.

When the battle completes, many kits are tired and weary from the whole endurance, but none near as bad as Chrome or Kyara. I pay no attention to the winner who Moonsight simply recognizes with praise, then dismisses everyone.

"I will take great care of your kits," Ankara promises to Evaron, as he escorts Aquila and her family back to their den.

"I do not want to leave," Aquila begs her mother. "I am worried about them." Chrome detaches from his nourishment to reassure.

"We are not invalid, Aquila. Just tired and hungry." With one final order, the red gryphon catches up to her siblings.

"I'll return later this evening," Chrome's father vows, before joining Adelhied and her kits.

"Trek safely," we bid them.

Now it is just Moonsight, Ankara, the kits, and I. But

to my immediate astonishment, I am taking in that there is one other.

Looking past the group, I see another Gryphon. A full grown female who appears bony thin and unhealthy; but there she perches quietly with no acknowledgment or care of what is happening. This golden Aquileian mother is the maternal individual of both Chrome and Kyara.

Hollice.

Scenic 31

Final Outcome

Being this weak, everything proves a difficult task including simple concentration. But I am catching onto Moonsight taking in mother's thoughts. Even Ankara scrutinizes her in a negative mood.

"Hollice . . . I am most unsure how to respond to this," For the first time, a cold feeling passes over my leader. His Queen trembles at his side, digging her talons into the earth. Anger for the first time in this Gryphon I admire so deeply. Only Hollice could match Ankara's at this moment.

"What is happening?" Kyara weakly falters, instantly detecting the frailty in her voice. Why is Kyara showing my same weakness? The moment of vocalizing her question, she falls back with a faint close of her eyes, having not seen her this way since . . . first finding her.

"The two are wasting," Ankara observes with her darkest look. When seeing her for the first time, my fear of her was intensely false before finding a gorgeous soul within.

"Now I know she indeed has a dark side."

"These kits," Moonsight introduces, "have absolutely no knowledge of how you are neglecting them. Of savagery that disgusts to the extreme." Finishing his statement, Ankara starts to severely pant in response to the mental images she is being fed. Do these thoughts belong to Hollice?

"I will not deny anything you pry from my mind," Mother interacts. "You may react in whatever way you desire."

"I am through being critical," Moonsight responds, momentarily turning away from us to drape wing over his mate. The two draw themselves into the secluded shadows of the ledge, privately converging together.

The sky disc is dipping below the trees; casting its remaining light through the branches; this day is coming to an end. My leader and Queen have been conversing below the stone ledge for a great while. So extensively, Chromium darkens its light rays with twinkling stars while my night vision begins setting in. Taking glance to Kyara, I find her shivering at welcoming the night air coming about. I huddle close in comfort and even wrap around her in my wings of down.

"I am so weak, Chrome," she painfully whines, "I cannot make it back to the barrier."

"We will," I positively urge. "I will help you and so will mother."

"NO!" Ankara protests with an alarming return. "This suffering will end." My Queen both angered and frightened most certainly knows of something Kyara do not.

"What would you do with them?" Hollice asks in a rather blank tone. "I do not desire either, never even from their first moment." With the remaining focus, I raise my ears in order to expand my hearing range. The words I have just received, I cannot process into my mind.

"I am unsure how your kits would react if they were informed," Ankara theorizes while casting a worried glance in our direction, "they think of themselves as your offspring."

Moonsight adds, "In truth, they are nothing more than victims of your actions." The feathers of his nape are on end from rage that was previously within his mate; having taken a direct transfer.

"How could you choose such evil," she snarls, "they are your gifts; yet, you see them as no more than little burdening creatures living off you." I think Moonsight is attempting to add something but holds back, allowing his mate to continue. "There is absolutely no love within you, Hollice. Your kit's have never received, because it does not exist. Never once thinking of their need for a mother who is meant to bring them up, having done the exact opposite."

An awful feeling comes over us all. Upon sensing it, Kyara presses herself ever closer than before.

Unable I am to take eyes off Ankara. Her frightening looks paired with anger, brings forth the hostile nature I did not believe to be real. Her talons are agitated, flexing into the earth beneath her.

"What is her reason for acting this way, what has Hollice done?"

"You could have given them up in the very beginning, but you chose resort of destruction." Now the two females are lock-eyed. "I know all your mind Hollice. It flows from within you as my anger pours out from within me." Drawing in a great breath, she continues, "You deprived Chrome and Kyara of their own needs. You harmed your own self in order to make them suffer and claim their lives." The feeling I am now coming over with is far worse than any to ever arise. A nausea is in my digestive system, as though an illness exempt of cure. There is no clear view of hope because I know deep down it is not there.

Before I am able to make any reaction, Moonsight pads past his mate approaching mother, Kyara, and I. "As your leader, Hollice, I order you to give the both of them up." The moment these demands pass his beak, my mother rises from her haunches and takes a number of pads away to leave Kyara and I unsheltered in the night fallen air. As her shadow withdrawals along with her, I take notice of the moisture drops in the grass. Tonight they may freeze just as Kyara and I now are.

Why has she gone? Why is she pulling herself away? So cold, even huddled close to my brother, for we are losing the body heat we do not have. All feels minimally different to the time Chrome had first found me weak and malnourished. My pleading sight to Hollice is empowered with everlasting desire for life, for it has been with me as long as I manage to remember. Having fought so hard alone in that tree, using pure will was the one way of staying alive until she and Chrome came. Now our endurance is equal.

Mentally strong and physically frail, I unsheathe my talons to grip the ground beneath myself and the dusk sky. Doing all in my power to reach her warmth, her milk, my mother.

Now looking at the kits I have had for so long, regret is with every moment of time I had wasted upon them. How they slowed me down from the moment Chrome had been sealed in my womb, wishing for nothing more than for him to never have been conceived; longing for that little golden Gryphon to remain no more than an egg deep within me. This one egg became one I do not call my own. If he never existed, Kyara would never have been found. If it had been that way, they never would have taken part of my life and invaded the rest. No desire came to pass these burdens onto anyone else; why gift something that is a load of pain?

Quite astonishing they remain here after starving

myself to malnourish my milk, attempting on killing them. Chrome and Kyara, the two kits depended on me like a pair of parasites. I look upon them at this moment and see Chrome observe his sister drag herself in my direction. This must end! Suffering must cease!

"Stop depending on me!" I screech. Kyara's spheres of pure black force themselves open, reflecting what little light remains of day and the particle approach of starlight. The horror I have placed into her expression shows upon realizing my true abandonment, just as her true mother did before.

"I never wanted either of you. You have taken advantage of me from your first moments. I did not intend to give any of my life, but you two have taken it away and ruined me too extensively." Leader and Queen place looks of disgust upon me while the kits who had once been my own severely shiver in the nightly air. Before departing, I conclude my finale with, "I am giving the both of you up. No longer am I your mother."

Astonished disbelief burns within my mind. Instinctively beginning to wail hard and mournfully, Kyara too joins crying to our calls ringing in the empty forest and into the mountains. Never have I felt so alone.

Usually this genre is cold as it is dark. That is why I huddle with my sister right now to share our body heat. We lay together in the darkening night as our energy begins slightly regenerating. When the light of day starts to overlap the dark of night, it is then we will be filled with power for a new day. Many claim darkness is always a sign of evil because that is when many nocturnal predators are on the prowl. But night benefits as well by safely concealing us in its shadows. Though we Aquileia are predators, even we have enemies. But I never thought an enemy could exist here, within the Gryphon race, within my mother.

I am stunned to the extreme; lost in both my mind and body. Abandoned as was Kyara when first encountering her with little remaining life. I am now no different, as she has returned to her original state. We are both without a mother.

"Chrome, Kyara," Ankara's guardian like voice comes over the two of us like a savior. She knows Kyara is in double my pain, for this is her second time. "The two of you are much too immature for understanding what has just now happened. I will only reveal my obligation in taking place of whom left you."

Every amount of energy within our bodies now transfers into our sense of smell. Taking in the pungent odor of what I know will save our lives. My night vision proves so limited this night, that I am only vaguely aware of Chrome at my side.

Hesitantly, I raise my head to the Gryphon I know as my Queen. My mind recalls when I first saw her, which caused fear to be my reaction to the dark fur and jet black feathers. But now I believe my brother, Ankara's true nature is that of a mother so different than Hollice. We find ourselves crawling toward our Queen, thirsting for what once belonged to her daughter. Thirsting for the life it holds.

After a time with her warm body and thundering heart, I withdrew from Ankara to surrender her my eyes. Maybe there is no need to add my voice, already knowing the thoughts arising into verbal's upon my tongue.

But the moment of meeting the dark pupils surrounded by deep blue, I bring forth with lack of purrs, "I want to know," pleadings reduced to cries of newfound pain, "what has happened? Why has she left my sister and I?" Every revelation Ankara conveys, comes along with a new wave of my heart collapsing deeper into my stomach.

Soon it will enter my digestive system, and I will die a slow suffering death. Exactly what mother wanted.

Chrome and I share so much. Even now, the pain is as much part of me as it is him. Claws threaten every organ within me, prickling against them as sharp talons with every intent of harm. I think of them as Gryphon paws; so soft at the appearance and even the touch. But secretly concealed, are the mighty talons ready to strike at any moment with deadly flesh piercing points.

Hollice is not any different.

I always believed she was good throughout with a golden well-groomed coat and such a soft succulent mammary. Loving her from the moment she saved my life, but the deadly talon has been released from the gentle paw; revealing its true nature.

I do have a full understanding of what has taken place. I am a kit just as these two siblings are, and even know the dreadful feeling of being separated from one so close to thyself; however, my mother mysteriously went absent. The mother of Chrome and Kyara has made a choice I could never expect from any mother. She has abandoned them out of the lack of love I have never known, nor seen before now. Taking in all that is happening here is an emotional poison to my mentality. It is making its way into my heart as a contamination, causing my body frailty from psychological damage.

I have learned in the Aquiliea's culture that a female gives part of her own life force in order to conceive and bare her kits. I have now come to realize that Skylar, my mother, did the same for me.

"I miss her more than ever before," I somberly boast. "But she must not have abandoned me as Hollice has her own. These two kits I know as friends are suffering far greater than I may never understand."

A great amount in point of perspective brings forth a theory out of my own survival experience. Back in Gauntlet, none were there.

"I shall be there for them as no one was there for me."

Scenic 32

Rising Malice

"It is pleasant for your thoughts to ring in mind after this occurrence," Moonsight thanks in projecting out to me. "You have been such a benefit to our race. As young as you are, you show incredible strength. Your own should be proud to have you." Lowering my muzzle to the ground without retort, the strangeness of Moonsight's thought hearing pricks at my side. But I am grateful to serve him as a psychological cleansing. All focus I input is optimism, for I learned since my early days to be strengthened by the worst rather than weakened. To adapt to the impossible, this is the way of the Vulpine.

This limit to leader and queen's ability is queer, but I know everything has a purpose. He and his mate just heard the thoughts of Chrome and Kyara's mother and accounted what they saw; not to forget it. If having not been blessed with this gift, I know for a fact the two kits would not have lasted.

I am thankful to have met and been accepted by the Aquiliean leader and his Queen because I too have become . . . blessed in my own non-visualizing way.

"Remember what I said, Fox!" Moonsight repeats. "Use what you see as a deformity to your advantage.

Reverse the curse." Now for the first time in so long, I draw back my lips to raise a positive expression.

Night transitions from dusk as the sky disk dips below the forest, shining eerily through the trees with its fire like glow. The remainder however reflects upon my friend's fur, and somehow, are the same shades as the sky disk itself. Why have I always felt that both he and it have some connection? Recalling, I think about the first time seeing that mysterious glow in the back of his throat, still having not brought it forth. This only serves my mind as a mend counteracting Hollice. Preferably, setting all focus on the night's approach with a chilled gale of hostile breath.

"There it is again," I announce with attempt of distracting all around, "that scary presence is approaching. The same I felt within the deep woods of Chromium." We all realize this now, but none are more alert than Fox. For the moment his ears receive my statement, he springs from knees into his four legged stance. Violet eyes accompanied by dilated pupils, ears motioning fast in every direction. He is hearing something, though not sure what. The time when my ears fully develop has not yet arrived, so I assume he is taking in something I cannot sense.

"Scat!" Fox announces with extreme concern, "Now!" Before I can react, Kyara is scooped up by Ankara, Moonsight grasps me in his own beak.

"No . . . not the mountains!" my partner protests. "I see them at this exact moment, right up there along the side, waiting for the chance to prey."

"They want the kits," Moonsight clarifies, tucking me protectively between his flanks. "Do you have any suggestions my Vulpine ally?" The dog pants with awful tremors, desperately searching his mind for an answer.

"I am not allowing Chrome or Kyara to meet the same outcome as Sanora. That is not their fate." My queen is more angered than ever, holding my sister so close against her belly, Kyara disappears enshrouded in her black fur. "We need a defense!"

I do not believe I could produce any greater fright than I am now, as my voice is fading into my own tremors.

"Do not fly!" Fox finally advises. "Stay here on the ground where you are least vulnerable." All us Gryphons give a bow with nothing else exchanged. Not one turns to look back as we catch the sound of rocks shifting on down the mountain's side. Something pursues us, something awaits ahead.

Moments into our path, the forest submerges us with the unwelcome entrance of two Gryphons creeping into view out from the shadows. Placing their terrifying eyes upon us, I can see they are content on Kyara and I.

Fox blockades himself between us. Long bushy tail pulsing in heartbeat tune, squatting upon hind legs, stretching arms in a defensive span. Dipping his muzzle, he snorts a black stream from his nostrils, making me jump in between Moonsight's beak.

This taunt is aggravating the two perching in our way. They are using no verbal's, only menacing expressions. To me, they appear as normal Aquileia but by Fox's reaction and the tightening grip on my leader's beak, I assume there is something beyond my eye's sight; as is a recollecting thought.

"Sanora was taken by Gryphons, but they had not been of our region according to her father." But I thought it was those silver metallic creatures only Fox can see. Yet these two here, I most surly do not recognize. "Could they be . . .?"

The wind continues blowing from the water, making it unable to detect the scent of these two. Yet, the harder I set my eyes over them, the greater my fear awakens within me. I am thinking back to when I had first found my sister and how it was the first time my fear came true. At the time, I had only been afraid for her life. Now I fear for us all.

These two menacing Gryphons fully realize they must pass through this Vulpine to even approach us; and they are intent on breaking barrier. Yet, before either of them make a move, something intervenes.

Fox is now a silhouette against a most unusual light brightening up directly in front of him. It casts flickering shadows almost like leaves in the wind. Now it is reflecting off the eyes of the enemy with gleaming shimmers, and I see their facial features change in the ember of this darkened night, glaring at my companion with newfound fear.

Now, Fox brings his paws out of span, directly into the light behind the silhouette of his head, where he lets out a deep puff of a breath into his paws, accompanied by the glimmers illuminating brighter than before. Holding his paws out once more, they cradle a wildly dancing gleam of orange, red, blue, and violet. As instantly as they formed, the two predators spring on either side.

With sudden reaction, he spits a great ball of light to his left, striking his opponent while springing to his right to catch the other by the legs with inferno grip. Both erupt great cries deep from within their bellows; yet I recognize neither as the shriek of a Gryphon.

Wasting no time in taking them down, I kill in order to prevent their claim of lives—Not only for Chrome and Kyara, but all Aquileia. Sinking both teeth and claws in the neck of this imposter, I find the meat is like nothing I have ever tasted. Similar to no mammal flesh that I know of and blood absolutely of no salt.

Quickly absorbing the remainder of the fire into my own fur; I leave the lifeless body by making a graceful leap into perimeter of its companion; fur already ablaze from my flammable saliva. Throwing hind legs into the air once again, they collide against the creature's chest, forcing it upon its back with every strength of restraint within me. My action is to put in them the same fear induced into my leonine allies. I have used Ankara's teachings of combat to restrain these foes, now is time for mother's psychological tactic—To claim dominance by fear and show who is now Vulpine Prince. Its eyes reflect my ember image in a dazed gleam, it will have to do for substitution of a mirror.

"You will not taste Gryphon blood," I roar. "You will only taste vulpine rage." My muzzle parts in a growl as drool descends from my exposed teeth in drops of ignited flares. Bringing tail between my legs, I breathed upon its thick fur setting it ablaze. Forcing my enemy into locking sight in my purplish gaze, I pry open its imitation of a beak, forcing my flaming spine extension down its throat.

Fire has only been described to me, and I do not mistake this visual, but being part of a living creature is beyond what my imagination could ever conjure. Flickering behind Fox's jaws in his hunter's grin, burning around his teeth and gums without apparent harm. Even his drools are in small drops of ember. When his tongue swipes out while panting, it too dances with flames flaring up brightly as his breath feeds the inferno. I overheard my brother claiming how the Vulpine hybridize and fuse according to their race exclusive blessings. Understandable, because we Gryphons are hybrids of raptors and big cats. Those are both animals, I am not sure what fire is.

All that remains of our enemy are two bodies lying

on either side of the clearing. There is a rather strong scent in the air that I fail to recognize, assuming only that it is blood. But even over the odorous result of violence, there is another pungent smell withering in this night air—the musky aroma previously warding me off like a skunk, intensified with the holder's ghastly appearance. One I now must classify pleasing to my nostrils, having even caused my heart to slow its rate and create a new sense of calmness. Relief I welcome with fresh flowing pride, and must express now!

With a great lurch of my body, I slip myself from the grasp in Ankara's beak with a thud of my paws against the earth. Now taking a long jump into his paws, which he immediately extinguishes.

I hug tight to the one whom frightened me from the first beginning. All my negative thoughts toward him exist no more, even the raging flames in his jaws do not bother me. Cradled here in their feverish grip, gently pulling me close to his chest, I pronounce "You saved us! My warrior of flame." Not sure where that came from, but it somehow acted through me. "Thank you." I conclude in finale, expressing by swiping tongue over his heart.

He is panting, with scent overwhelmingly bitter of the deep forest. "I trust you not to breath fire on me. Now that I know you are a friend."

"I am here for you all, Kyara." The volume of his voice rises as does his ears, but it is as though my heart is collapsing into my stomach out of what my hero brings next, "Our battle is not yet over. I need you all to carry on," he projects anxiously at a high speed. "They will attempt something different. I feel we should do the same in order to gain advantage."

The vulpine of the group again searches his mind for another answer while cradling me closer against his chest, both Ankara and Moonsight join to create a small huddle.

"Take Chrome and Kyara," Moonsight orders after placing my brother protectively between Fox's flanks. "Ankara and I will fight in return. When you are approached by one of these creatures, do everything in your power to defend our young."

"Think of them as your own," The Queen adds. This new perspective strikes Fox at her request. This is not only an altered view for my new friend, but a whole new realization entirely.

Scenic 33

Blood and Adrenaline

Time rushes my fear on the power of my own adrenaline—But not mine alone, for it emits from the five of us.

Shifting muscles, I transfer into two-legged form to take Chrome and Kyara into either of my arms. Their weight does not feign me, because strength beyond my adrenaline is coming forth. Beginning from what the Queen has asked of me . . .

"Think of them as your own . . ." this verse is now captured within my skull, echoing in my mind, never to be released. Filling with whole supernatural energy, burning with unlimited love to fuel every muscle; forming me into the Vivacious Vulpine I had not expected to be. In the beginning, I saw these kits as nothing more than helpless young. But now I understand, they are filled with life just as I am.

I found it hard to understand birth from the beginning of my life. How mother conceived and bore me into father's paws after his life force fertilized her own. My body formed within her out of pure natural conception, all six limbs and tail. But what about my spirit, had her womb formed that as well? Or is that something beyond understanding?

Three newcomers descend upon our group emerging from the faded black of night. Before getting a chance to land, Moonsight hurls into the air. Taking down two at once with unsheathed talons. Our Queen tackles the remainder; severing the victim's neck with both beak and talons. In seconds, the three fall dead within the undergrowth. Blood stains the trunk of a pine, withering over the ground fallen needles.

"Amazing," I comment. "How they went for their opponent's weak points.

At my angle, it is nothing but bare tree trunks with burrowing roots. Many are pines and the soil is much like sand. Through the trees, I now see the white crescent igniting the sky as the night grows ever darker. From this distance, I am hearing the bending river's flowing weave.

"This sudden tranquility is not right," I bark out in my moment of envisage, not caring if overheard. I am fighting like never before, and will not be taken advantage of.

"They are plotting ambush," Moonsight confirms, ears raised in hearing the enemy's mentality. Yet none of us stop, we continue into the wood. Two quadrupedal and one bipedal.

"We require a new plan," Ankara proposes. There may just be more fear within the Queen compared to the kit's we are risking our lives for. At times, the mind is unable to work with time itself; as it is not always in tune. Time is far ahead of my thinking as I am only beginning to understand every moment significant to our survival.

In brief moments, I as well as Moonsight and Ankara receive the thundering sound of pads. Turning muzzle only slightly, my eyes glimpse a blurred image of they . . . now every defensive instinct burns hotter than ever before. It is time to be a hero.

Throttling my legs out so hard, joints pain at the force. They attempt to sprint ahead of me, none daring attack my flaming tail. Holding both Chrome and Kyara tightly, we enter back into the brush. Various plants rip away as my paws forcefully cut through every obstacle. Leaving a trail of burning vegetation behind. The greater my progression takes me into the forest, the more I am in need of a new strategy. The pain of my entire form may as well cease existence, for all of me is in tune with guarding the kits I carry. Carrying on like a machete through the wood's undergrowth grants me a new idea as instantly as it claims my faith.

With throbs in my mind, I generate every new thought outside, sending every mental transmission out to the minds of Moonsight and Ankara. Miraculously and to my astonishment, they have kept up with my speed, following closely on either side of my rear. When the entire plan is transmitted, they couple cry out in response.

All while gripping the two in my forearms, I take a sharp right turn. Bellowing out a great breath to pour out upon the plants and paws of these rogue Gryphons.

Ignoring the cries to focus on my fire trail, my Aquliean allies prepare for their partake. Doubling back east and west, I create multiple flame walls by swishing my tail in the brush. In moments that simulate eternities, there are less pursuers and far more sufferers. The origin of the enemies pain continue rippling down my spine; bridging out onto my tail in pain not near as extreme.

"I may create a forest fire, but will patch that later."

Upon turning back to the destructive strategy, I find some are taking flight over my walls, but even that is challenging to succeed without burning their undersides. Along with the hurdles of these imitation Gryphons, comes

Chromium's leader and Queen as they too pass over the flame walls. It is now time.

Outstretching my arms, I hold out Chrome and Kyara in either of my paws. Moonsight grasps Kyara, while Ankara springs forward swiping Chrome from the opposite. The couple now disappear into the nightly forest.

Raising focus to the overhead trees that have just granted a new idea. I inflate the entirety of my cardio heavily with oxygen. Another roar flares on my breath adding a flaming coat to the tree branches. Despite the uproar these creatures are making in their imitation bodies, they are not alone in making foreign cries. For the voice in my roar is not Vulpine.

Over the sound of my heart throbs and the beating of Ankara's paws, my ears sense the crackling of fire now distantly behind us. "It is so astonishing to know of the great power Fox withheld for so long. Now it rages outward against our enemies." Because of his unleashing, others are beginning to awaken. Squirrels trail down tree trunks and other small critters emerge from all around. Is it the fire they run from, or the wrath of these predators in bodies similar to our own? Why do they want Kyara and I so bad? I only know this fierce running and intent to protect she and I is strong within our guardians. But this sense of safety is rapidly evaporating from within not just me, but everyone.

At an instant halt, I am let go from Ankara's beak and tucked tightly between her flanks the moment she settles upon her haunches. I only hope Moonsight is doing equally the same with Kyara.

My Queen is panting hard as I now see the limits of these miraculous Gryphons. Her thighs compact me close against her body as the one shield and barrier against our enemy. Her body heat is overwhelming against my own. Somewhere beneath the flesh, is her womb. Resting my paw here against her belly, I allow it to warm my pad, wishing it was from her I had come. What if I had been born alongside Sanora; would I have met her deadly fate?

But my biological mother is Hollice, who saw me as a curse; attempting to dispose of me from the beginning. Ankara prevented the loss of both Kyara and I by proper nourishment and love in the way it was meant to be. If I was not meant to form within Hollice, I would not have begun there. It would have been in the womb of another. Then why was I meant to be born out of her?

That dreadful electric charge is returning, as always when these creatures are near. The same who have been preying upon us this whole evening in the form of Gryphons.

"Ankara?" my voice only being a whimper accompanied in several tremors.

Tauntingly purring in creepy chatters.

The only reply they get is a flare of wings and the unsheathe of talons. Both leader and Queen are prepared to fight.

"Why don't you give us the reason for assassinating our daughter?" Moonsight challenges. "Your intent of murder upon her is just the same upon these two." At his voice, a good-sized female approaches. Her pelt and plumage a rather unusual shade of red, much like blood, while baring absolutely no common likeness of an Aquileia. At her entrance, his mood turns to anger as the enemy eyes bare down on us. Reminding me much of Hollice, the Gryphon I can no longer call mother. I only hope Fox and my brother are both safe.

The red Gryphon takes a lunge in my direction but Moonsight beats her away with beak hook and talons. Taking me up, he dives into the grass with determined might to get us to safety. Along with the sound of scars tearing into his flesh from above, he grunts in agonized suffering as these bad Gryphons attempt ripping him away from my guard. Ankara's wails are equally filled with excruciation as she hurries to our side, Chrome in her beak.

She charges her head beneath Moonsight's wing, forcing my brother protectively between his haunches, joining me under his shelter. The Queen then pulls away and screeches into combat, returning her own thrashes and wound inducing cries to these savage foes.

Moonsight opens his forepaws before us; beyond them an ever-growing forest of vegetation. It is now we realize our small size as a huge advantage. Sprinting forward and out from under Moonsight's belly, we rush under the thick brush plants, concealed beneath and away from the danger above. We hear our leader now joining his partner in battle, while our opponents have no idea we are making a furtive escape.

But where is Chrome leading me?

Scenic 34

Heart's Will

My mind overloads with so many thoughts, it begins to hurt. Pure instinct tells me that getting my sister to safety is most important right now. My sibling and I are running faster than we know possible, but do not dare call back for fear of being overheard. Her only reliance is in me; meaning it is I who must guide her.

The Aquiline instinct as a kit is the same as any other. When fearing for our lives as we now are, we only have a single desire. I know this impulse has been with me from the moment of my conception. That small spark of life awakening in the beginning, expanded into my full development, a Gryphon named Chrome.

When Sanora's birth arrived, her mother gave the love I never received from my own. It was then that she was taken by them . . .

But they must of known of Hollice's killing with deprivation. Only when she gave us up to Ankara and Moonsight, did they make finality of this murderous assault. The heroism of leader, Queen, and Vulpine triggered our bounty.

Memories are flowing through my mind repeatedly

as water washes upon our shore, entering my head through sight and scent. The marks of my father's territory have been there as far back in time as my mind is able to go. My eyes receive what I have come to know in the past as my home. Possibly I should not have these feelings any longer, but cannot let go because these sensations will not let go of me. Flaring my ears back, I take in the beat of Kyara's paws forcefully keeping her speed with my own.

The thorn barrier is before the both of us. Wriggling ourselves under and behind its protective brambles, we blast into the den.

"Chrome!" Hollice throws out my name in total disgust, "Kyara."

"Those creatures are after us," I wail. "Having not the slightest idea of what to do, I just followed Chrome."

"And you come here?" she growls. "What is going through your head Chrome? Have you not accepted I care nothing for either of you?"

"I have," my brother verifies. The moment the revelation comes past his beak, he rests both paws upon her own. Laying head overtop, I can only observe and wonder what he is doing.

"I love Ankara as the first to treat me as her own. But this night, they have come upon her, Fox, and Moonsight because they stand between us and them. Taking in every wound and scar meant for Kyara and myself, I could not stand to see three that I love suffer in our defense. We ran from the attack when the chance was granted, I hoped these creatures realized there is no point in fighting our friends for a target they do not have."

"Then why do you come to me?" our former mother demands.

"Because," Chrome begins, "I could not be under the guard of Ankara, Fox, or Moonsight. I do not want them to suffer any more. Out of my own instinct, I came to you. Having depended on you from my first beginning, I care not that you have no love for me. But it was your choice alone that brought me to life, and I thank you for choosing to bare me, mother. For taking in Kyara and for giving us to a mother who gives love. You may not love me, but I love you. Because you are the one alone who made the choice to give part of your life to me. You alone chose my life over death in the beginning. It is because of that, that I enjoy prosperity. Just by my mother's doing of that one right choice."

I am feeling a quite odd sensation pass over my barrier. To now see a whole new perspective toward the kit who came from my womb, as he has just revealed that he . . . loves me. Never has this come to my mind, nor the faintest hint of consideration. Chrome feels for me in a way I have never for him. He is right, it was my choice at the moment of his birth, having even optioned to let him die in the beginning. Later amounting to my incentive action of depriving myself to bring he and Kyara to death.

"You love me? Despite what has happened and what I have done to the both of you?"

"Yes mother, because you are my beginning. It was you alone who could, and did make the choice of allowing me to live on. I forgive what wrong you have done."

"Loved by my own son," For the first time, it is pleasing my mind. Before now, I had not believed he cared anything for me. I felt used from the first beginning of motherhood. Yet now, here is my Chrome: my son. Thanking me for being the mother who I denied myself as.

"I now understand," I begin with renewed spirit. "I thought nothing of either of you; just a burden and nothing more." Kyara joins her brother, snuggling at my paws while I take in their love for the first time.

"Please help us mother, I do not want more harm. We need you as our guard." Kyara is only a whimpering ball of black down while she hugs herself tight against me. Drawing Chrome close as well, I obligate to the both of them.

"I . . . am here for the both of you." Now understanding I could not have loved them before; not until revealing they themselves love me all on their own.

Scenic 35

Young Hybrid

Genocide is only one term for mass killing. To now have the enemy's blood on my paws is a rather different feeling. "I have prevented the blood of my friends falling upon theirs," I ponder by taking into mind, kneeling to the earth, bowing head to catch in my paws. "The lives of my friends have not been claimed this day." I breath, attempting to ignore the bodies who lay here at my doing.

"Living to fight for my life." Which is reason enough for being immortal. With my immunity to death, I will give every part of my life force to defend. Exactly what Castige began in his life. "It is now the duty of every Vulpine to carry on those deeds."

So not to harm any more of Chromium; I absorbed the fire back into my body, accepting in every last flame from this parched land. "This forest has made a great sacrifice this night," I project out, "Thank you, and just as you have, I sacrificed my own self to protect my allies. Using our power to its limits, you and I have defended the life of the Gryphon's here tonight."

All is so tranquil; the hissing smoke of burnt vegetation proves to be the one isolated sound. It does not matter if no one is listening, because I know someone is— Whether it is the passed on spirits of either Vulpine or Aquileia.

Returning to a gallop on four legs, I sprint ahead before the rushing river. Hurling myself into the air, angling my leap so to land in the river. Breaking the surface, water submerges my overheated body in its chilling depths. Steam evaporates into the air directly overhead while my external flames extinguish to the soaking of each individual hair. Refreshing is my lone description to this sudden temperature change. Feeling satisfied with my cooling, I shift to into biped form and inversely surface up.

For the first time, I know mother loves Kyara and I. In the beginning, all was assumption that she cared for us. Now it is certain.

"Are they still after us?" Kyara asks in a single breath.

Coming close to her, I caution, "I no longer hear the crackling of Fox's fire; yet, it is too quiet to know." Having no desire to further frighten her, an agitating feeling suggests we are not yet safe entirely. With Hollice sheltering over the two of us, I should have no reason to be afraid.

So much has happened in this short period, as the sky disk disappeared not too long ago. With our hunters and guardians, my first official destruction on Chromium has made a full presentation. Though I am grateful my sister and I have not become part of it, I can only pray my friends have not meant their own final fate. "I feel this is not over, Mother. They are still after us . . ." my voice falls away the moment our ears take in the heavy beating of approaching paws. My sister shrieks, having every right to. To anyone's eyes, they are Gryphons. But even my heart knows they are not of the Aquileia heart. The sides of our barrier's entrance break apart as two charge in side by side. The moment thier bloody talons unsheathe, mother reacts with true Gryphon reflex. Flanks spreading on either side of Kyara and I; Hollice impales her own talons into either throats of the attackers. Blood pools from their necks and onto the bedding only a minimal length away. It is only slow moment before the two bodies fall limp over the earth floor, deeply gashed in the necks, a quite disturbing imagery of gore.

"Chrome," Kyara sobs, hugging me ever tightly.

"We must remember," I force out, comforting her in my wing embrace, "these are not Gryphons. Our kind would never do such morbid things."

"Right," Hollice validates, wrapping her great leonine tail protectively around us. "A true Gryphon does not choose such evil." Mother is obviously mesmerized by her own clarification as both her eyes part open in awe. The blood on her paws emits a rather unusual odor unlike any red mammal blood I know of.

"Did you really shed this blood for Chrome and I?" Kyara pleads.

"I did," Hollice verifies. "Your own is not meant to be so."

"Why do so much, for us kits?"

"It is out of love," I jump in informing. "Ankara explains we are the outcome of love alone. A great sacrifice made to bring by our mother's and father's." Her bead like eyes cannot be any more firm. Giving me the strength to carry on, "We are not products of biological components. Not a clump of cells coming together at random. We are . . . miracles!"

"That is what I did not see in the beginning," Mother informs, "That was my mistake, I could never be anymore sorry for what I did to you, my own kits. The miracles of Evaron and I."

Pain now rings through the forest. I only hope these cries are of our enemies and not allies.

"Hollice!" My mother's name erupts from outside. I know who's the moment of its coming. Evaron, my father. But to my striking reaction, the first Gryphon to enter is . . .

"Aquila!" Announcing as she throws herself over the bodies and into my wing's embrace, groaning hard with a heaving breast. Tauro follows with Avalon, along with Adelhied urging them inside. Evaron's fatigued form concludes reason for the group smelling of his exposed blood. However, my father is alive beneath his scars.

"Moonsight? Ankara?" I plead.

"Here," comes our leader's call of reply as he comes in following his Queen. Yet Fox is absent, "Alive." Moonsight declares in answering my thoughts.

My father's wounds seem to be doing all to counteract his vitality; but guarding Aquila and her kin is making him feign being alright.

Leader and Queen now take position at the entry; preventing any attack from this obvious target. But everyone here cannot keep ears locked in one position, for every sound claims our attention like a leech. None voice or move as these interrupting noises spread around now in every direction.

In ending these silent moments, Moonsight wearily predicts, "They are ambushing all sides of this barrier. They will tear through your walls, Evaron. Every thorn and vine until they reach us."

"We will not allow such a future," Ankara exclaims. All agree and take position on all sides of the den. Kyara, myself, Aquila, Avalon, and Tauro are forced into the very center with five adult Gryphons at our defense; risking flesh and life for the five of us. Optimistically, this love and care proves a powerful comfort even in this dreadful cataclysm.

The barrier I call my den is of dry bramble walls, kindling sensitive to being parched. It alone prepares to smite the darkness as our barricade against the enemy, ready to enflame its guarding light in absolute penetration.

But where is the flame?

Letting my mind go, I absorb in all that is taking place. Are these really my last moments in life? Will excruciating pain be what ends it all? First seeing those I care for gored to death, then feeling the claws and beak points of my enemies impale me like a piece of prey meat.

I want to know what is happening outside; fortunate I am capable of finding out. Using the same instinct I had when searching for Kyara, I cast my spiritual senses outward. Projecting as far as possible, though I am visually blind, I travel outside the barrier to make out the biological forms of these imitation Gryphons. They feel so different, convincing me ever more that they are not true Aquileia.

"So many," I whisper, "How are we to match these opponents?"

But amount is not our only concern. We all know these creatures are supernaturally stronger than ourselves, which only frightens me ever more. Yet now comes a thought from an unknown source, as fate has brought it to me. Projecting myself even further across the land, I feel the electrical waves of a friend. His aura almost identical to the false Gryphons, but his brain is unlike any I have ever known before, simplifying my chance of contacting him. Energy of rushing water is what I am feeling, then finally comes the electrical impulse of my Vulpine ally, pleading.

"Fox! Please!"

I am received.

I am received.

Scenic 36

Organic Barrier

The once strong walls of the barrier are failing at the tare from the outside. At a speed faster than a Gryphon could react, a hole in the roof bursts open directly over Mother. The moment I turn head to the attack, the two are already locked together by talons, nearly crushing Aquila and her sister as they impact on the barrier's floor. Cries ring throughout the fabric of existence so numerous and great, I do not know if they are of friend or foe. Painful determination throws me into my own purpose, reacting by leaping to the one whom I love and depended on from my first beginning.

"MOTHER!" I wail before the talons penetrate her thin frail body. The lack of food has made a target out of her form, as though she is nothing more than a fragile substance at risk of disintegration. "NO . . . I am instantly cut off as she throws her wing over me, holding it between myself and this attacker. Creating a blanketing feathery wall I cannot pass.

Moonsight and Ankara continually barricade the entrance, Adelhied and my father attack at the now ripped holes in the structure; clawing anything that comes through. Finally, it is she who manages to strike out and leap to mother's aid.

The shelter is there, up ahead. Producing such sorrowful cries, surrounded by evil murderous intent. "There, fading into the ground. The entrance." The bramble thorns prick my pads while I add my own grunts of pain; nothing will stop me. Ankara locks on to my own mind, where our plan is immediately becoming one.

Knocking out an imitation Gryphon from entering the den, just enough time provides my charge with flames ready. Inside the barrier, I join both the youth and adult Gryphons; but it is the one whom wrestles both Hollice and Adelheid that captures my defensive action.

The right moment arrives to pry open this creature's beak. Parting my lips, my jaws open right before its exposed mouth. The false Gryphon's eyes are dark with a newfound horror as I am now entering its visual. This individual is not able to cry out as the kits now are in their shrieks. Because I am safely passing my inferno breath into its body, away from harming my friends.

Adelhied loosens her defensive grip on the villain, pulling the dead form off Chrome and Kyara's mother which limply collapses to the side, smoke exhausting from its mouth in a peculiar burnt odor. The kits are paralyzed at the sight of this, but the oncoming attacks from the outside cause immediate ignorance. They know I am balancing the ferocity of this attack.

Upon hind legs, I make a biped stance over the center of the den. Chrome comes to the fallen Hollice, Kyara throws herself upon me, huddling securely between my hind paws. In return, I protectively curl my tail fluff around her just as Skylar did for me. Her scent nulled my stress and fear, comforting me in pure security. Now my own must perform this same task by assuming her duty. I am the guardian now.

Adelhied's kits are unsure if to be afraid or relieved, but I gift them a toothy grin with absence of fire and soften my purplish stare to reassure I am a friend. Without delay, I raise my arms and head to the roof. Drawing in a great breath to exhale my flares.

"Fox is here! Oh what pure, true, relief," I have come to know his facials so well, as it is now coming upon his expression as he stands two legged over us kits. Not wasting a moment, the dog inhales to give his lungs an ember glow beneath his hide to silhouette his ribcage. Shining awe penetrates this darkened moment as he bellows out hot raging light. Setting fire to the brambles, and in moments, the entire structure.

"To the center!" Moonsight orders. Every Gryphon huddles tightly in the middle to shelter us. The barrier could collapse any moment, but I see Fox is in complete control. Chrome, Aquila, Tauro, and Avalon join me in the soft surrounding of Fox's tail. Clinging to his heated paws, cold and trembling. Mother is there beneath the guard of father, fighting her wounds with strength I may never understand.

"I do not want to think about all that is happening only just outside." Now burrowing my head beneath Fox's tail, I find that his body temp has risen excessively to his internal flame. Roaring so greatly, I hear it flow beneath the fur and flesh of his spine extension. It is a comfort attempting to only concentrate on this and the crackling fire overhead; blocking out the last screams of our enemy is the challenging task.

Finally, I manage to clasp paws over my ears, folding them over and sealing away as much sound as I am capable of.

I pray, "If this is my end, let it be silent."

"Kyara," comes my name in Fox's spicy breath. Reopening my eyes and uncovering ears, we are returned to reality. Rising up from the coil of his Vulpine tail, I find the only sound is the hissing of burnt wood and bramble surrounding us in the ruins that was once our barrier den. Ash flurries into the air of thick, gray dust—Soiling everything it takes landing upon, including each of us.

But there is another sensation in the atmosphere as well. It is not I who was silenced, it was the Gryphon imitators. A feeling has come I was not sure I would experience again, but here it is. The relief of security; our safety has rejuvenated.

A S A P u b l i s h i n g C o r p o r a t i o n

Scenic 37

Chromium Departure

Everything is now granting me Deja vu as I pull little Kyara into my paws. "Our victorious survival is not by my paw alone," I pant out to the kit I am cradling, acknowledging each of the adult Aquileia. My friends and I are rising up in the remains of this Gryphon's barrier, reduced only to a crater of ash—Much like my home, Gauntlet.

Yet this time I am not alone in survival. Rescued by my own paws, guarded by my own breath, I long for this joy and peace to be blessed over other races. I know what I have done is right, but I desire to do so much more. For I am seeing something I desperately want to change, but is there anything I can do? First, the familiar aroma presents as my eyes fall upon its scarlet source. Following its origin trail to our fallen victim.

"Hollice," Evaron calls softly to his mate. Dipping his head low to rest the side against her, she receives him with lids sealed and tongue exposed beneath his eye; tasting her mate's presence. Chrome and Kyara's mother is showing her stamina much like my own, but I and the others understand the life left in her is too frail. Not even Moonsight's blessed abilities are enough to heal. This is her last end.

"Mother?" Chrome's calls in no more than a breath. At such an immature state, it is remarkable that even he knows. Kyara hesitantly follows her brother's path before Hollice. The golden Gryphon gives her two kits a gaze they have not received before—A first loving glare from mother. The same I know from my own.

"Kits," comes her hushed expels, fighting past the severity of the wound. "I did not understand your love till you revealed it for me. I am now able to return it."

Chrome's paws are wetting themselves in her scarlet discharge, caring nothing for its intrusion, as it is his own. Kyara is with him to share incentive on taking in all Hollice is bringing forth. "I was wrong to choose your death," now shifting her line of sight, I find it falling upon myself. "You saved us with both your spirit and body, Fox. I thank you." In correct response, I give the mother a bow and place a paw over my heart, then extending it out to her. Flexing her own, the Gryphon pad meets mine in midair. Now I take this thanks from her leonine foot by touching paw pad over my chest once again.

She continues her battle while her body drains both blood and life, for as long as she is able to. But I have bared this traumatizing scene to the extent of my own emotional grip. Pulling myself away is the right choice, attempting not to bring up fire or stomach contents. This scent of true Gryphon blood is even more overwhelming, bringing me down emotionally and physically in a repetitive fashion I am coming to know. As my body falls to its knees, my muzzle descends into my paws with wet eyes. But my ears remain open for this final witnessing. Her mate lays beside, gripping her close. Adelhied shields her young while leader and queen attend these final moments. Chrome and Kyara rest themselves within their mother's paws, allowing to be claimed by slumber; temporary slumber. That of Hollice's is eternal. Being awake for such an endearment is woe to the extreme, a suffering that pains each of us. She does not want this for her kits, Chrome and Kyara ought to be celebrating their survival in vitality, not being weighed down on Hollice's . . . departure. My one hope is that this will strengthen and not weaken. What did not perish me in Gauntlet, will surely empower my fellow allies, just as I fused with fire.

Evaron's hasty breath accompanies the palpitating of he and his mate. In a struggle past his suffering, he presents to Moonsight.

"Thank you, for saving her in the beginning, preceding our son's birth."

Chromium's Leader is somberly heaving what little breath he has by answering

"I so desire to do more."

"You saved each one of us," Chrome's father testifies, "I know you and your mate have done all in your power. For us, and the Aquileia." With his extensive appreciation, the Gryphon begins to clean away Hollice's neck wound, which has ceased flowing. Moonsight gives a strong shallow bow, then descends the remainder of his body to the ash crater. Ankara joins him as the two can finally rest.

A short heart beating period passes while the kits are claimed by fatigue. Now just small bundles with sides rising and falling, tuckered out from this extensive night of horror. With failing physicality, Hollice cradles them close within embrace of her leonine paws. Yet her last ounce of spirituality remains to close her ending.

"I finally know that life is a fated gift. A belief only has meaning when it is right and true." To live, seeking the purpose. Only to find it at the conclusion.

This conclusion, is her final.

These last moments of are spent in silence. Evaron, Chrome, and Kyara sleep along with her. Only she will not reawaken to this reality. Leader and Queen of the Aquileia groom each other, tending to their scars. Adelhied nurses her three kits under my close watch. After all that has taken place, I do not know if predators will even attempt an ambush. Dearly I hope having terrified them. Resting on my haunches, I seal my wounds in saliva while my body cools its steam. The dawn will bring a whole new day, granting the opportunity for a new beginning.

A S A P u b l i s h i n g C o r p o r a t i o n

Scenic 38

Mourning Flame

"It is ready," Evaron announces as he and the other Gryphon's back away from the burial. The mother is left where her last end occurred, hidden beneath the tinder amongst the already parched wood that once made her den. My Aquileia colleagues are ready, I am as well.

Perching before the brush mound, the sorrow in me cannot be held any longer. Hot tears form in my eyes again, but these drops burn against my eye balls with the familiar heat I am coming to know well; fire forming its flares directly in my vision. These tears fall from their ducts in drops of fire, splashing into my paws to set ablaze. They combine to form a perfect fire cradled in my paw pads. Holding them before wood, I exhale to forward my breath into the tinder, setting Hollice free from this life.

The fact my birthplace has become mother's final rest is hard to take in. She lived irritably, now deceased and loving. But the relief of being loved by her for the first time eases the pain of absence.

"You understand that even in the time after this life, she will always love and support you. The bond as her kit is everlasting," I could have heard this from almost anyone.

Ankara, or even my sister, but this comforting voice originates from the heart of another.

"There is so much truth in your voice. I am only beginning to understand it," Aquila engulfs her red wings over me, followed by gently tracing her beak through my neck feathers.

"Let it come to you naturally," she advises. "It will take time, just as you will."

"At the moment, I am unsure what to do next."

"I had the same experience," now it is Forjah, perching directly before me flexing his wings in a great stretch. "I lost my mother and had no idea what to do then. So I made the choice on returning to my birth home. There, I made the decision to move on to an entirely original existence. Instead of extensive mourning for her, I put myself forward into a new life as I am doing here in Chromium."

"How were you able to let go?" The Vulpine gently drums against the air by giving his two cross species limbs a confident stare.

"I have not let go," he details. "I have held on to her from the moment my life began." Turning muzzle to the side, Fox inhales to catch his breath, careful to not release any flares. "But now that she is gone, I understand more than ever her meaning to carry on. While always keeping her in heart, I forever remain in her own."

"Do you mean you allowed that event to help you, in a way?" Kyara queries with interest while jumping into the conversation.

"Yes," my combat partner confirms, "we have the gift of adaptability, so I allowed this traumatic event to change me in a good way. Pressing forward, as she fed my desire to."

"It is as if you are turning it all around to make the

negative into positive. Using the last end as the new beginning."

Massaging his claw gracefully against the side of my sister's beak, he praises, "You are right on, Kyara."

What was once broken is now on the mend. Just as our Vulpine declared, Mother's death has brought forth renewed life, and I thank her to the greatest extent for the sacrifice. My father will continue supporting Adelhied and her kits, Kyara and I have even been offered a home. Temptingly, it would be great sharing a den with Aquila, but I do not believe that is meant for me yet. Evaron knows it is his calling to provide and protect the fatherless kinship.

Now comes my choice. Where I will go is not a question in my view. I know what I want, and who I want.

Proceeding to where the Queen is settled, I begin by echoing my Vulpine friend's view.

"Forjah is right. This tragedy has resulted in much good." Fighting so hard to hold back the grief to make her proud. But those same trembles from when Hollice abandoned us in the cold are returning. My Queen's action is the swipe of her tongue over my figure, cleansing me entirely of the soot and dirt from the long night. In gratitude, I purr forth . . .

"Thank you, Mother." Only a breath passes from her beak before I annunciate, "That is how I see my Queen. You are my first true mother, even before Hollice. So dearly, do I want to be your son." My entirety goes quiet, having fulfilled my intention. Still breathing difficulty, my head dips low in utter embarrassment to the strong emotion now radiating from within.

The light touch of my Queens paws come on either side of my body. Taken up and cradled in her leonine grip, I am granted her gentle acceptance of, "My son, you are."

"What about me?" Kyara brings up. I return to ground level, privately consulted by bringing her beak before my ear. She has always looked to me for guidance, but this is not a choice I am meant to make for her.

"Kyara, my sister, what would YOU like to do? Who do you feel you should be with most?" The black kit lightens up astounded by my grant of responsibility, but appears fully ready to independently decide for herself.

I am looking from Chrome, Evaron, Ankara, Moonsight, and Tauro's family. In need of dire help, I bring focus to Fox who supportively holds out black pads with bright violet eyes and toothy canid grin. Now, the dog draws back his paw to rest over his chest, which symbolizes his heart.

"I understand," it is time to feel my true internal desire. Moments only last before I know exactly what my choice is. Flexing out my own black paw, I rest it upon that of the Queen's. Raising her attention, I have not a single fear toward her any longer.

"May I call you mother?" I request. Ankara's lids gently touch her blue surrounded pupils. Moonsight gives his voice as she erupts in purrs.

"If we may call you daughter."

Miraculous, is my best definition of this current event. Kyara is coming with me, we are to live in the mountains with our leader and Queen. Kyara and I turn to Evaron at the moment, he approves of our choice, but not before bidding us a gentle but temporary goodbye.

"We will see you at the next tournament, and I bet you will have even a greater joy of training in the mountains. I know the two of you will make me proud!"

"Most certainly!" We praise together.

Scenic 39

Into the Coals

So fast, emotion and atmosphere can shift entirely in a direction both unexpectedly and unpleasant. Time does not seem to be in agreement now.

"Fox!" It is Moonsight who breaks this glorious silence, once again with negativity in his voice. Not caring what devastating knowledge he has, I must take it in.

"They are leaving," he concludes, "departing from Chromium, set on a new mission of malice." Now the Aquiliean leader gives a sorrowful dip of the neck, and finalizes. "They are shifting their attack, attempting control over the Vulpine." Having not the convenience of a mirror, I have never seen my expression of terror. What is it like, the same, or worse?

"An unanswered question is finally fulfilled," I breathe in dismay. "The one who plagues control and genocide against all Vulpine, is not alone as we believed. This further feeds the theory that these false Gryphons and my races enemy are one and the same." I have no regret of sharing my thoughts with Moonsight. "Because of the gifts my race withholds, we hybridize with powers unique to all existence; I showed them that kind of power this night," I say gesturing with a flare escaping my breath. "It is because of my incredible fusion to fire, that has further fed their hunger for such advancements of miraculous hybrids and tribrids. They are selfish and desire to control the Vulpine's power. Whether making sure we never prosper, or using our energy for their own."

"From all that has taken place, I feel your foes are indeed part of these Gryphon imposters." Moonsight completes with his own perspective, "I do agree with you Forjah." Everyone but Ankara and her kits are taken aback by the use of my true name. But the use is serious, as this is a matter of great importance.

"Their desire for dominance is strong, we are the only ones blockading their way."

"My pure instinct informs we have the same enemy," Evaron jumps in. All around, everyone is on the same level.

"We are in more danger than ever before; even our great inspirational hero died in defense. Our enemy is a whole army, while my side is no more than a few survivors of the endangered." More afraid than ever before, how are we able to fight when so few remain? We may be hard to kill, but not impossible. Castige died, proving our immortality is limited.

"You desire to return, Forjah. I know you do." All I manage is giving Moonsight a ratified bow.

"I am the cause. Unleashing my fire adaptation is what set them off. Now the bounty has transferred between our races."

The danger has shifted, now I must do so in response. Hurling over the thorn barrier in a dive, I shift into quadruped, disappearing into the east wood at increased speed. My paws are not quitting, even after the excruciating night of battles. The rising disk appears, shining its weaving rays, trickling around the trunks and into my pupils. The tree line marks the break where I am crossing over.

But the moment reality touches my eyes, it does so by contacting my ears and nose. Waves sound over the soil, spreading their fresh scent into my nostrils. Viewing the shoreline defies all my intentions of reaching my fellow Vulpine survivors.

As though faint, my legs collapse from beneath me. Muzzle buries in the sand like trying to avoid a skunk's musk. To pass, is my desire. Why do I remain here? Please, take me out. Bring me away.

Moonsight has come to my side, closely followed by everyone else. Each are feeling my stab. I am not worrying for them as before; it is they concerning over me. Helping my allies has led to a terrible outcome. Focusing on the good of losing only one is a great difficulty. Moonsight's paw comes over my growing mane in a pleasant massage, followed by equally gentle exhales of, "Forjah, the purpose this tournament serves is not only for the Aquileia ourselves?" My ears jump as does fire surfacing behind my uvula."

"You mean . . .

"Yes, we Aquileia are building up an armada. A force beyond willing to side with the Vulpine. Our fore-generations were once enemies; now we share the same enemy."

It is one of the few times I am unable to make a response, for I can only extend my thanks. "All of you, fighting at my side . . ." I could not ask for anything more. The remaining Vulpine, I know will welcome it.

"This is a sad revelation," continues Moonsight. "Yet it must be known. A new generation is awakening into this war. We are now part of it."

"But Forjah gave all to defend us," Kyara announces. "He deserves our help."

"His entire race deserves our help," enlightens her father, "I feel it is time for us Gryphons to expand outside of Chromium's territory."

"Correct Evaron," Ankara inputs, "Living in the mountains, we see there is so much beyond. Whether over the land, water, or sky."

So much to take in, overloaded with facts, unable to make my own choice. Which trail to follow is a mystery; yet my energy is close to its limit. I require rest and the chance to set my mind at ease.

Padding on alone in quadruped, tail slightly held above the ground, I prefer this stance as my greatest tributes to the Wild Inheritance. The Vulpine Instinct carries me to the shoreline. Waves pleasingly dance over the sand, emitting the most pleasurable sound—ending with its cool fresh aroma.

Leaping from the warm sand upon a solar basked rock; I perch upon my haunches and open my wings. Flexing my leathery limbs into a great stretch, I fix eyes carefully to view my third pair of limbs in a whole new way, as Skylar does. Now, I see a pair of large black hands I only know bats to possess. Strong and majestic they are, a gorgeous work of art all on their own. Miraculously formed in the studio of Skylar's womb by the paint of Sy.

"I realize now, I am a marvel of life. An artwork almost extinct." Once locked against my shoulder blades, I lay on my side to absorb the heat of the stone. Taking the disk rays into my fur as it now peaks over the eastern horizon. Curling up, holding tail over my eyes, both mind and body enter the visionary world by the bestowal of my Vulpine Instinct. To later awaken and return to this reality. "We all have our limits," I repeat, "Meaning our enemy must have their own."

"Forjah," calls a voice most familiar. First my mind awakes and then my body. Summoning my eyes to open before the dawn of day, pupils narrow in response to the risen sky disk.

"Rested?" Kyara inquires with a prod of her paw into my side. At first, I only raise my head in greeting of both she and Chrome. I have slept through the dawn and morning with midday still ahead. "I'm beginning to feel nocturnal," I bring out, "my body and mind are roaring with energy that could even make me airborne."

"Can you?" Kyara begs in excitement.

Bowing my shameful head, I tell her, "If only that were more than a metaphor."

"Time will reveal the true purpose of your third limb set, our Vulpine ally." The waves seem to carry the echo of Moonsight right into my ears. Straightening myself up, I take a great feline stretch in my spine and six appendages.

"You are immature as we are, but your wings are far more majestic than that of any kit." This comment of Kyara's astounds me.

"Your wings are that of raptors, predatory birds. While my own are that of bats, the first of flying mammals."

"And look what we have become," Ankara joins in, "We are Gryphons who attain flight as fledglings."

"I am sure you will one day be a flying Vulpine," motivates Kyara who causes a grin to pass across my muzzle which I am not sure a Gryphon beak can do.

"I believe my positive side is inherited from Skylar, my mother."

"I bet she is as nice as you," Kyara wagers on the assumption of my joy.

"She is far more genuine," I verify. All this joyful

energy is pleasing after what took place the night before.

"It is time to move on to the next path in the trail," Moonsight starts, drawing up his paw which clutches my pack. "By hearing your thoughts, Forjah; I find the will to return to your race." Raising my head to meet the Aquileia's leader straight on, I then lower it in acknowledgement.

"Yes," I confirm, "Because of what I have learned and become; my kind is in need of this new dog." Rising up and shifting into biped, I conclude. "I have advanced from a hybrid into a tribrid and may fuse yet again. But for now, my race needs the miraculous blessing of my inclusion. Reciprocate to their defense, I must."

"Calculation predicts my return will be before dawn," consoles Moonsight, pressing beak hard against his mate. Both Chrome and Kyara are in awe that I am leaving. Exactly as I.

"Chromium will be so different without you, I just began to see you as a friend, Forjah."

"Chromium is now safe because of him," Ankara adds, pointing out the good of my actions to Kyara. "The outside lands will also be safe upon his return."

"Mother is right!" ratifies Chrome, "The Aquileia have been saved. It is now the time for those beyond Chromium to experience his strong heroism." My battle partner is doing an extreme attempt at being mature, but I see the dip in his neck and dampness in his black beady eyes.

"No, it is on my promise that this is not goodbye," Positioning myself before the kits, I extend paws forward, gripping their diminutive bodies and bringing them close. There is no ending, I assure this. "It is a meaningful challenge to learn and prevail together, but an even deeper goal of doing it alone and independently. It is now time to learn by relying on ourselves, exactly as we do each other."

A S A   P u b l i s h i n g   C o r p o r a t i o n

Leadership can only be obtained by guiding both you and your team. Did I learn this from mother? Ankara? Or all on my own? All that is for sure, is truth of these statements.

The despair and loss of striding Moonsight's back is heart wrenching, for I have just taken my paws off Chromium's earth; despite knowing it is not my last.

"No, it will not be the last," he softens his voice upon answering my thoughts. "I am also certain we will come to your land." His reassurance is as powerful as his spirit alone. In temporary departure, I touch paw to my heart, then extend it out to Evaron, Adelhied's family, Ankara and her two kits. They too extend their paws in receiving me, returning to rest them down over their own hearts. I'm not saying goodbye because my Vulpine instinct impulses it is not so. A reunion will take place somewhere ahead in time.

"From the land to the air!" I call out. By the power of lion and raptor, Moonsight leaps, taking out over the fresh water body. The great wings expand on either side, propelled by paddling the water's surface before arising. With one last glance, I look back to Chromium; the Gryphon's home having become my own. How this reflects on my personality is beyond coincidental. How mother always described that I never stay in one place too long, always moving on to the next level once ready. Now riding on the back of the Aquiliea's leader, soaring over the dark water to my next destination, I know I am going for my next level. Not knowing what this next demesne will be, I do know I am ready for it. Ready for an unknown future.

Spreading wings, I allow them to carry over the night air, gently gliding over and under the leather folds. Visualizing what it must feel like to fly again.

"I feel I could just lift off right now," but the Vulpine Instinct has no clear information for that. I can only carry on with my adaptability, and use my Wild Inherited personality in response.

Resting lids of my fire singed tears, I allow my mind to clear and expand. My tail flutters along with my sails; and my internal flame brightens with newfound hope. "I will make it mother, I will be a Miraculous Freak."

Thank You

for Reading

Chromium Birth

A S A   P u b l i s h i n g   C o r p o r a t i o n

ABOUT THE AUTHOR

Thinking beyond the realm of imagination is an arduous endurance to the mentality; this is the challenge that David Talon accepted. He is an Eagle Scout of the *Boy Scouts of America* and a certified Archery Instructor; yet writing is where he fleshed out his hidden talents. Like the protagonist in the story, David wasn't well developed at the beginning of *Chromium Birth*, and only toward the book's completion did he transition from immature hybrid into fused adulthood.

As a kit, he vowed to trek the isolated journey of becoming independently unique; purely imitating how the vulpine (Fox Genus) deviate from their canid relatives at the most unusual. This chosen goal began to influence his writing; fuzing with it to create an original world of fresh characters and ideas beyond the limits of thought. Inspired by animal companions and anthromorphic literature, Mr. Talon aspires to tell these new stories with a full cast of beastly characters.

The temptation to keep things simple and repetitive was extreme. But setting paw and talon on the fresh trodden trail, this author takes lead down the winding turns and fluctuating altitudes of this alienated reality. He lives by this same goal today, to challenge and inspire that original ideas continue existing on just waiting to be unearthed.